The Protector
Book Two of the Sophie Lee Saga

by Stormi Lewis

STORMI LEWIS

The Protector
Book Two of the Sophie Lee Saga

The Protector
Book Two of the Sophie Lee Saga

ISBN: **979-8-9856999-1-3**

Library of Congress Control Number: 2021917513

For information, contact Stormi Lewis

cspresspublishing@gmail.com

Discover us online:

www.chasingstormi.rocks

Find us on Instagram and TikTok:

@chasingstormi

Praise for

The Protector

"I was sucked in completely! I couldn't put this book down and I was in SHOCK!! With the ending and I just cannot wait till the third and last book! Please give yourself a treat and read this saga!"
- Amazon Review

"I loved loved loved this book. I could not put it down. The action in this story carries you away with it. Sophie is a character that you fall in love with right away and keep on rooting for her to win. I love how the relationship between Sophie and James continues to grow as they try to figure out who the man with the cane is. Ben and Tina are also a great couple and I love how they help Sophie I loved the Anne of Green Gable reference as I loved this TV show growing up. I enjoyed learning a new word - oneironaut. The ending of this second book is going to make it impossible to wait for the third book. I can't wait to read the next book."
- Amazon Review

"Another fast paced fun read with all the feels by Stormi Lewis. "The Protector", book two of the trilogy pours on the excitement, romance, and mystery. If you love a good cliff-hanger this book will leave you searching for the release date for book three."
- Good Reads Review

"Stormi Lewis does not disappoint in the second of her trilogy. This thriller is filled with twists and turns and romance. You most definitely will want to read The Key which is the first in this wondrous trilogy. I highly recommend this book and give this a 5/5 stars."
- Good Reads Review

"We finally get a little background story on the man with the cane,

Clarice and Sophie's parents in this one!! As I learn more, I'm finding her character more relatable and my distaste for the man with the cane has grown stronger. After this cliffhanger, I can't wait for book 3!!!"

- Santana Saunders, Author

To the OG Storm Chaser, who gave me my love of stories and books, always made sure that I knew she loved me, was always proud of me, and the spirit to all of my writing. I will see you in my dreams whenever you can take a break from chasing around Elvis and drinking coffee with your loved ones in Heaven.

To Shyera McCollugh Thomas, who convinced me to go back to my roots, and gave me the greatest gift I could ever ask for. Pure happiness, pandemic and all.

To my Instagram Support Team, who let me reach out for the good, the bad, and the breakdowns to help build me back up and get me back on track.

To Booktok and Authortok, who are forever teaching me new things and helping me reach my author goals.

To Katherine, who took the time to help me get Sophie into even more hands, and keeps me going when I get overwhelmed.

To my beta readers, that gave me valuable feedback to make this book the best version of itself for you.

Lastly, to my Storm Chasers, who never stop conquering their personal storms while supporting my passions and personal growth. I would not be here without you.

MATURE LANGUAGE
AND
CONTENT
18+

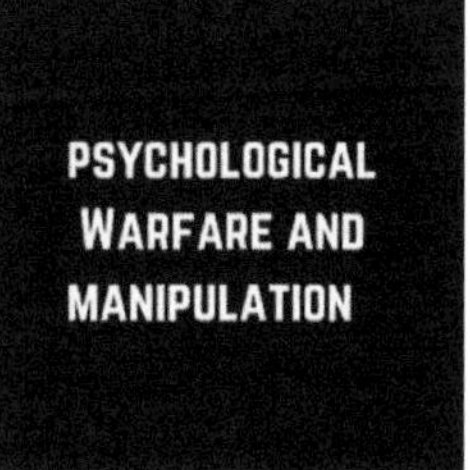

VIOLENCE, KIDNAPPING,
AND OTHER
PSYCHOPATHIC AND
ASSASSIN TENDENCIES

One

As a mother, you take great pride in being able to produce life. To have a part of you that will live on long after you are gone. Someone that you can instill your morals, values, and traditions into. Someone you can help shape into representing what you stand for, and to continue the fight to make the world a better place.

At least, that's how Angie viewed motherhood. She had married her high school sweetheart, and life couldn't be better. Jim was even more excited than Angie when they found out she was pregnant. Even though they had both come from simple families, they were determined to give their first-born son as much as possible to help him succeed in life.

They named him Nicholas, after Jim's father. Jim had lost his father unexpectedly to a heart attack in high school, and it had left a mark on his heart that Angie was eager to help heal.

Nicholas was a quiet and well-behaved baby. He slept often, hardly cried, and was a blessing of a first child. He was such a calm child that it made Angie and Jim eager for a second one. Jim had been an only child growing up, and wanted his son to experience brotherhood. Angie agreed wholeheartedly, because she was very close to her brother and two sisters. They would name their second child, Peter, after Angie's grandfather.

Nicholas was excited to be a big brother. He pointed to Angie's belly often and said, "Mine!" They assumed that despite not fully understanding the concept of pregnancy, Nicholas knew he would be Peter's protector. They didn't realize that Nicholas had other plans at his age.

Angie was getting closer to her due date. She stayed at home with Nicholas while Jim worked for a local insurance agency in their small town. They had a simple home, which they were quickly outgrowing. Jim was pulling extra hours before the second baby came.

Angie had put Nicholas on the floor in front of an educational tv show with their trusty black lab, Sam, before going into the kitchen to grab some water and a second of peace and quiet.

It would be Nicholas' excessive glee and giggling that would catch her ear. She didn't hear him express a lot of emotion, so Angie was eager to see what had caused such an emotional outburst out of her son.

She stood in the doorway to the living room, but nothing seemed out of the ordinary. Sam was curled up around Nicholas as a protective barrier as usual, and Nicholas was giggling and clapping as he stared at Sam. Yet, something was not right. Angie felt it in her bones.

Shortly after, she dropped her glass of water and glass shattered across the living room floor. Sam's eyes never blinked. His chest never rose. What was even more frightening was the look of pride that Nicholas gave when he looked back at her as he continued to giggle and clap his hands at his greatest accomplishment.

Angie told herself she had been in the kitchen longer than she realized, and it was only an accident. She told Jim that Sam had passed unexpectedly, and they would have to deal with the body. Jim came home and took the dog to be disposed of by the vet.

When he returned, Jim looked at his wife with curiosity. "How did you say you found him?"

"He was just in the living room. Why?" Angie had asked.

"The vet had said, his windpipe had been crushed," Jim said, deep in thought.

Flashes of her constantly telling Nicholas to be gentler around the dog came before her eyes, but Angie simply shook her head before saying, "What a weird thing to conclude." She held her hands protectively over their unborn child. "It was just an accident," Angie whispered under her breath.

However, it wasn't an accident. That would not be the only life Nicholas would take, including her own. Angie stared at her oversized belly in the mirror, not knowing what she had created with her first child. Or that he would sacrifice the baby inside her for nothing more than pure fascination.

Nicholas now sat in a large red leather chair, rubbing the

symbol etched on his gold ring, deep in thought. It turned out rather easy to have your name legally changed when there were no parents to declare otherwise. Nicholas never suited him anyway. He was as far from any kind of saint as humanly possible, so he chose his own name. A name that truly represented him and what he stood for. A name no one would suspect until it was too late. But for now, Sophie only knew him as "the man with the cane."

"I can't believe you lost her, AGAIN!" screamed Clarice, holding Eddie by his shirt and preventing his feet from touching the ground. For an anorexic-looking thing, she had some serious strength in her. Sophie had been MIA for over a week.

"Stand down!" she heard her father yell from the shadows.

"Edward, here, has lost your 'pet', AGAIN!" Clarice said, through her clenched jaw.

"Stand down," the old man repeated, giving a final warning from the shadows. Clarice resentfully put Eddie down.

"Maybe if you stopped sending incompetent people in to get Sophie, we'd have her by now," Eddie snapped, while massaging his chest.

"You think you can do better?" Clarice hissed, glaring down over him.

"Edward is correct," the old man said, annoyed. "You really must find better help."

"You always take his side!" Clarice shouted at the darkness.

"Watch your tone, Child," the old man threatened. "And if you didn't let him always be right, I wouldn't have to point it out constantly."

"UGH!" she screamed and stormed off to her quarters. Clarice slammed the door shut behind her. Her room was simple, with a steel desk and a basic twin-sized bedframe. The mattress was worn and hard, just the way she liked it. Thin black sheets, a military hunter green fleece blanket, and a feathered pillow made for her bed. There were no posters, no pictures of Clarice with family or friends, no sign of personal affects. Just a single reading lamp on top of the desk with a folding chair for her seat.

"Little twerp!" Clarice screamed to no one as she bent down, grabbed the knife hiding on the outside of her ankle, and threw it at the door behind her. It landed square in the middle of Sophie's head. It was a picture of Sophie with her parents at her fifth birthday party. Right before Clarice tried to drown Sophie in the pool, per her father's request to get Jess' attention.

"You're no better," she muttered to the figure with a knife sticking out of her forehead. Clarice sighed heavily before going to the door and retrieving her knife. She paused to look at Sophie's mother before stomping over to her bed and lying down. She stared at the ceiling and thought about the first time she had met Jess.

Clarice hadn't minded her in the beginning. She even thought they could be friends one day. Jess was kind to everyone, but her heart would be her greatest downfall. Clarice's father made a point to show more interest in Jess, even back then, and made sure Clarice knew her work never could measure up. He always said healthy competition was good for the soul, however, it would forever be one-sided with Clarice on the losing end every time. She grunted and rolled on her side.

Clarice remembered the day Jess came in on cloud nine. She was going on and on about some nerd scientist she had met and declared in front of everyone that she, Jessica, was "in love." Clarice made the same face of disgust that she had made the day she found out. She never understood what Jess saw in Jack. However, it made her father furious, and for that, Clarice was glad.

Things grew even worse once Sophie was born and Jess demanded to quit. It was music to Clarice's ears, but her father wouldn't stand for it. He even ordered Clarice to kill the little girl on her fifth birthday. The sooner the better.

Clarice was excited to accept the challenge. Sophie was too smart for her own good, and Clarice was tired of being second best. However, Jess had interfered before she could take the child's last breath, forcing her father to re-evaluate. If Jess wasn't willing to be his number one team member, then her daughter, Sophie, would take her place. Clarice would never cross his mind. She never had, so why start now?

A tear rolled down her cheek as Clarice remembered the day she, herself, had announced she was walking away from his business. Clarice gathered the courage to enter his office unannounced. He laughed in her face as if she were a clown performing for the king.

"Who would take you?" the old man sneered at her.

"Some people find my skills extremely helpful," Clarice said, putting her hands on her hips in defiance as he sat in his large red leather chair behind his redwood desk.

"Your mother thought the same thing and look where that got her?" he said, giving a hard laugh and waving his hand dismissively in the air before going back to writing on whatever he had been working on.

The image of her father strangling her mother up against the kitchen wall, simply because for the first time in her life, Clarice's mother demanded that he be a father to his children, played clearly in her head.

The old man held her high as her feet dangled beneath her, and her hands desperately clawed at the hand that held her neck so tightly. Her mother's eyes were wide and full of fear as they became blood shot. Her lips swelled up, and she gasped for air.

"Got something to say, Child?" the old man had growled at Clarice, as she stood in the living room at the age of nine, watching the life of her mother be drained right before her eyes.

"No, Sir," Clarice responded, knowing if she did, she would be next. Then her mother jerked convulsively before going limp under her father's out-stretched arm. He let go, letting the body slide down the kitchen wall, falling face first onto the hard tile floor. Her mother's eyes were still open, but no life left in them.

Clarice swallowed, waiting to see if she would be next. Her father just stepped over the dead body and got a beer from the fridge. He eyed Clarice with suspicion as he continued to sip his beer.

Clarice had stared at her mother's blank expression. She tilted her head to study it before mimicking it and walking away.

Her father always brought up her mother as a reminder of what he was capable of, but Clarice was already well aware. She had killed, tortured, and hunted for him with the hope of one day being accepted. That would never be the result. Clarice knew that at twenty-one, and she wanted to be free and find the love that Jess had claimed existed for everyone…even Clarice.

"So, go then," the old man had said flatly to her face. "It's not like you're any good here," he shrugged.

Clarice sighed heavily in defeat and turned to leave the office.

"Of course," the old man had teased. Clarice froze immediately.

"Of course, what?" she had regrettably asked him.

"Of course, someone will have to train the child properly," he had stated, tapping the pen on his chin.

"Isn't that what your 'pet' is for?" Clarice chided, keeping her back hazardously exposed to her father.

"If Jess wants out, I will give her an out," the old man had shrugged, but Clarice knew that meant he was going to murder Jess. "Her daughter can take her place, and who better to teach her than you?" he had taunted.

Clarice knew it was bait. She knew if she didn't leave then, she would never have a life to call her own. This opportunity would never exist again. However, her desperate need for her father's approval engulfed her, and Clarice gave him her heart to crush, yet again.

It was Clarice's sole mission to bring the child in and make Sophie into the soldier her father desired. Jess had other plans, though, and the mission was becoming more of a pain than Clarice thought it was worth. Nonetheless, her father would never accept the reality of the situation. His obsession grew with each team's failure. Sophie was already in her early twenties, and Clarice was tired and over it. No one was worth chasing for over ten years. Not even this brat.

Sophie evaded every team Clarice had ever sent, and she did it with a sickening smile. Although Clarice couldn't blame the girl. She would do the same if she was on the winning side of the fight, too.

However, Sophie wasn't the average girl, either. You didn't need a big fancy doctor degree to notice Sophie had lightning speed, genius level intelligence, and God knows whatever else they hadn't uncovered yet. The girl was trouble with a capital T, and Sophie would be her father's downfall. Clarice wondered if, given the chance, which side she would take. She sighed heavily and rolled back onto her back.

Her father never gave her an opportunity to dream of what she wanted to be when she grew up. Only that it would be by his side, like a loyal dog, constantly seeking her master's approval.

Her mother had been murdered. Her brother's neck snapped like a twig, without any sign of remorse because he became too "difficult". A dog that was kicked to death, because it barked too loud one day. A sister, gone, for simply wanting something different. Clarice gave her father everything he demanded, but he still couldn't give her any respect or something remotely symbolizing love.

Someone like Jess had a husband who adored her and died for her. A daughter that was her world, and would survive it all, while Clarice had no one at all.

Her own father still had a soft spot for Jess, even after she demanded to be set free. Blood meant nothing to him, especially if Clarice's was spilled in the process of achieving his plans. She closed her eyes and tried to get some rest. All she found was darkness and a heart that desperately wanted to be loved.

Clarice fell into darkness quickly. When she opened her eyes, emptiness surrounded her. Minus the wooden door that seemed to stand randomly in the middle of nothingness.

"What the hell?" Clarice said, out loud to no one.

"Open it," whispered a forgotten voice.

"What the hell for?" Clarice demanded.

"Stop being such a chicken and open it," said the forgotten voice, a little more sternly.

"There's nothing behind it," Clarice scuffed, but curiosity took over as she reached out to turn the handle. Light filled the room as a force pushed Clarice through to the other side.

"Hey!" Clarice yelled. No one answered. It took a minute for her eyes to adjust to the light.

She was standing in the middle of the old training room in the bunker. A large black mat consumed a majority of the floor and tables with various fighting equipment lined the back wall. The century sparring BOB boxing bag sat in the far corner, and they spread out punching bags between the various support columns.

"About time," laughed Jess as she came out of nowhere from behind Clarice.

"This isn't real," Clarice whispered to herself.

"No," Jess said, calmly. "But it's a suitable substitute when needed."

"When needed?" Clarice asked, confused and forgetting her anger.

Jess began pulling her hair up into a messy bun. "Come on, Clare Bear. For old time's sake," she said, with a mischievous smile as she took stance.

Jess put her left foot forward, carefully balancing on the ball of her foot, and put her right foot directly under her right hip. She held her left hand out at waist level, preparing to block any strikes, and placed her right palm facing up in front of her chest.

"Seriously?" Clarice asked the ghost from her past.

"Scared?" Jess taunted.

"Never," Clarice said, with her own wicked smile, mimicking Jess' stance.

"That's my girl," Jess murmured. She waved at Clarice to come.

Clarice tilted her head and assessed her dead friend before her. She never seemed to beat Jess in combat during training, but a lot had taken place since Jess had been alive. Clarice started with the usual kick jab combo they had used in training as kids. Jess spun and blocked every attack.

"That's all you've got after all these years?" Jess teased.

"Just getting warmed up, Sweetheart," Clarice sneered. She had a plan to win this time. She would need her energy to get to the final blow.

"How's life?" Jess asked casually as they continued the dance.

"You, know. The usual," Clarice responded casually as she increased her striking momentum. "Tracking down your daughter to bring her in. Dad won't let me kill her and put us both out of our misery, so I'm doing what I'm told," she shrugged.

Jess knew better than to stop her. "You deserve better," Jess said, as she barely missed a punch from Clarice.

"Probably," Clarice shrugged as they continued in combat with each other.

"I have to ask," Jess said, slowly, as she barely missed Clarice's jaw with a kick. "Why do you hate her so much?"

"I have my reasons," Clarice snarled as she attempted some of her new maneuvers on Jess. She quickly slid under Jess when she jumped into the air to do a swing kick, catching her off guard. Clarice rolled on her back and pushed herself back to her feet into an immediate stance.

"Good to see you've been practicing," Jess said, with a hint of pride in her voice. "You'll need it," she added smugly, and winked at Clarice.

Jess took off at a run and flipped over Clarice's head. She spun around and gut kicked Clarice, forcing her to fall back a few steps.

"Practicing in your grave?" Clarice grumbled, catching her breath.

"Something like that," Jess shrugged in response and took stance while studying Clarice carefully.

"Why do you care if I like her or not?" Clarice snapped as she stood up and put her hands on her hips. Why was she fighting a ghost, anyway?

"Because she's my daughter," Jess said, sternly, mimicking Clarice's stance. "It would be nice if you two could get along."

Clarice laughed out loud and shook her head. "Not happening."

"What reason do you have to hate her so much? You don't even know her?" Jess asked, dropping her hands and pleading with her.

"I know her well enough," Clarice retorted back before turning on her heels, walking through the door, and slamming it behind her.

Clarice opened her eyes to see she was back in her room, alone, and now furious. "Nice try," she mumbled to the ceiling before rolling over and going back to sleep. There were no more wooden doors or ghosts to haunt the rest of her dreams.

"Well, that went well," said a tall man with short brown hair and sad bright blue eyes, coming up behind Jess and putting his hand on her shoulder.

"Clarice isn't one to convince overnight," Jess muttered with a frown of disappointment.

"Is it honestly worth the effort?" Jack asked.

Jess turned to glare at her husband. "She's just really lost at the moment," she snapped and shrugged his hand off her shoulder.

"Hey," Jack said, more softly. "I just meant that it's been a while, and she's not been in the best environment." He gave his wife a concerned look.

"What's the point in being able to reach them if we don't try to make a difference?" Jess sighed in defeat. "And yes, I think she's worth it," she added stubbornly.

"Honey, I'll stand by you. Nothing will ever change that. However, there are rules, and we need to be careful. It does no good if we cause more harm than good," Jack added with a warning.

"Our daughter wasn't the only one that got left behind," Jess said defiantly, with her arms crossed.

"I understand that," Jack assured. "We just have to be careful is all, my love," he said, walking over and kissing her on the top of her head gently.

"I'm not giving up," Jess mumbled with determination.

"I would expect nothing less," Jack chuckled as he took his wife's hand and they walked back into the light.

James watched Sophie in awe. He had so much appreciation for her stamina! Being on the run constantly was exhausting, and he missed his warm, comfy bed immensely. There was nowhere else he'd rather be than by her side, though.

Sophie observed Tina and Ben from the shadows of the third floor of the State Library of Pennsylvania. The building stood four stories tall, with the typical grey brick exterior. Large marble columns lined the inside of the walls with gorgeously white laced balconies and a spiral staircase in the back center to match.

Each level held multiple bookcases filled to the max with books. The main floor was comprised of large wooden tables and chairs down the center of the entire floor for studying. It was full of the warmest oranges, yellows, and golds, and large chandeliers hung from the ceiling. It was definitely a bright spot on this gloomy and rainy day.

They had already visited several libraries along the east coast, but this particular library had one of the top genealogy websites in the country. Both Tina and Ben had insisted that it needed to be visited for the cause.

Sophie wasn't a fan of being in the larger cities right now. However, Harrisburg, PA was proving to be a very interesting place to visit. Broadstreet Market had provided a nice array of local culinary delights, conveniently crowded Thursday through Saturday every week with forty different vendors to choose from. Riverfront Park was beautiful, no matter what time of day it was.

Sophie also loved their current hideout. They had located a quiet bed-and-breakfast on Airbnb located strategically off the grid from the city.

Her friends were exhausted and frazzled. Yet, they had kept up with her at an impressive rate. Tina had done nothing but live, eat, and breathe the information that had exploded from the SD card.

Whenever someone offered to help, Tina just waved them away. So, Ben took to looking into the doctor aspect of Sophie's life searching for clues, and James usually helped Sophie to keep watch from a far.

"I want to do something for them," Sophie whispered to herself softly.

"What did you have in mind?" James asked curiously.

"Suggestions?" she asked, looking deeply into his eyes. His knees nearly buckled underneath him.

"I'd say a date night, but they can't really go anywhere," James said, tapping his finger to his lips as he thought. "They'd probably just settle for some extra sleep," he chuckled to himself. "But Tina won't do that until she solves this puzzle," he added matter-of-factly.

"We're going to have to force her to take a break," Sophie said, frowning.

"Good luck with that," James snickered and rolled his eyes.

Sophie stared at her friends, deep in thought. Within seconds, she grabbed James by the arms, full of excitement. "I've got it!"

"This should be interesting," James teased.

"I'm going to make you a list of things to grab," Sophie said, while frantically searching for some paper and a pen out of the backpack that rested at her feet. "Just don't get caught," she added sternly before feverishly scribbling items on the paper.

"On it!" James said, taking the piece of paper from her and saluting her before kissing her gently, grabbing the backpack, and rushing out the door.

"Nerd," Sophie giggled to herself. She went back to watching her friends from a far. They had come so far in such a short amount of time. She giggled thinking about the day they all decided they wanted her to train them....

Tina had grabbed Sophie after they reached their first bus stop and insisted that they needed some self-defense training. Sophie had thought about it and came to the same conclusion.

They had met in a vacant warehouse in the middle of downtown. It was supposed to be boys versus girls. However, when James walked over to partner with Ben, it didn't go very well. Ben threw his hands up and backed away immediately.

"No offense, Bro," Ben had stated as politely as he could. "I love you and all, but if an assassin is going to take me out, I think I'd rather have Sophie training me on how to survive."

"Hey!" James shouted, insulted. "I was top of my class for the CST Program."

"Yeah, and you dropped out," Ben murmured back. James glared at his friend. "I'm just saying, Sophie's been chased by these goons since she was in her teens. She has a little more experience, is all," Ben said, shrugging.

Sophie had seen the hurt in James' eyes, so to stop the fighting, she had Ben and Tina pair up and they both taught them. James remained disgruntled that his skills had been so easily dismissed by his friend. Sophie was impressed by some of his moves and incorporated them into her training as well.

Every couple of days, they worked on the physical aspect of their new mission...surviving. Sophie made sure that the partners rotated, because "you never know who is coming for you or what they're capable of" she had pointed out. Despite Ben's hesitation, James had quite a lot to offer. Sophie reminded him of that fact every night before bed.

There was so much still to learn about James. Quite frankly, Sophie was still in awe that he loved her so much, man with the cane and all. Yet, James didn't exactly give his secrets away freely.

Outside of learning that they recruited him out of college to join the CIA, there wasn't an explanation of why he quit. James had more walls than maybe even he realized, but as long as they didn't die on this mission, Sophie was fine spending the rest of her life helping him dismantle, brick by brick. Heck, she still had her own gaps to fill in.

Although an IT guru, Tina also had extensive self-defense training. She talked little about her situation, too. Sophie was pretty sure that was determined by the government more than Tina herself. She took the time to share everything else with Sophie, and it was enough to make her feel like a sister.

Ben's only secrets were those imposed by James and Tina. He hadn't officially started working as a doctor, so he didn't have any specific patients to attend to. Sophie found him the easiest to talk to.

Ben was definitely the brother she never had. However, spending time with him made Sophie think of Edward. She wondered if he was still alive, if he was okay, and if she would ever see him again.

The last couple of days had brought memories of their time together as children to the surface. Sophie had nightmares about how much Edward suffered abuse, both at school and at home. His dad was not a pleasant person and looked for any excuse to take his frustrations out on Edward.

Sophie knew he preferred everyone else call him Eddie. However, she always felt like he had earned the right to have a more proper name. Edward was a survivor on so many levels and deserved the respect of having a formal name like the characters in the books Sophie always read. She smiled fondly at the memory of kicking Tucker's ass just to get him to stop torturing Edward at school. She'd almost gotten suspended, but it was absolutely worth it.

Sophie couldn't stand bullies. They always thought they were better than everyone else. She understood that most bullies were usually bullied somewhere else in their own life, or simply weren't taught to be decent human beings.

Sophie had hated how it had somehow become acceptable

behavior. No one ever wanted to stand up to the bullies for the fear of the repercussions. It was just easier to let them be mean and nasty than to tell them to knock it off for some reason. A reason Sophie didn't agree with and had no fear of helping the bullies learn that their behavior was unacceptable.

It was the start of a short but beautiful friendship with Edward. Her dad had forced Sophie to take him under her wing, so to speak, and Edward quickly became a part of the family, whether she approved or not. Sophie knew her dad well and had loved his loving heart for the less fortunate.

Jack had always supported her fighting, because he knew Sophie's heart was in the right place. Her mother was a little stricter, and a lot less understanding about getting caught. Still, Sophie had been put in charge of keeping Edward safe. A job they forced her to abandon the night her parents were murdered.

She wondered if they were disappointed in her for not keeping her word. Sophie hadn't seen the wooden door or anything else from her parents since they had left Maine. She didn't want to think about if it was some sort of punishment. Or if, even worse, Sophie wasn't meant to see them again.

She gulped down the lump in her throat and went back to watching Tina and Ben do their research below in separate corners. Man, did her mind wonder more when she was surrounded by books!

Before the sun went down, each person left by themselves in 20-minute intervals. It helped them not look like they were together. It impressed Sophie at how well James, Ben, and Tina could all ignore each other in public. Yet, they were so close and loving once they reunited in their rooms. James was already waiting for them when they arrived back at the Airbnb.

"Did you get everything?" Sophie asked him eagerly.

"Of course," James shrugged with ease and confidence.

Sophie excitedly rummaged through the store bags laying on their bed. "Thanks, Babe," Sophie said, smiling her Cheshire grin and kissing him softly on the lips.

"What's in the bags?" Tina asked as she entered the room with her husband in-tow.

"Well," Sophie stated slowly. "I know being on the run constantly isn't easy, and I wanted to reward you for all your hard work."

"Oooo!" Ben clapped his hands in excitement.

"Soph, you don't have to," Tina said, laughing, shaking her head at her husband's response. "We would do anything for you," she added, taking Sophie's hand in hers and squeezing it tightly.

"I know. I still wanted to," Sophie said, smiling shyly.

"Well, spill it already!" Ben said, unable to contain his excitement.

"It's not much," Sophie said, giving Ben a warning look. "But we're going to have a spa day in!" she exclaimed as she used some jazz hands, hoping that it would add excitement to her minimal surprise.

"Ooooo!" Tina squealed.

"A what?" Ben asked, confused. Tina elbowed him in the ribs, forcing him to backtrack. "Oh! A spa day! Sounds great!" he added, forcing a smile.

"I've got you covered," James winked at his friend.

Sophie's face dropped a little. She knew she couldn't take them out like she wanted to. It was a lame idea. Tina glared at her husband before rushing to Sophie's side.

"Don't let him fool you," Tina said, giving Ben the evil eye. "He loves spa days even more than me. He's just trying to be macho and not show it."

"Can't I look at least a little manly in front of her?" Ben grimaced for good measure. James gave him a thumbs up behind the girls' backs so they couldn't see.

"I know it's not much, but since I can't take you out because of the circumstances, this was the first thing that came to mind," Sophie said, staring at the floor.

Ben felt guilt overwhelm him and went to give her a hug.

"Tina's telling the truth. It's my favorite thing. I just don't want you thinking I'm a sissy," he whispered quietly in her ear.

Ben felt Sophie relax immediately in his arms, so he stepped back, grinning from ear to ear, and went to join his buddy on the bed while he waited to see what torture lied ahead.

"We thought we'd start you off with a wax job," James teased as he elbowed his friend.

"Anything for my girls," Ben winked at Sophie, while continuing to pray to the heavens that he would survive tonight with no scars.

"Actually, you and I are going to start with beers and getting caught up on some football," James smiled at Ben. "Dinner is being delivered."

"And we're getting our hair done, since that takes the longest,"

Sophie smiled at Tina.

"Score!" Tina said with excitement. "I'm ready to trade the blonde for a bit."

"Really?" Ben asked in both surprise and alarm.

"We have to change it up some, so we're not so easily traced," Tina answered before Sophie could. "And I can always go back to natural once everything is done," she assured her husband.

"You might find her in a color that drives you even more crazy," James offered as he cracked open some beers.

"Not possible," Ben said, smiling at his wife, hoping to smooth things over with her as well.

Tina sighed dramatically, grabbed the bags, and dragged Sophie into the bathroom before the boys could say any more.

"Lots of options," Tina said with excitement once they were in the bathroom. Sophie laughed.

"We'll have to be careful. Permanent dye can be a real pain, and this is a nice place," Sophie added, studying Tina.

"I know I'm in talented hands," Tina winked.

"I wasn't worried about mine," Sophie laughed as she dragged everything out, including some cheap towels, to help spare some unwanted damage.

"Do me first so I can watch, and then I'll do you," Tina added with authority.

"Yes, Ma'am," Sophie saluted. "Now, which color would you like to be this month?" she asked, doing her best Vanna White impression. Tina picked out their colors, and Sophie got to work.

"This should be interesting," Sophie said, before rolling up her sleeves and prepping the color.

"What do you think they're doing in there?" Ben asked, with a hint of concern.

"I try not to think about it," James answered with a chuckle, and took another sip of his beer.

They laid on the king-size bed that was covered in a brown and gold 70s style printed comforter that matched the mauve vintage carpet and curtains. The flat screen tv they watched the game on looked incredibly out of place compared to the furniture, décor, and the lime green telephone on the nightstand.

"You and Sophie seem to be doing alright," Ben said, trying to distract himself.

"Nothing to complain about yet," James shrugged, not sure where this was headed.

"I'm just happy for you," Ben assured as he laughed and took a sip of his own beer.

Just then, they heard the bathroom door open and turned to see what the girls had been working on for so long. Ben expected to see his usually blonde-haired wife. Instead, he was greeted by a 5'4" brunette, whose hair Sophie had cut into a chin-length bob with the occasional blonde highlight poking through. His mouth dropped open, unable to find the words for such a drastic change.

"You hate it, don't you?" Tina whispered, crushed by her husband's lack of excitement.

James elbowed his friend quickly in the ribs, forcing Ben to stutter out, "It's just a bit of a shock since you've been blonde since we met in the first grade."

James gave her a reassuring smile, but Tina never took her eyes off of Ben, begging for his approval.

"We had to change it," she stammered grimly. "It's just hair. It will grow back. I thought you would like it," Tina said, staring at the floor, both disappointed and hurt. "I thought it looked really cool," she added, sulking.

"Cool is not the word I would use," Ben said, with no emotion in his voice. No one moved or spoke for what seemed like forever.

Then, out of nowhere, Ben strutted over to his wife and threw her over his shoulder as she giggled like a schoolgirl.

"We'll be right back," he announced, as he carried her to their bedroom and shut the door.

James chuckled and shook his head at his friends. It was good to see them in good spirits. They had been working so hard, and everyone needed a break.

"Well, that went over well," James hollered in the bathroom's direction. "I think it's safe to come out," he shouted to Sophie. "They're going to be a bit."

"You may change your mind," he heard Sophie shout in dismay.

Oh crap, that meant she had changed her appearance, too. Well, he would not hesitate as much as Ben; he told himself. However, the fiery redhead that emerged from the bathroom had him unable to move.

Sophie's hair had grown some since they had first met, and now was just about an inch above her shoulders. The color was a bright, dark red wine that forced James' jaw to nearly hit the ground.

"It's way brighter than we expected," Sophie said, wrinkling her nose up in uncertainty.

"Well, it's definitely going to be hard to blend in," James whispered as he tried to slow down his pulse and force the blood to come back to his brain. "You always stick out," he added hurriedly after seeing the concern on face.

Sophie retreated into the bathroom to see what she could do about her hair, when she heard James shout, "Oh no you don't!" He ran in after her. "Please don't change it again," James begged. "I," he stumbled, "I really like it."

"It's too bright," Sophie said, in confusion. "There's no way I will blend in! I need to try and fix it," she said, grabbing at the remaining boxes and checking the color options left.

"Babe," James whispered softly into her ear as he gently wrapped his arms around her waist and pulled her close. "It's absolutely stunning," he said, kissing her on the cheek.

"This is why I have to stay dark. The red just makes me stick out too much. I told Tina going natural would not be the best idea, but she insisted," Sophie said, frowning while she looked at her other options.

"That's your natural color?" James asked, surprised.

Sophie looked at him and raised her eyebrows. "Not every red head looks like Orphan Annie," she said, shaking her head and trying to come up with a solution.

James laughed against her neck as he nibbled on it. "What better way to hide than the original version?" he offered, praying desperately that she would decide to keep this color. Sophie had always stirred up desire in him. He was learning he just might have a thing for redheads.

Sophie's knees were growing weak with his touch, and her core was warming with desire. "Got a thing for redheads, huh?" she laughed, trying to get her focus back on the task at hand.

"Nope," he murmured against her neck. "Just this one."

"You always know how to save an argument, don't you?" Sophie giggled as she closed her eyes and moaned with pleasure at his touch. "What about Tina and Ben?" she asked, letting her hands roam.

"Ben's admiring your handy work," James smirked, twirling her around, so she was sitting on the bathroom counter. "I think they're going to be awhile," he added with his usual boyish smile.

"Well, then you should probably lock the adjoining door," Sophie whispered with her Cheshire grin.

"Yes, Ma'am," James saluted and ran off to lock the door.

"Can you believe that's her natural color?" Tina asked in excitement as she took another bite of pasta.

"No," Ben answered, unable to take his eyes off his wife.

"Ben!" Tina giggled. "If I would have known, I wouldn't have waited until we were on the run to change my hair," she laughed and shook her head.

They ate, watched a movie, and the boys offered the girls massages after attempting to paint their nails for them. Spa night had definitely turned out to be a bigger success than Sophie expected. There was plenty of time to work on the puzzle. Well, not really. However, they would have much greater success by taking a break.

A light flickered in the bathroom, and it caught Sophie's eye. Her instincts went into overdrive, but Sophie shook her head, assuming she was just seeing things.

The bathroom hadn't been updated to current code and matched the décor in the bedroom. She went back to watching the movie, assuming it was old wiring. After she did, the light continued to flicker at a more rapid rate. Sophie focused on the bathroom door that remained cracked open.

"What is it?" James whispered to Sophie, as he felt her body tense up hard against his.

"I don't know," Sophie said absentmindedly before getting up slowly and heading to the bathroom.

Tina and Ben also turned to watch her as she cautiously walked towards the flickering light. James grabbed the gun on the nightstand next to the bed. Something wasn't right. They could all feel the temperature drop a couple of degrees.

James came up behind Sophie and signaled her to wait while he went in first. Sophie shook her head no. She pushed open the door and remained on the other side of the doorway. She looked around the obviously empty room. The light went out completely. Sophie's eyes adjusted quickly. She stared at the familiar face that looked back at her. Only, it wasn't her own.

"Run!" her mother screamed at her, before a large skeletal hand pulled her back. Sophie couldn't believe what she had just seen, but knew better than to ignore it.

"Grab your stuff! We need to move now!" Sophie shouted, slowly backing away from the bathroom.

"What's going on?" Ben asked, confused and alarmed.

James couldn't believe what he had just seen either. He also knew if Sophie said it was time to go, questions would have to wait until later.

"Now!" Sophie yelled, before going to grab her own stuff.

They had learned the lesson to never fully unpack, so it was easy to grab what they had left out and shove it back into their bags. Sophie had already carefully disposed of the hair dye earlier so there would be no trace of their changed looks.

As rehearsed, everyone met in the one room within three minutes, and they quickly used their assigned escape routes and headed for the next meeting spot. No one hesitated. No one dared to look back.

Something more dangerous than usual had to have found them for her mother to appear before Sophie like that. She was chilled to the bone.

She continued to push on with the look of horror on her mother's face ingrained into her mind, followed by the large skeletal hand that gripped her mother tightly and dragged her into darkness.

The sound of his cane echoed on the sidewalk as it pounded against it. He rarely left his home; however, this was a trip worth making. He stopped to stare up at the secluded bed-and-breakfast in the middle of nowhere Pennsylvania. Its siding needed to be replaced, and it was a sickening yellow. Probably to entice people to choose it for their getaway.

The flowers were dying, and the trees were losing their leaves. Summer was long gone, and a crisp fall breeze replaced the summer heat. Plenty of greenery surrounded the isolated building. There was nothing owners could do to make this cold, rainy weather look enticing. The carved pumpkins on the peeling antique white porch reminded him that his favorite holiday was around the corner.

"Hello, old friend," growled a familiar voice from the bench off to the side of the yard, under a tree that was clearly dying.

"Bates," the man with the cane replied, lacking any emotion before sitting down next to the man waiting for him.

"I found him like you asked," Bates answered nonchalantly.

"That's good news for you," the old man replied, staring off into the abandoned street ahead of him.

"What do you need an oneironaut for?" Bates asked curiously.

"Testing a theory," replied the old man dryly.

"Anything I should be concerned about?" Bates chuckled.

The old man remained silent. He was quietly debating if he still had use for Bates, or if maybe he should be the first test subject. He settled for simply replying, "Don't ask me questions." He hated questions, yet everyone seemed to have them.

Bates knew better than to keep pushing. He merely pulled the piece of paper out of his jacket pocket, handed it over, and got up to walk away. He had stayed alive this long. He wanted to keep it that way.

The old man watched Bates sleek back into the shadows. Two could play this little game, he thought to himself. Jess and Jack wouldn't suspect he would have figured out what they had been doing. Jess never gave him enough credit. She would learn the hard way, even in death, that he always got what he wanted. And he wanted Sophie. Now.

Two

The next meeting spot was Buffalo, NY. There was something at the FBI location that Tina needed to get. Buffalo was a hard place to go back to, though. Sophie contemplated if putting flowers on Bill's grave was going to be too risky. Despite all of her efforts, the vision of her mother being dragged away by a large skeletal hand continued to haunt her as she looked out the bus window at the passing dreary scenery.

Everyone was traveling different ways to get there for precaution. However, being alone was the last thing Sophie wanted right now. She knew she couldn't be selfish and put them all at risk. It didn't make the ache for her friends any less severe. Sophie gave a deep sigh, crossed her arms across her chest, and tried to rest while she could.

The wooden door appeared in the middle of the darkness, and Sophie eagerly grabbed the handle and flung open the door.

“Mom!” she yelled into the light. There was no answer. “Mom?” Sophie asked, full of concern.

“She’s not here right now, Peanut,” her father answered, walking towards her.

“Is she okay?” Sophie asked in full blown panic.

“She’ll be fine,” he answered, but the uncertainty came through his voice.

“What happened?” Sophie asked him urgently.

“There're rules in death, Sophie,” her father answered gloomily, staring at the floor. “Your mother broke one, reaching out to you like she did, but it was an emergency. Don’t worry about it. I’ll take care of it.”

“Don’t worry?!” Sophie exclaimed. “How can I not worry about it?”

Jack looked sternly at his daughter for the first time in Sophie’s life that she could remember. “This is not your world. I will take care of your mother,” he responded firmly.

Sophie knew better than to argue. “Well, at least tell me why she had to break the rules,” she requested more softly.

“He was coming. She didn’t have a choice,” Jack said, deep in thought.

“The man with the cane?” Sophie asked, confused. “I was so careful.”

Jack put his hand on his daughter's shoulder. Sophie immediately felt his warmth. "It had nothing to do with you," he assured.

"What do we do now?" Sophie asked, pleading for guidance. She hadn't heard from them since they left Maine. Maybe she was off course.

As if sensing her hesitation, Jack answered," You're on course. Just keep going."

"I haven't seen you in so long. I thought you were mad at me or something," Sophie said, avoiding Jack's line of sight.

Jack lifted her head up to look into his eyes with his free hand. "You were doing just fine without us," he chuckled. "You didn't need us."

"I always need you!" Sophie cried out.

"And you will always have us. However, right now, I have to help your mother," Jack said, backing away. "Stay on course. Keep your friends safe. And Peanut..." he said, smiling. "We're so very proud of you."

Before Sophie could respond, she was pulled back through the door, and it slammed in her face. She opened her eyes to rain pounding against the window. Everything swirled around in her head, making it impossible to relax.

"Sleep, Peanut," she heard her father call before she felt his finger whisk her forehead and she fell into a deep, empty sleep.

James sat on a bus from a different carrier and stared out the gloomy window while he watched the rain make intricate patterns as it streaked down the pane. That was bizarre, he thought to himself as he replayed the image of Sophie's mother being dragged back by a large skeletal hand.

James had recognized Jess' face from the picture behind Mario's bar. This was not the first time he had seen Jess. Jack and Jess had come to James in a dream. Or at least he thought they had. It was a surreal moment indeed. He hated the thought of Sophie being alone right now, most likely replaying the same image James was trying to figure out the meaning of it all.

He always felt like a huge part of him was missing when they weren't together. James hated the emptiness. He thought his world had shattered after Helen had left him at the altar, but nothing compared to the loss that being apart from Sophie gave him. James had thought he would never find love again, only to realize that he hadn't found it in the first place until he met Sophie. He kicked himself for not recognizing it right off the bat.

Life hadn't exactly gone as planned for James. They recruited him right out of college to join the CIA. He assumed it had a lot to do with his remarkable test scores and ability to hold his own. James was much smarter than most gave him credit for. Although his dad most likely wanted James to follow in his own footsteps and also become a doctor, it just wasn't what James wanted. Not that he really knew what he wanted. Serving his country just seemed to be a better fit. His dad never gave him grief, though.

However, James wasn't willing to play the political games that came with the job. If someone needed help or to be saved, James couldn't figure out why any red tape was needed. Or the constant lying it took to accomplish the simplest of tasks. So, he walked away.

There was a lot of talk about how he couldn't "cut it" or "do what needed to be done," but that wasn't the case at all. He understood lying was necessary in some situations. However, lying just for personal gain was completely different. And there was a lot of lying for personal gain in the CIA.

Tina had tried to get him to switch to the FBI, however, James needed a break from the government gig. Not that he didn't have offers. They were piling up in his old apartment, and he had to disconnect his phone so it would stop ringing long enough for him to get sleep at night.

Then James met Helen. She was of money, too, but Helen didn't have a problem spending it regularly. Her dad was a CEO of a huge oil company. Her mother was a stay-at-home charity stay-at-home parent. In the beginning, Helen had been sweet and wanted to save the world like James did. Protect the weak and stop the bullies of the world. Or so he thought.

Helen volunteered at the animal shelter, protested for animal and human rights while saving the planet in her free time. She was full of confidence and always said she loved James for his "simpleness."

After a year of dating seriously, James proposed. That was what you were supposed to do when you found someone that loved you for being yourself. Helen had jumped at his proposal for marriage and began planning immediately.

Despite the bride's father traditionally paying for the wedding, James noticed that his family was covering the bill more often than not. Suddenly, Helen had an expensive taste for everything that was "required for a wedding" as she put it. James wanted something small and intimate. Helen wanted the Cinderella ball.

She spent a lot more time away from him stating that she was planning, but "planning" turned out to mean that she was having sex with Curtis from her father's corporation.

Helen tried to get James to commit to her father's business. When he didn't, the arguing only increased. James saw all the signs. He just wasn't willing to admit it.

Then the big day came, and they filled the seats to capacity. Over 6,000 people, most of them James didn't even know, shifted in their seats uncomfortably as they continued to wait for Helen to walk down the aisle with her father.

However, Helen would never come. She had left a note in her dressing room stating she had found true love with Curtis, and he was going to be able to provide her with the life she deserved. Whatever the hell that meant.

James thought he was going to have to lock Tina up once she found out. James' parents and friends took care of the guests while he remained on his spot at the front of the runner in his tux and his hands crossed in front of him. Everyone tried to get him to move, but he just couldn't.

He continued to look out at the lake behind him in shock that life had gotten so far off course. Once he heard the clock from inside the reception hall chime midnight, James finally turned around, walked right out the door, and got in his car and drove.

He found himself outside the graveyard where his grandparents laid. "I'm sorry," James whispered to them both. "I tried." He curled up between the gravestones and fell asleep.

The town had plenty to talk about. James heard the whispers

behind his back. No one dared to talk about it to his face, and James was glad for that.

He worked odd jobs here and there, despite his family having plenty of money. James enjoyed doing different things and helping those in need. He avoided the corporations and spent his time with his friends while they worked on building their new careers. James helped Tina and Ben study to pass all their exams required. They also had plenty of movie nights and good times.

After a year, Tina decided it was time for James to move on and started setting him up with just about any person with female anatomy that breathed. It would be the night that James found Sophie in the woods that would change his life forever, though.

At first, Sophie was just a blurred shadow, running deeper into the woods. She was faster than anyone James had ever raced against. Just when he thought he had lost her; Sophie had reached out and grabbed him to push him up against the trunk of the tree she had been hiding behind. The move was swift and graceful, and once his eyes had adjusted again, James was looking at the most beautiful woman he had ever seen.

Sophie's bright blue eyes seemed to look directly into his soul. Though her short, chin length black hair was messy, and her face a little dirty, Sophie was the most beautiful thing James had ever seen. She was thin, athletically built, and pale as the moon's light, with black clothing that clung nicely to her curves. James did not know why Sophie was running, or who was after her, but he found himself instantly drawn to protect her at all costs. What a bizarre sensation, since Sophie hadn't even spoken much to him yet.

It wasn't just about her looks. There was an electricity that seemed to course through his veins when they touched. An instant feeling of need and desire spread from his core. Sophie was different. She was special. She would give him a run for his money, as he would find out later.

Sophie challenged him to be the best version of himself, even when he didn't know what exactly that meant. James wanted to make her proud of him. He liked who he was when she was with him. James finally knew what love was actually supposed to feel like. Sophie didn't just tell James what he needed to hear, or what she thought he wanted to hear. She called him out constantly and kept him in line.

She gave him strength when he felt weak, and valued his opinions and advice, even if she did not intend to take any of it. Sophie could take care of herself. There was no doubt about it. However, she had innocence and curiosity that needed to be fed and appreciated.

Finally, a woman of equal intelligence that didn't have James clenching his jaw in annoyance. And her Cheshire grin was to die for! James had heard of girls saying that love gave them butterflies in their stomach and made their knees go weak. Sophie would be the first to prove that it could happen to men, too.

She consumed his thoughts and dreams, and when she wasn't around, James couldn't function or breathe as well. If he thought of Helen, it was simply as a reminder of how little he really knew what he needed before meeting Sophie.

James knew she had to be hurting and being by herself just made him worry more. Sophie would remain tough on the outside for his friends and him, but the image messed with his head and Jess wasn't even his mother. He closed his eyes and used all his strength to send his love to Sophie as she traveled.

James prayed she wouldn't shut him out. He prayed Sophie knew how much he really loved her. What he would do for her. How much he needed her. He concentrated hard on her new image. Sophie with her dark red-wine hair hanging around her face, smiling, and waiting for him to get to her.

Sophie had a hoodie on and hid as much of her red hair under it as possible. She had been born a ginger, just like her mother. That didn't help her not be an easy target at school. The bullies always picked Sophie out first, but regretted their decision shortly after. She smiled her Cheshire grin as she thought of all the nasty kids she had put in their place.

Even as a baby, Sophie seemed to have showed a substantial amount of intelligence and plenty of sass to go with it. She was faster than most, both mentally and physically. She remembered her parents watching her intensely and spending a lot of time whispering behind her back. Although most of her memories as a teenager were still blurred, one thing Sophie knew for sure…she had always been different.

She didn't fit in with any of the kids, and spent her time escaping into books. Sophie loved *Anne of Green Gables* because she felt like Anne understood her pain. Despite getting into trouble at a young age, Anne could still find love, which gave Sophie hope her differences didn't make herself incapable of enjoying love too.

However, something had happened on her fifth birthday that really seemed to change everything. A woman tried to drown her in their pool, and the man with the cane stood back and watched. A scene that was still blurry but made her shiver all the same.

After that, Sophie was suddenly on a vigorous training schedule. They taught her to fight off any attack. She started seeing a ton of doctors and received what felt like a thousand shots a week without being sick. A fact that still bothered her today. What was in the shots? Why did she have to have them?

However, other questions needed to be answered at the moment like "what did the SD card have to do with anything?" and "why did her parents have to be murdered?" Of course, another important one to solve was "who the hell was the man with the cane?" and "why did he want her so badly?"

Sometimes Sophie wondered if fate hadn't stepped in to wipe her memory in order to have her be vulnerable enough to let James and his friends into her life. It was a gamble that Sophie still struggled with daily. Was helping Sophie putting their lives in more danger? Or was staying with her keeping them alive?

Sophie couldn't bear the thought of losing any of them, but losing James would mean she would lose part of herself. Was it selfish to allow them to stay with her, just so Sophie could keep James? Probably. Sophie never allowed herself to think about it too much. Most likely because she would eventually make herself follow through with what was best for James. She just wasn't ready yet and doubted if she ever would be.

Sophie got off the bus and looked in the direction that would eventually lead her to Jumping Jack's Power Plant. She instantly became nauseous and fought the need to throw up. Even if Sophie could physically make herself go back there, whoever was tracking her would definitely watch to see if she would return.

Sophie kicked the rocks on the sidewalk as she weaved between the people and avoided being caught on any cameras. She could change her hair, but there was nothing she could do if they captured her face. Facial recognition software was more advanced these days, and it only took a partial shot to flag her.

The image of Bill, confused and scared while being held hostage by Simon, flashed before Sophie's eyes, causing them to tear up. She had a strong desire to leave a flower by Bill's grave and stop to say hello. However, that wasn't a safe option either.

Sophie wondered if his family could give Bill the burial he deserved. Guilt consumed her. After everything that had happened, Sophie couldn't even go to pay her respects.

Bill was dead because of her. Sophie and her desire for human companionship while she tried to save James and her friends. When was she going to stop choosing whose life mattered more? A tear ran down Sophie's cheek and she wiped it away swiftly before it dropped from her chin.

"I'm sorry," Sophie whispered to no one.

"I know," she heard Bill's voice ring in her ears. Sophie went to look up, but Bill urgently whispered, "Don't!" so she kept her head down and continued to weave in and out of the crowd.

"I miss you," Sophie whispered to him.

"I miss you too," she heard Bill's voice crack. "You're doing great, Kid. Just keep going. Don't worry about me. It's nice up here. And I'm giving them hell," Bill stated with pride.

Sophie smiled. She wasn't sure if she was just imagining Bill's voice to help her get through Buffalo, but she would take it. "Don't get caught," Sophie chuckled as she kept moving towards the meetup.

Sophie was the last to arrive, as usual. She did a walk around, checking for all possible quick escape routes and making sure they were secure before entering the Quality Inn. The word "quality" was being used loosely.

The neighborhood was not ideal for tourists, which made it perfect for Sophie and her friends. The inside was clean, and the staff was polite. This was not a location that people were dying to stay at, which suited Sophie just fine.

When she got to the room, Tina was already working feverishly on the secured laptop at the small wooden desk across from the bed. Ben was leaning over some books spread out across the king-size bed on a tan comforter, and James stood in the corner holding the beige curtains back and staring out the window into the alley. Relief flooded him once he saw Sophie standing in the doorway with her backpack in hand.

"I was worried," James whispered as he kissed Sophie softly and passionately.

"I'm better now," Sophie breathed once they parted. "So, where are we at?" she asked Tina and Ben.

"Basically, I could decode about three-fourths of the card," Tina said, frowning at the laptop in front of her. "I just need to get something from the office, and I will be able to crack the rest."

"What are we dealing with?" Sophie asked, sitting next to Ben's books on the bed.

"Most of it is about the logistics of how a satellite in space can be used to offset the environmental pressures of the atmosphere, causing such things as hurricanes and tornados. There's also a way to set off earthquakes and tsunamis, but I'm still trying to figure out that part," Tina said in annoyance.

"You mean, someone can actually control weather from a satellite in space?" James asked with distress.

"Apparently," Tina answered, matching his concern. "Sophie's father designed a satellite that could help control weather. Only Jack's plan was to keep the planet safer with the supposed ongoing effects of global warming, etc. He never intended it to be used for evil," Tina added for assurance. "With the insane hurricanes of the past, like Katrina and Sandy, Jack was looking for a way to save lives. He honestly thought he could offset what Mother Nature threw at us. However, something changed his mind after a while, and it doesn't seem like Jack ever finished the project."

"So, why make such a big deal about keeping it safe?" Sophie asked with a hint of irritation.

"Because it's not just about the satellite," Tina said, deep in thought.

"What do you mean?" Ben asked, finally taking a second to look up from his own books.

"There's a puzzle within this puzzle," Tina said with a hint of admiration.

"What?" everyone seemed to ask almost in unison.

"Yeah," Tina said, smiling. "There's some sort of puzzle within this puzzle. That's what I can't figure out. I think there's a message for Sophie, but it's too hard to see until I decode the rest of the documents.

Don't worry," Tina said, taking Sophie's hand and squeezing it. "I'll get to the bottom of it," she said, winking at her friend.

"I'm not worried," Sophie lied. Her head was already buzzing about what possible explanation all of this had, and why lives were being taken for it. "What about you?" she asked Ben, trying to distract herself.

"Well, I believe that Dr. Moore was genuinely giving you immunizations to help you fight off as much as possible," Ben said, assuring her. "That's why you got as many shots as you did from him. He was just building up your immune system." James winked at Sophie for assurance.

"I wasn't really worried about Roger," Sophie laughed.

"I know, but he was part of MY puzzle," Ben said, with a little pride. "You said the other person was a woman, right?"

"Yes. A brunette, I think," Sophie answered, trying desperately to pull those lost memories to the front, but they were still missing.

"I actually think the Dr. Cox you mentioned is Dr. Elaine Cox," Ben said triumphantly.

"Who is that?" James asked, sitting on the other side of Sophie on the bed.

"Well, from what I gather, she's very well-known in the science community as the first genome surgeon," Ben stated casually. Everyone stared at him. "She's heavy into the CRISPR tool," Ben added, as if to make it clearer. Everyone just continued to stare at him.

"English please?" James asked, shaking his head at his friend.

"Don't you guys ever read anything?" Ben asked, blinking rapidly at them in disbelief. "CRISPR is the new tool they used to dispatch into living cells, and they can manipulate any gene in any tissue in any organism," he said excitedly. "Basically, any alteration in your DNA can lead to disease or disabilities. There's a group of scientists in San Francisco that are working on trying to figure out how to alter damaged DNA. For example," Ben continued without waiting for questions, "if someone has some sort of genetic disorder such as autism. Instead of just learning how to cope with it, a genome surgeon could simply go in and surgically remove the errored DNA and possibly even cure you. They're not as close as they want to be to achieving it just yet, but it's very exciting news for patients that suffer from rare and incurable genetic diseases!"

"Wow," Sophie said, stunned.

"So, are you saying Sophie was a test subject?" James asked cautiously.

"I'm not sure," Ben said, truthfully. "It seems like she just collects samples in order to practice manipulating it. Nothing points to the fact that she ever works on children though."

Ben had a theory about why that probably wasn't completely true. He just wasn't ready to share it yet.

"But didn't you say your dad gave you shots too?" Tina asked Sophie.

"Yes, I do remember him giving me something," Sophie said, deep in thought.

"What would your dad be giving you if he didn't study medicine?" James asked, confused.

"No clue," Sophie said, frustrated.

"Hey," James said, lightly stroking her arm. "We'll sort this out."

"I honestly don't know if there is a bottom," Sophie said, standing up in frustration. "The more we figure out, the more questions that need to be answered. It just feels like there's never really an end," Sophie said, enraged, as she stormed off to the bathroom to throw some water on her face and cool down.

James got up to follow her. Tina quickly grabbed his hand.

"Give her a second," Tina warned. "This has to be ridiculously hard for her."

James looked longingly towards the now closed bathroom door and sulked back onto the bed in defeat. He knew Tina was right, but all he felt was desperation to help Sophie feel better.

"Maybe we should quit for the night and watch a movie," Ben offered, also staring at the bathroom door. Sophie was the little sister he never had. His heart ached as he watched her struggle. Ben wasn't sure the truth was going to be any better. He knew he would have to tell her what he knew. Ben worried if it would be the straw that broke the camel's back. He loved that camel, and he didn't want to be the reason it broke.

James volunteered to get some dinner while Tina and Ben worked on finding a movie that would be a suitable distraction. Sophie remained in the bathroom looking at an image she hadn't seen since her teenage years with her new red hair.

Why had her father insisted she find the key if the project was unfinished, anyway? If the man with the cane couldn't use it, then what was the point? What were all the shots for? What was any of this for? Sophie splashed some cold water on her face and looked back into the mirror.

She willed her mother to appear once more and give her guidance, but all she saw was her own sad, exhausted, frustrated eyes looking back at her. Was her mother okay? Sophie felt sick to her stomach and hunched over the bathroom counter.

"Get up," she heard her father's voice order.

Sophie was too irritated to move.

"Get up!" Jack warned her. "I have enough to deal with right now.

Don't make me worry about you too."

Sophie's head shot up, and she saw the alarm in her own face. So, her mother wasn't okay.

"Don't," Jack cautioned. "She's fine. Now focus and go be with your friends."

"Seriously?" Sophie yelled madly. There was no response. "Fine," she muttered, and did what her father asked her to.

Sophie was pretty sure she had lost her mind anyway, talking to ghosts from her past, and playing God with people's lives. She didn't want her father to worry about her, angel or imaginary. So, Sophie put a smile on her face, opened the bathroom door, and went to join her friends.

Three

James laid silent as he felt Sophie toss and turn in the bed next to him. He had tried to give her the space she usually needed to process things. However, neither of them was going to get sleep at this rate. He rolled onto his side, gently wrapped his arms around her, and pulled her close to him.

"I'm sorry," Sophie breathed out in frustration.

"For what?" James asked casually.

"I just can't seem to get my brain to shut down enough to sleep," she sighed heavily.

"Wanna talk about it?" he offered.

"I don't even know where to start," Sophie whined.

"The beginning usually helps," James suggested.

"You saw what I saw, right?" she whispered softly.

"Yes," he assured.

"I don't think she's okay," Sophie choked out. Panic consumed her.

"Your dad will not let anything happen to her. We both know that," James stated bluntly.

"Is it real? Are they some kind of ghosts? Or am I losing my mind?" Sophie whispered with her voice cracking.

"First of all, if you're going crazy, then I'm going right along with you," James chuckled, kissing the back of her neck. "I have never believed that people just leave you after they pass. I think they remain our guardian angles and come in any way that we need them to," he added softly. "I think that your parents clearly knew what you would be up against, and went to great lengths to make sure they would never truly leave you to fight it all alone. You hear all the time how loved ones visit those in need in their dreams. It doesn't make you crazy, Babe. It makes you loved and protected," James finished.

Sophie rolled over to face him, remaining wrapped up in his arms. "Dad said she broke the rules and had to pay some sort of price," Sophie whispered. "She did it because the man with the cane was too close." She lowered her eyes to stare at James' bare chest. "I wasn't careful enough, and now I may never see her again," Sophie choked up again.

James pulled her even closer to him. "Do you really think Jess is going to let that be her only option?" he whispered softly and kissed Sophie on her head. "We both know where your stubbornness comes from," he said with a smile.

Sophie laughed, and his heart warmed at the sound. "No," she replied softly. "Probably not."

"So, why don't we get some rest. We can come up with all the plans you want to tomorrow. Right now, I just want to hold on to the girl that I love more than anything and fall asleep with her in my arms," James whispered softly and kissed Sophie on top of her head again.

"You keep talking like that, and you'll be stuck with me for good," she giggled.

"Let's talk about it in the morning," James smiled against the top of her head.

Sophie nuzzled into his body and found the peace she needed to finally fall asleep. James sighed and ran his fingers through her hair.

He knew she wasn't ready just yet, so he would keep the engagement ring in his backpack a little longer. Not that running from a psychopath and dealing with ghost parents left a good time for proposing. And James wasn't exactly sure how he was going to get Jack's permission from beyond the grave, but he knew exactly what he wanted. And he wanted Sophie. Forever. If the man with the cane didn't get her first.

Jack stood before twelve hooded figures in black cloaks with his head bowed in respect. Black fog circled around his feet as he stood before the council of death.

"There are rules," boomed a loud, scratchy voice in the center.

"We are aware," Jack said, keeping his head down while trying to remain calm.

"She broke one!" the cloaked figure on the left shouted, shaking the ground beneath Jack.

"She understands and won't do it again. She only did it to spare her child from death," Jack pleaded without making eye contact.

"The living do not outweigh the rules of the dead!" yelled the center cloaked figure as it stretched out a large skeletal hand pointing down at Jack.

The ground beneath him shook so violently that he almost lost his footing, but Jack continued to stand his ground.

"I promise you, my very soul, it will not happen again," Jack pleaded, knowing what the promise actually meant.

No more Sophie. No more Jess. And no opportunity to tell them goodbye. Yet, if it meant keeping his family together for a little longer, then he will make the sacrifice in a heartbeat.

"You have made your case," screeched the last cloaked figure on the right. "Be gone!" it shouted.

Jack turned on his heels and left immediately. Once in the middle of a clearing, he dropped to his knees and clasped his hands together. He didn't know if God could hear him in the in-between, or if He could even help Jack to begin with. It never hurt to try when his family was in jeopardy.

Jack silently prayed, not only for the safe return of his wife, but for the strength he knew he didn't have to help Sophie survive what was to come if Jess didn't return. There were no answers. No reaching out to Sophie. Just a helpless man pleading to keep his family together a little longer, because if the man with the cane got Sophie, then all hope was lost for the world and Heaven itself.

Sophie woke up oddly rested, despite all that was going on. Then again, James was always the peace to her chaos. It was one thing she loved most about him, despite how absurd dreaming of any kind of future with him was. There were priorities.

First, they had to figure out what the point of having the key was and beating the man with the cane. It didn't mean that she didn't dream of her forever future with James. Sophie smiled and bit her bottom lip as she walked across the bedroom to brush the morning tangles out of her hair.

"You're killing me, Smalls," she heard James growl in a low voice.

Sophie giggled in response, only making his pants grow tighter with a need for her. He got out of bed and stalked across the bedroom floor to spin her around and pin her up against the bathroom counter. She immediately felt his erection up against her, between her thighs, making her core heat up quickly.

"Good morning, Beautiful," James said, deep with desire, as he took her mouth with his.

Sophie moaned with acceptance, and eagerly wrapped her legs around his waist when he lifted her and gently set her on the bathroom counter.

"How is it I can never get enough of you?" Sophie breathed as she threw her head back to give him access to her throat.

James immediately began kissing and nibbling down the side of her neck as prompted. "Because I can never get enough of you," he murmured against her neck as he worked his way down towards her chest.

Sophie pulled him closer with her legs and filled her hands with his hair. She gasped as his erection came closer to where she needed it.

He moaned against her neck when he felt her rub against him, full of need and passion.

"Hold on," he whispered in her ear, as he placed his hands under her thighs and carried her towards the bed, feverishly kissing her and claiming her mouth with his own.

James gently sat Sophie on the bed, only to yank her pajama shorts and underwear off in one swift pull. Sophie giggled with anticipation and glee.

"Shhhh," James whispered. "We have a lot of work to do today, but I need you so badly I can't stand it. This will be quick," he said, smiling down at her with pure hunger and need. Sophie nodded to confirm, and bit her bottom lip, waiting.

James grabbed a condom before climbing onto the bed like a cat stalking its prey. He gently slid his hand up her top to caress her bare breast and tease the nipple between his fingers. Sophie arched and moaned in acceptance. James licked his lips while looking deep into her eyes. She was wet and waiting.

Sophie gasped and arched again when she felt his tongue twirling inside her. Her mind quickly melted as she moved her body to match his rhythm. She never knew every time could be just as amazing as her first, no matter how pressed for time they were. "James, please," Sophie whined. She was shaking and ready to erupt.

"Not yet," James whispered against her, his hot breath making her need him even more.

"Please!" Sophie begged, and he didn't have the heart to keep torturing her.

He kissed his way up her body as he straddled her. She was so warm and ready for him. James took pleasure in watching her gasp and arch her back as she accepted him into her.

It didn't take nearly as long for Sophie to adjust before she was eagerly setting her own pace for him to keep up with. James smiled at himself, realizing he may have created a monster, but he didn't care. He wanted her as badly as she wanted him.

James went in quicker and harder with every thrust, and just when neither could take any more, they exploded in unison as he took her mouth to his in order to keep her screams of pleasure from escaping to wake up their friends.

He needed her. All of her. And nothing would stop him from keeping her. Not even the man with the cane.

When James and Sophie met up with Tina and Ben, Tina was wearing a navy business suit with matching heels and a blonde wig that was twisted up into a messy bun.

"What?" Tina said, in response to James' quizzical look. "Can't exactly go showing off my new doo to the FBI cameras, now can I?" she huffed.

"What if something goes wrong?" asked Ben, his voice full of concern.

Tina stopped stuffing her backpack to place her hands on her worried husband's face. "Nothing's going to happen," she whispered before kissing him gently. "The FBI doesn't want me. It's a simple mission, in and out, no dilly dallying. And I have the A-Team watching my back!" she added with extra enthusiasm.

"I still don't like it," pouted Ben.

"That's why I'm going as her assistant," smiled Sophie.

"Yeah, I don't like that either," frowned Ben. "Are you sure these wigs are going to be enough to fool them?"

Tina smiled wickedly. "Who said all we were going to be armed with were wigs?" She hurried James and Ben out of the room. "Let me do my work. We have to be on time for this to work!" Tina shouted as she closed the door in their faces. "Now..." Tina said, tapping her fingers together like a mad scientist. "Let's get to work!"

When the girls emerged, the boys both gasped. Sophie was in a short, bright red wig. The prosthetics on her face hid her natural features completely. No one was going to mistake this figure for Sophie, minus her unusual gracefulness, of course.

She wore a matching black business suit and heels. James couldn't speak. He had never seen her dressed so formally before. He swallowed the lump that seemed to be stuck in his throat.

"You look good, Kid," James choked out, unable to take his eyes off of her. "You're going to have to move less gracefully. It makes you stick out like a sore thumb."

"Seriously?" Sophie asked in shock.

"Yes!" they all exclaimed in unison.

"Huh," she said, deep in thought.

"Come on," Tina interrupted her. "We need to get going."

"Are you sure about this?" Ben asked, pleading one last time.

"We need this," Tina said in her motherly voice. "And nothing is going to happen to me with Sophie by my side, so please relax and focus. I need you to have my back just in case." She leaned over and kissed him gently on the lips.

"Watch yourself," James ordered as he puckered up for his own kiss.

"Who said you're getting a kiss?" Sophie laughed.

James' look of shock was priceless. Sophie smiled her Cheshire smile and kissed the man she loved with all her heart. Hopefully not for the last time.

The outside of the FBI building in Buffalo, NY was an almost "L" shaped building made of beautiful, creamed stone and tall vertical windows. The FBI symbol was prominently located off to the middle right of the front of the building, to remind you of where you were before entering. It was clean, modern, and beautiful all in one.

"Badges," said the very serious 6'3" French roasted, brown-haired muscular tree before them.

"Right here!" Tina smiled as she handed over her actual badge, and the fake one she had made for Sophie. "Just visiting from the Oklahoma office," she added. The man could have cared less. He was too busy thoroughly inspecting their badges.

Sophie tried not to fidget. She knew Tina had made sure that it would pass for the real thing, but it didn't make it any more comforting watching the stranger go through such great lengths to triple check the small plastic badge. Then again, this was national security headquarters, and they had to keep everyone safe, she reminded herself.

"Where are you headed?" he asked, his deep voice echoing in the entry way.

"The second floor to meet with Lisa Doubleman," Tina replied confidently. He looked them both up and down three times from the rims of his thick reading glasses before frowning and letting them through.

"Good grief!" hissed Sophie once they were out of ear shot.

"That's nothing," giggled Tina as they headed towards the elevator.

"Who is Lisa Doubleman?" asked Sophie.

"No clue," smiled Tina as they followed the herd in front of them into the elevator.

"What floors?" asked the short, mousy brunette that wasn't much taller than 5'3". Everyone was telling her various numbers.

"Top floor, please," Tina said politely. The girl pushed all requested numbers, and everyone rode in silence to their designated floors. Sophie knew better than to ask questions. She was in Tina's world and needed to follow her lead in order to blend in.

The elevator emptied down to just Tina, Sophie, and a male and female. Once the doors opened, Tina hit the floor in large strides and Sophie hustled to keep up with her. This was clearly "all business, Tina" from what Sophie could tell.

Tina strode with even more confidence than usual in her own work environment. Being in a different office made no difference. Tina knew these were her people, and she blended in perfectly.

Sophie was a little jealous that her friend could feel so

confident no matter what, but this was where she clearly belonged. Sophie wondered if she would ever belong anywhere outside their private club of four. She quickly shook her head to get focused on the task at hand.

Tina leaned into the opened door that was full of agent desks. "Jeanette?" she asked casually.

"Yes?" answered a blonde female of average height and build in confusion.

"Douglas wants to see you immediately in his office. He said, to give me the file you're working on that needs to go to the lab," Tina said, with authority, not even batting an eye.

"We're not supposed to meet until later..." Jeanette trailed off, in deep thought.

"I can tell him you're not ready," Tina said, shrugging her shoulders.

"No, no!" Jeanette said, hurriedly. "Here," she said, thrusting a file into Tina's hands before grabbing her own badge and rushing out of the room to the elevator.

Sophie tried not to look at Tina. She knew if she did, she would lose it. Tina was amazing! She flipped through the file for a minute or two, then started strutting through the hallway again with Sophie in tow.

"How did you know there'd be a Jeanette? Or Douglas?" Sophie asked in amazement.

"There's always a Jeanette and Douglas," Tina shrugged and headed for the lab.

Once they got to the clear door marked "Lab" Tina swiped her badge to gain access. Sophie followed her friend eagerly to see what other tricks she had up her sleeve.

"Here," Tina said, shoving the folder at the nearest lab tech. "Jeanette needs this for Douglas by this afternoon."

The 5'7" red-headed girl with thick glasses in a lab coat eyed Tina suspiciously. Her hair was in a messy bun on top of her head, and she looked as pale as Sophie and covered in freckles.

"Do you want me to tell Douglas he'll have to wait?" Tina asked, looking down at the tech. After a few seconds, the lab tech shook her head "no" and headed to her desk to get to work.

"Follow me," Tina told Sophie with the same authority she had used with the lab tech. Sophie nodded and followed suit. They headed to the back of the lab. Tina used her badge to get into the back room that looked similar to a bank vault. "We will not have a lot of time, so cover me," Tina said, a little softer as her brows frowned in concentration while she looked for whatever she needed. Sophie kept watch at the door.

"It looks like security is coming," Sophie warned after a couple of minutes.

"Got it!" Tina exclaimed, and shoved the object into the backpack on Sophie's back. Security entered before they could sneak back out.

"What are you doing in here?" demanded the gigantic tree that had checked their badges when they entered.

"Sorry," Tina giggled like a schoolgirl. "We got separated from Lisa and got all turned around. My apologies," Tina shrugged shyly.

"We don't have a Lisa Doubleman," he said, with authority.

"Oh, that's not good," said Tina, wide-eyed. "Someone by the name of Lisa Doubleman was showing us around. I don't know what's going on. You should really look into that. It's not safe for strangers to be walking around in here."

Sophie fought hard not to giggle at her friend's impressive ability to play victim suddenly. Boy, did Ben have his hands full with this one!

"You're the strangers!" the tree shouted. Sophie went to stand in front of Tina, but Tina just held her arm out so Sophie would stay in place.

"Listen," Tina said, offended. "You're welcome to call my director. She sent me here to check out the facility because you guys have been getting so much recognition for your stellar work, and she wanted me to take notes and report back. Now, I can let her know how we were treated and that you let someone that isn't even an employee show us around the facility, or we can find out who gave us the wrong name to begin with."

"We don't want to be in trouble with Oklahoma, Sir," whispered a slightly smaller guard with blonde spikey hair and a chiseled chin.

The tree stared long and hard down at Tina, who didn't budge her innocent act for even a second. Sophie heard him growl in resignation as he opened the secured door and ushered them out.

"Where else do you need to go?" the tree asked, very annoyed.

"I think we have enough, don't you, Susan?" Tina asked Sophie, who just gave a single nod of acknowledgement. "We'll let the director know the rumors are true," Tina added with a smile.

"Brian will escort you out," the tree huffed and stood with his arms crossed as poor Brian lead them all the way out the front door.

Neither said a word as they hurried across the street to catch the bus.

"Well?" they heard Ben's voice in their ears.

"She was amazing," Sophie said with pride.

"Piece of cake," Tina said with confidence. However, her face wavered a bit, showing the toll stealing from the FBI had taken on her.

Sophie put her arm around her friend as they rode the bus down a couple of blocks before hopping off and heading to the alleyway to remove their wigs and double back to the hotel.

Four

"What's all the fuss?" demanded Clarice as she entered the tech room.

At the front of the room, there was a wall made of large 43" computer monitors, each showing a different scene. Rows of metal desks and chairs lined the room, leaving two desks in the center facing the wall of monitors. One with a triple monitor setup that Eddie toggled control over everything. It was cool, dark, and the only light was provided by the various monitors in the room.

"They're in New York, Ma'am," said an eager, early twenty-something blonde agent walking up to her with a clipboard in his hands.

"Where?" Clarice snarled.

"They WERE in New York," sighed Eddie, crossing his arms in annoyance.

"Where are they NOW?" Clarice demanded. She stared down at the blonde eager agent.

"Oh, uh, we're not exactly sure, I guess," the blonde agent flustered.

Clarice whipped her head to throw daggers through her eyes at Eddie. He shook his head at both of them.

"Tina used her badge at the FBI branch," shrugged Eddie.

"What were they doing there?" Clarice hissed with a mixture of irritation and curiosity.

The blonde eager agent went to speak, but Eddie cut him off.

"She showed up with an assistant to inspect the facility for her local branch," Eddie replied, lacking any emotion.

"Sophie?" Clarice demanded more than she asked.

"Most likely," Eddie said, turning his back dangerously to Clarice to pull up the footage.

"The facial recognition didn't identify her," the blonde eager agent attempted again.

The look from both Clarice and Eddie had him retreating to the corner and keeping his mouth shut.

"Which direction?" commanded Clarice.

"They went down an alley and most likely doubled back. We have located no footage to determine which direction yet," Eddie stated flatly.

"Find her!" Clarice ordered.

"Working on it," Eddie said, with a hint of annoyance.

Clarice stormed out of the room, glaring at the eager agent as she exited.

"And that's why we don't call anyone until we have ALL of the information," Eddie said over his shoulder in irritation. This kid was going to be the death of him. Literally.

Tina tried to pretend that she was fine, but her friend knew better. Sophie sat on the bed and watched Tina work quietly at the desk on the other side of the room. Ben came in and sat next to Sophie.

"How goes it?" he asked cautiously, while he watched his wife work feverishly on the laptop.

"It's a hard place to be," whispered Sophie. "However, Tina was amazing," she said, with a smile creeping across her lips. "You would have been so proud to watch her command everyone she came across. She didn't miss a beat."

"That's my girl," Ben whispered back, full of pride.

Just then, James entered the room with a bag full of supplies.

"Thought I would grab dinner," he said, laying the bag on the table.

"Oh, COME ON!" yelled Tina out of nowhere.

Everyone rushed to her side. "What?" Sophie asked with hesitation.

"It's the second puzzle!" whined Tina.

"What?" Ben asked in confusion.

"I can't figure out what it's supposed to be!" exclaimed Tina with a bit of hysterical laughter. "It's just some random sentences. There's no digital code or anything," Tina said, throwing her hands up in the air and walking away.

"Let me take a look," said Sophie.

Together, they made little sense, but there was something about them that sounded familiar. She just couldn't put her finger on it at the moment.

"Well, that's good, right?" asked James. "We need to move tonight now that we have invaded the FBI, anyway." Tina flinched at the statement.

James hurried on. "So, at least this is something we can work on while we travel, and we can get that device thingy that we borrowed back to where it belongs, right?" James finished with a hopeful smile towards Tina.

Sophie began scribbling the information down. "I think I'm going to take this with me. There's something memorable about them. I just can't quite place from where," said Sophie, shoving the piece of paper into her pocket. "We need to leave soon," she added with a hint of urgency.

"I hope you got mine to-go," Tina said, as she packed up the laptop and grabbed her bag. "I have a bus to catch," she sighed with frustration.

James got her a bag to-go while Tina carefully put the device into an envelope with the address to Jeanette. She figured it was the least she could do for most likely ruining her afternoon at work. Tina handed it over to Ben.

"Drop this off at the front desk please, Babe," she stated before giving him one last longing kiss. "See you on the other side," Tina said, winking before going out the front door.

"See you on the other side," Ben called after her. He ate quietly with his friends for about 45 minutes before grabbing his own bag.

"See you on the other side," Ben said, waving to them and went out the door, dropped off the package at the front desk for his wife, and headed in the opposite direction once he got outside.

Sophie sighed heavily. James got off the bed and held out his hand to her. "What?" she laughed.

"Come here," James said with his boyish grin that could make her do anything.

Sophie pushed off the bed and took his hand. He pulled Sophie into his arms and began slow dancing with her in the middle of the hotel room floor. James hummed gently as he occasionally kissed her on the top of her head.

Sophie giggled. "You're mad," she laughed.

"Mad for you," James said, smiling against her hair and kissing her again.

"Do you wonder what your life would be like if we had never met?" Sophie asked quietly.

"Nope," James said, and continued to hum as he danced with her.

"Why not?" Sophie asked, pulling away to look him in the face.

"Because I already know what my life was like without you," James said, smiling. "And I hated it," he winked before tipping her head back to kiss her passionately.

"You need to go," Sophie whispered when they came up for air.

James sighed. "Okay," he said, smiling and shrugging. He grabbed his own bag and threw it over his shoulder. "I miss you already," he said, kissing her gently.

"See you on the other side," Sophie whispered, smiling against his lips.

"You'd better," James winked back, walked out the front door, and headed for the bus station.

He hated leaving her. He knew it's how it had to be. Yet, the life was always sucked right out of him the second he closed the door. James was dying to ask Sophie to marry him, but he knew she had to be ready too. He hoped she would get there soon as he bought his ticket and climbed aboard.

Sophie looked around the room. Only her bag remained. She used to be fine traveling alone. Since meeting her new family, she always felt empty when they separated. Sophie wasn't entirely sure if keeping them close was selfish or what was keeping them safe. All she knew was that they had changed her life forever.

Sophie threw on the hoodie that James gave her on their first date and breathed in his scent. She tossed her own bag on her back and looked around the room.

"Goodbye, Bill," she whispered. "I miss you."

Sophie pulled the hood over her head, climbed out onto the fire escape, slid down the railing, and landed gracefully, like a cat, to the ground. She looked carefully around before strolling down the back alley on her way to the train station.

James watched the rain beat against the bus window as it traveled late into the night. He held his bag firmly close to him and jumped when he felt it vibrate against him. James scrambled to grab the burner phone that was currently going off. "Hello?" he asked, full of confusion and fear.

"Jamie, it's Mom," he heard Sally's voice come through the other end.

"What's wrong?" James asked in panic.

"We're fine, Dear," Sally assured. "We have to return to the states. Your father has to give the keynote address at the national conference this year."

"Okay," James said, patiently waiting for the other shoe to drop.

"It's a masquerade party on Halloween in New Orleans," Sally stated matter-of-fact. James didn't respond. "We will get you guys the invitations to get in."

"Mom, I don't think we should..." James started, but was cut off immediately.

"Jamie," Sally stated more sternly. "We haven't even gotten to talk to you in months, and a mother needs to see her children and know they are safe," she said firmly.

"Mom," James tried again.

"Have you asked her yet?" Sally asked, quickly changing the subject.

"How did you know?" James asked in shock.

"A mother always knows," Sally chuckled. "Why do you think your dad put your grandmother's ring in the bag for you?"

"There hasn't exactly been a good time," James sighed.

"Jamie, in this situation, the timing will never be good," Sally stated bluntly.

"She's not ready, Mom," James replied more firmly.

"How do you know until you ask?" Sally meddled.

"Mom, I have to go," James sighed, shaking his head.

"Alright, Son," Sally conceded. "We'll see you in New Orleans on Halloween."

The phone went dead before James could protest. He turned off the phone and put it back in his bag. How the heck were they going to pull off seeing his parents for Halloween?

Granted, the masquerade lent good coverage, and it would be nice to do something normal and in public for a change without worrying about being caught on tape. The right mask would keep them safe. Besides, Sally wouldn't stop until she got her way, and her calls alone would put them at risk.

James sighed and pulled the phone back out. He typed a quick message and pressed the send button before putting the phone back in his bag. Now, to figure out how he was going to get the girls' dresses for the ball.

Sophie bought her ticket for the train and climbed aboard. She was thankful to see the cars mostly empty as she worked her way back to the last car. A mother held onto her sleeping daughter towards the front, and a man more interested in his paper than his surroundings sat by the window in the middle of the car.

Sophie passed them all quietly and picked a seat by the window in the very back. It was the perfect place to watch what came at her and giving her a quick exit to her back if needed.

She slid down into the seat, thankful to find it very comfortable. It surprised Sophie when she felt her bag vibrate against her. She quickly scrambled to pull out the burner phone buried inside.

See you in New Orleans on Halloween. Explain later. -J

"What the heck?" Sophie said out loud.

The man lowered his paper and gave her a glare before going back to his paper.

Sophie knew James wouldn't change the plan unless it was necessary. She was dying to call him directly, but communication needed to be limited. She looked out the window as the train pulled away from the station.

Sophie was supposed to head to Atlanta, GA to draw any team away from New York. There was no way of getting around having to use Tina's badge at the FBI headquarters, and Sophie knew the man with the cane would be hot on their trail. She needed to get them going in the wrong direction.

Would Atlanta be far enough away if they are to be in New Orleans by Halloween? Sophie watched the buildings whiz by and contemplated her options.

It was definitely a different pace to be traveling with three other people versus being alone. Sophie deliberated often if she was actually keeping them safe or putting them in more danger. Was her motive to stay together purely selfish? Probably. It was nice knowing that she wasn't alone anymore. She honestly wasn't sure she could go back to it.

Sophie closed her eyes to view the map of the United States in her mind and quickly calculated where to go to draw them in the wrong direction that would still get her back to New Orleans in time for Halloween. The vision of James tipping a cowboy hat at her made Sophie giggle out loud. She covered her mouth immediately and got a second glare from the man with the paper. Nashville, Tennessee it was.

Sophie closed her eyes again and rested her head on the seat as she quickly drifted into darkness.

Darkness surrounded Sophie. No wooden door appeared. Something wasn't right. Her senses were in overdrive.

"Mom? Dad?" she called out. Sophie got no response.

There was a soft, dark, and almost evil chuckle coming from in front of her. Sophie took a step towards the sound when she felt a small hand slide into her own and tug on her arm.

"Don't!" her mini me yelled, glaring into the darkness ahead.

"What is it?" Sophie asked her.

"Nothing good," the little girl muttered.

Sophie could feel the little girl's tension radiate through her own adult body down to the tips of her toes. The evil laugh was growing louder. Sophie went to take a step again and was yanked back by the little girl.

"There's no door," the little girl demanded, as if that was to clear everything up for Sophie. She looked at the little girl, full of confusion. "There has to be a door," stated the little girl without taking her eyes off of whatever lied ahead.

"What if it's mom?" Sophie asked her as a sickness consumed her being.

"That's not mother," the little girl stated defiantly, never taking her eyes off the darkness ahead.

Sophie went to pull her hand away and go see if she could save her mother when she heard Jess's voice come from behind her.

"No, Peanut," Jess pleaded.

Sophie turned around immediately and saw her mother standing behind her with a skeletal hand on her shoulder. Sophie went to run towards her, but the quick nod from her mother had her stopping in her tracks.

"What's going on?" Sophie asked in a panic as fear consumed her body. "Where's dad?" she demanded.

"I don't know," Jess answered honestly. "You cannot go into the darkness," she pleaded desperately. "Nothing good is down there."

"I don't understand!" Sophie cried as she became overwhelmed with emotions.

"Calm down, Peanut," her mother soothed. "You must not go anywhere without a door," her mother stated firmly. "Do you understand me?" It was the same urgency she heard from her mother when promising to hide in the closet before the man with the cane murdered them.

"And watch you die again? No!" Sophie shouted.

The skeletal hand gripped tighter on her mother's shoulder, and Jess surrendered into the pain. Sophie went to run to her, but Jess shoved out her hand and blinded Sophie with a stream of light. Sophie stumbled backwards and nearly fell on top of the little girl.

"Sophie Lee," her mother ordered. "You must not go anywhere without a door," Jess stated firmly. "Do you understand me?" she commanded.

"Yes," Sophie said, still rubbing the light from her eyes.

"Get some sleep," Jess sighed. "You need the rest."

"Mom," Sophie pleaded. "What's going on?"

"We're sorting that out at the moment," Jess half lied. She honestly didn't know what was going on. "Please," she pleaded to Sophie. "Rest. We'll be with you soon."

Jess looked down at the skeletal hand on her shoulder that seemed to signal for them both to disappear.

"Mom!" Sophie yelled. The little girl grabbed her arm and wouldn't let her move.

"There's no door," the little girl whispered. "We can't go."

"What's going on?!" Sophie demanded to the little girl, but she looked blankly back at Sophie and shrugged her shoulders. She wiggled her finger for Sophie to bend down to her level, so she bent down to look the little girl in the eyes.

The little girl gently touched her on the forehead, and with no chance to protest, Sophie was forced into a deep, peaceful slumber. She would not remember the darkness. She would not remember the wicked laugh that seemed to call to her. She would not remember her mother being controlled by a skeletal hand that didn't seem to be attached to anything. The only thing she would remember would be the warning that was given with significant force.

You must not go anywhere without a door....

Five

Jack paced anxiously in the solid darkness, keeping his eyes on the floor. The black fog danced around his feet as he waited to go before the council.

"Come," a tall, cloaked figure ordered.

Jack followed nervously behind, not daring to look up. He took his place in front of the council once more.

"Jessica Harris broke one of the sacred rules of this realm," boomed the center and tallest figure of them all.

"We are aware, and give our deepest apologies," Jack stated, keeping his focus on the floor out of both fear and respect.

"Deliberation is complete," howled the figure furthest to the left. "We will return your wife."

Jack jerked his head up immediately to look at the twelve cloaked figures before him. Once the shock had passed, he dropped his head once more.

"I'm ready," Jack said, solemnly.

"That's not necessary," hissed the figured on the far right. "There's more pressing matters at stake."

Jack stared at the floor, unsure if what he had just heard was correct.

"They will be the destruction of us all!" shrieked another on the left.

"It is not their doing," warned the center figure. "It's the living forcing their way in. He is to blame."

Jack jerked his head up once more, and his stomach dropped as if he was riding a roller coaster that had just plummeted towards the ground.

"What does he want?" shrilled another figure on the right towards Jack.

"It's not possible," Jack whispered to himself.

"What does he WANT?!" screamed the figure again at Jack.

"Our daughter," Jack said, shaking his head into focus. "That is why my wife and I remain in this realm."

"We must force him to stop!" screamed another figure.

"Let him have the girl!" demanded another.

"You cannot!" hollered Jack as he reached out his hands in his plea. "If he gets her, all realms will be destroyed," he added quickly. "He follows no rules, let alone respects those in place. No one will be safe. Not even you," Jack asserted.

"No one can harm us!" boomed another figure.

However, the center figure tilted his hooded head in what Jack hoped was consideration of what he was telling them.

"He will not stop once he has our daughter," Jack said slowly. "You know her powers. If he can control her, not even death is safe."

Arguing erupted before him, shaking the ground and nearly knocking Jack off his feet, but he remained steady with his eyes locked on their hooded figures.

"This is NOT our mess!" one finally declared.

"You brought this upon us!" yelled another. "You fix it!"

"How am I to do that?" asked Jack in desperation.

"It is not our concern," rumbled another.

"He will break the rules," pleaded Jack. "It may take breaking them to resolve this in return," Jack warned.

"Then pay the price when all is done!" boomed another.

"Please!" begged Jack. "If we're to break the rules to save you, should we not be spared?"

"We have already spared you once!" demanded another.

"The counsil has spoken!" announced the last figure on the left. "You are dismissed!"

The black figures faded away. Jack noticed the center figure remained in hesitation before disappearing with the others. Jack could only hope that it was the one that understood fully what was to come. He could only hope that maybe it would come to favor his wife and his own fate when all was said and done.

First, Jack needed to talk to an old friend without breaking the rules. There was no need being punished before Sophie could be saved. Jack turned on his heels and ran into the darkness ahead of him.

Sophie woke up just in time to change trains and head to Nashville, Tennessee. She made sure to get caught on the occasional camera to help direct the current blood hounds that hid somewhere behind computer monitors, watching her every move. When they could see her, that was.

Sophie smiled her Cheshire grin to herself. She bought two tickets and headed for the ladies' rest room. She brushed her hair in the mirror and waited patiently for the train to board.

The ticket master held out his hand once she stepped on, and Sophie placed the ticket for Montana into his hand before she headed to the back of the train. She quietly slipped off undetected through the back door, and boarded the opposite train on the platform to find her usual seat in the back. No need to show them where she was headed before she could actually get there.

Sophie pulled out the paper with the random sentences scribbled on it. She knew them all, yet she did not know from where exactly. She scanned her memory of the billions of books she had read over her lifetime, only still to remain blank on their origin.

Frustrated, Sophie folded up the piece of paper and put it back into her bag. An unusual chill ran down her spine. Something else had happened to her recently, but all she could remember was a statement:

You must not go anywhere without a door....

Seemed like an odd thing to have stuck on her brain. She had only ever seen a door before passing through to see memories or visit her parents when they could come to her. Sophie shook her head and shoulders to shake off the unwanted chill, leaned back, and rested her eyes. It was a long ride to Nashville, and she had to make sure she got caught on as many cameras as possible before she disappeared to head to New Orleans. Sophie wasn't sure what was coming. Something told her to rest as much as she could. So, she did just that.

Ben surprised himself when he was the first to arrive in New Orleans, but then again, he had been the closest when they received James' text message. Ben knew he would be in charge of finding them a place to hide out since this was not a preplanned scheduled stop, so he scouted for the best location to keep them together without being detected.

He was proud of himself and felt like he was getting quite the hang of this "living life on the run." Although he was pretty sure his future job offers wouldn't quite feel the same way.

Ben also worried about Tina's job. He was sure breaking into the Buffalo office would carry great consequences for his wife, but Tina had insisted that she had it all covered.

Not that he regretted helping Sophie. She was the sister Ben had never had. Their sacrifices would never outweigh hers of keeping them all safe from the douche bag man with the cane. Ben knew that and never complained.

He was also very excited to see his best friend find the love of his life finally. Helen had done such a number on James. Ben hadn't cared for her since the beginning, but you can't tell love where it should go.

Ben believed deeply in fate and knew that heartbreak led James to Sophie. She was the best fit for James, even if he wasn't eager to admit it in the beginning. Ben just hoped that they would outlive all of this so James and Sophie could settle down and be a family like James always dreamt about.

James never mentioned the ring in the bag. Ben already knew it had been in there for a while. He also knew that James was respectfully waiting for Sophie to catch up to his feelings, which Ben agreed was best for everyone.

However, there were things about Sophie that even Sophie didn't realize herself. The girl had been genetically altered. Ben just wasn't a hundred percent sure how. She mentioned receiving a ton of shots as a kid, but the alterations that he had noted couldn't have happened through simple shots alone. Her DNA had been altered completely, and that could only have happened during gestation.

Ben hadn't discussed his suspicions with his wife. That was because he knew he didn't have to. Tina saw what he saw. She trusted Ben to get to the bottom of it and let them know what he found out.

However, Jessica Harris was a ghost that couldn't be tracked. There was no way of knowing Sophie's past, because only Jack's scholarly accomplishments were recorded. An impressive amount at that, but too many things didn't add up.

Ben knew it was driving his wife just as crazy as it was him. Clearly, animal genes had been added to Sophie's own makeup, but Ben did not know how many had been added, or to what extent. There was no tracking down Jess to ask her what she knew, yet he wondered if it was by the man with the cane or some other sick soul that they may not even know about.

Ben shook his head and checked into the Olivier House Hotel. In the heart of the French Quarter, the hotel was a deep red wine color, with white doors and black shutters to protect it against oncoming hurricanes. Three stories high, with white laced balconies and large green plants hanging over each door from the outside. Once in the room, he pulled out the burner phone and texted the address with nothing else and pressed send.

Ben looked around and appreciated the security that the inner brick walls provided against passing storms. The hotel had survived everything thrown at it since 1836, and the carpet and furniture looked like it hadn't been upgraded in decades based on the floral patterns. It should be easy to hide in plain sight in the French Quarter on a holiday that gave them perfect cover by hiding behind masks.

He knew exactly what James was up to. Ben was well aware of the doctor's annual national convention. He was also aware that this was most likely Sally's idea more than Roger's. However, it would be a great place to locate some people that might be able to give them answers to Sophie's origin.

In the meantime, Halloween would be here in two days, and they would need dresses, suits, and masks. Ben grabbed his wallet, put the hood of his jacket up to not only hide but fight off the chill, and went to search for suitable costumes.

Tina beat James to the hotel. She knew Sophie would arrive

last. Knowing Sophie, she most likely headed somewhere other than Atlanta, Georgia, to give them more space between the blood hounds and them. Tina was curious where she went, that allowed her enough time to get back to them. She was also curious to know what James had up his sleeve to be changing course in the middle of the game.

Tina saw Ben's bag and shook her head before putting her own on the bed. They had two separate rooms again, so Tina explored her own surroundings. She had never been to New Orleans.

Although living on the run was stressful, it was an excuse to get her traveling again. Since she had worked at the FBI, traveling hadn't been much of an option outside of her yearly summer trip to the Moore's.

Tina slumped down on the bed. Thinking about the FBI made her sick to her stomach. She remembered the day they had recruited her, well before she was due to even graduate college. Tina had always been a wiz with whatever her fingers touched. Puzzles were her specialty, and the FBI drooled over that fact.

She had finally felt like she belonged with her lab crew, instead of being a complete outcast for being way too smart for her own good. Ben and James had been the only ones to never allow her to feel like an outcast with her overactive brain.

Tina spent most of her childhood making sure the other two clowns stayed out of trouble. Ben had been really shy back then, minus his time with James. James was the only one that seemed to break Ben out of his shell instantly. Tina had to earn the right.

Tina, of course, had feelings for him long before he was ready. However, she had patiently waited for him to catch up. She knew from their first accidental kiss they would be together for life. She also knew she would always be ahead of the boys, maturity wise, and so Tina bit her tongue and waited for Ben to realize what she had already known since they were six years old.

Tina had never been more thankful than when he finally did. They dated through most of high school and remained sweethearts as they both excelled through college, ahead of the typical schedule of most college students. Everyone had given them grief for getting married so soon, but when you know you've found your soulmate, why wait? Their wedding was small, intimate, and the best day of her life.

She only wanted the same for James. Nevertheless, when he settled for Helen, Tina had to do the most faking she had ever done in her life. That girl was nothing but a spoiled brat. Helen put up a good front. However, all she wanted was to spend someone else's money, even though she had plenty of her own.

Helen used people until she was bored. Luckily for James, she grew bored before he was stuck with her for life. It's just a shame she purposely waited until their wedding day to let him loose. Tina would never forgive her for the heartbreak she caused James.

Like her husband, Tina knew fate had bigger and better things for her friend. She did not know it would come in the package of Sophie. It surprised Tina that it took no thinking about throwing away everything she had worked for to help Sophie out, but that was the power of Sophie. She never asked Tina to. Tina was fine doing it all the same.

She also knew of the engagement ring James hid in his bag for her. This was the family she had always wished for the four of them. Tina, like the boys, was waiting for Sophie to come to the same conclusion.

It wasn't Sophie's fault, though. The girl had been through more than any of them would ever be able to imagine. Tina's heart broke more for Sophie than it did for herself and her silly FBI job.

Sophie was special. Ben had never told her exactly how special, but Tina knew it was because he was still trying to piece his own puzzle together. No normal human could do half the things Sophie succeeded at.

She heard what no one could hear. She moved like a cat more than a human. Sophie was faster at everything she did, both mentally and physically. Tina had never struggled to keep up with someone mentally before. Sophie had been the first to give her a run for her money. Tina knew there was more to discover about how special Sophie was exactly, but the bigger question was why and by whom?

Then there was the issue with the key they had found. Tina realized long ago that Jack was also a very intelligent man. Definitely giving Sophie an added advantage over most on normal circumstances. Then again, so many things didn't add up about her own puzzle.

Why give Sophie something to carry for life that wasn't complete? Was she not supposed to carry it the whole time? Or was it supposed to be a bargaining chip during desperate times? Or did Jack not have enough time to complete his plans before he was murdered?

Despite her best efforts, Tina knew little about the man with the cane. He didn't seem to be the kind of man that gave up. At all. And he clearly wanted Sophie more than anything.

For Tina, too many questions remained unanswered. Jack was extremely smart. Too smart for his own good, like Tina. Surely there was more to this puzzle. She just hadn't found the other pieces yet.

Jack also knew the man with the cane would never stop coming for Sophie. Tina knew Jack had Sophie altered out of love. She couldn't blame him for that. He had designed her to survive anything thrown at her, but Jack also made sure it wasn't an obvious alteration, either. Sophie still took time to heal, which would help keep her undetected by a typical doctor if she landed in one's hands.

Tina suddenly felt exhaustion consume her. She laid back onto the bed and found darkness once her head hit the pillow.

It shocked Tina when she opened her eyes to darkness minus the wooden door before her.

"Open it," she heard a strange female voice call to her.

Tina hesitated and looked around, but saw no one.

"You're safe," the voice called to her softly. "Open it," the voice repeated. "For Sophie."

Tina reached out and opened the door. Instantly, she was engulfed by a flood of bright light. She covered her eyes and waited for them to adjust.

"Hello, Tina," a shadow figure spoke as it stood before her.

"How do you know my name?" Tina asked in frustration, unable to focus on the figure before her. Her eyes seemed to take forever to adjust.

"I know you, because you help to keep my daughter safe," the female voice said softly as Tina felt a soft hand reach out and remove Tina's hand from her eyes. A beautiful woman, who was the spitting image of Sophie in so many ways, was smiling back at her.

"Jess?" Tina said in much disbelief. Clearly, she was having an intense dream, or she had officially lost her mind.

"Yes, Dear," Jess replied softly.

"How is this happening?" Tina asked as her brain tried to rationalize what was happening.

"Let's just say that occasionally even death allows us to help the living," Jess smiled back at Tina and headed to the kitchen, that seemed to appear out of thin air behind her. Tina slowly followed her.

"Is this about the key?" Tina asked. "I'm working as fast as I can, but all we found were random sentences that don't seem to go to anything."

Jess shook her head as she poured hot water from the kettle that had whistled out of nowhere. "Jack did always love his puzzles," Jess chuckled.

Sadness fleeted across her face for a split second before being masked with another smile. This one less genuine.

"Why am I here?" Tina asked, sitting down at the table before her as Jess set down a cup of tea for each of them. Jess held her cup to her lips and blew the steam away.

"Because something is coming that I don't think even Jack and I can help her conquer, and we're going to need your help," Jess said, with a now weary smile.

"Is it the man with the cane?" Tina asked with renewed focus.

Jess noticed no one had spoken his name and knew it wasn't her truth to tell, so she just simply nodded.

"Who is he?" Tina questioned.

"A very mad and determined man that will stop at nothing until he has Sophie under his control," Jess said, with much anger in her voice.

"WHO is he?" Tina tried again.

"He will let you know soon enough," Jess said, as her eyes glazed over into emptiness.

"Why not just tell me?" Tina demanded in frustration.

"Because there are rules, and I have already broken one. I will not get a second pardon, and Sophie will pay the price," Jess said sternly. "Do you want that?"

Tina looked at the untouched tea before her. "Of course not," she resigned.

"Jack gave her his own puzzle pieces to help keep her safe," Jess continued, trying to sound less harsh. "I know you're the puzzle queen, so be sure to solve those for her and help her with the tools she needs."

"You didn't have to pull me into...this," Tina stated, waving her hand at the dream kitchen that currently surrounded her. "I would have done that, anyway."

"I know, Honey," Jess assured as she lifted her eyes back up to meet Tina's. "That's not the only reason you're here," Jess said, looking down at her tea again.

Tina stared at the ghost before her and knew whatever was on Jess' mind was big enough to scare her. Dead or not. And if it scared death, it had to be serious. She remained quiet and waited for Jess to confess whatever she felt she needed to.

"Something terrible is coming. I'm not sure what exactly, but it's going to take all of you to help fight it," Jess continued. "Jack and I will do what we can from our end. Although lines have already been drawn, I'm doing my best to blur them and get you more help," Jess rushed on. "Jack is looking into the specifics to see what he can figure out in the meantime."

Jess turned the cup round and round again in her hands, obviously bothered. Tina reached over to touch her hand gently and felt nothing but amazing warmth when she did.

"It might mean we have to break rules that will bear serious consequences," Jess said, biting her lip and blinking away the tears that threatened to form in her eyes. Suddenly, she looked up at Tina with urgency. "No matter what happens, I need you to promise me you will always stand by her. No matter what happens. In case Jack and I are unable." The last part came out as a broken whisper.

"No matter what," Tina promised as her heart broke for the ghost before her. Jess smiled weakly back at Tina.

"They will toy with her. They will make her second guess her choices and she may even lose her way," Jess said, more firmly setting the lukewarm tea down on the table. "They thrive on the cat-and-mouse chase and will fight dirty. Physically and mentally," Jess warned. A chill went down Tina's back.

"So how do we beat this asshole?" Tina asked, full of commitment and determination.

"He will never stop," Jess said, as her eyes turned the deepest shade of black Tina had ever seen.

"Death it is," Tina said, understanding immediately.

"It won't be so easy," Jess said, in more of a growl than anything. "He has no conscious. He has no soul. He knows nothing of love. First thing first. Solve the key. My husband gave it to her for a reason. That puzzle I cannot help with," Jess added, looking down at the table again.

"I will," Tina confirmed, once again laying her hand over the ghost that felt more real at this very moment than her own touch.

Jess jerked her head up and looked over her shoulder. "Don't let James lose faith," she added without turning her head back. "Go now," Jess ordered.

She quickly faced Tina, reached out to touch her lightly on the forehead, and forced Tina back through the door as it slammed shut before her face. Tina woke up gasping for air.

"Hey," Ben said in concern as he rushed over to her and stroked her arm. "You okay?"

Tina blinked her eyes several times as they focused back on the reality before her. She turned to look at her husband.

"We need to solve both our puzzles, Ben," Tina said in alarm. "The man with the cane is coming for her, and she's going to need all the tools we have given her to fight."

"What do you….?" Ben trailed off as he studied his wife with grave concern. He had never seen her so agitated before in the entire time of knowing her.

"We need to keep this quiet for the time being," Tina added, challenging him to silence, knowing her husband would want to share with his friend.

"Tina, what's going on?" Ben ordered.

"I don't know," Tina answered honestly. "But it was bad enough for Jess to haul me into a one-on-one conversation, and even death is nervous about what that asshole has planned for Sophie." Tina swallowed the lump in her throat and took Ben's hands in her own. "So, let's find out what gifts Sophie truly has so we can beat him once and for all," she said, staring at Ben intently.

He knew better than to question his wife on a normal day. And this was far from normal.

"On it." Ben finally nodded in confirmation. "I'm pretty sure we're here to attend the doctor's national annual ball, per Sally's request. I got the tuxes and masks, so when you're up to it, I will leave the gowns to you," Ben winked at his wife, knowing that she loved shopping almost as much as she loved her puzzles. The break would allow her mind to flow more freely as an added bonus.

Tina smiled and held out her hand for the black credit card that had a bogus name and plenty of money that the dresses they required wouldn't even make a dent. Ben chuckled and shook his head. He was glad that she was getting color back into her cheeks.

Ben could no longer question the existence of ghosts. He had already been visited by one himself and was told not to mention it. Jack had reached out to Ben while he was on his way to New Orleans. It was brief, and the message urgent as well.

"Find Dr. Corbin Dallas, and Edward Sterling," Jack pleaded once he had convinced Ben to open the wooden door before him.

"Who?" Ben asked in confusion.

"Dr. Corbin Dallas and Edward Sterling," Jack repeated, looking constantly over his shoulder. Something had him terrified. Even Ben could tell. "Please, Benjamin," Jack begged. "For Sophie."

Then he had touched Ben's forehead lightly and pushed him back through the door as the door slammed in front of him.

Ben had woken up instantly confused, trying to determine what he had eaten before he had fallen asleep on the bus. "For Sophie," Jack's voice echoed in Ben's ears. It sent shivers down his spine and made his blood go cold.

Ben had been studying up on the powers of dreams since Sophie had first mentioned the wooden door. Dr. Corbin Dallas was what some called an oneironaut. A person who could supposedly control the dream world, especially through lucid dreams. Ben had found the doctor title to be laughable until he looked into Dr. Dallas' credentials, which contained much more than just some "dream walker."

He had a few PHDs that included psychiatry and neurology, although Ben did not know how he had found the time to accomplish so much at a very young age. In fact, he was getting lost in Dr. Dallas' credentials when Tina had stirred from her nap. Ben had figured she was just tired from all the traveling and stress of breaking into the FBI. Knowing it was a ghost visit, he knew first-hand how much energy it took from the living to speak with the dead.

It was hard for the logical doctor's side of Ben's brain to register, but a previous visit from a dead grandmother at an early age had already proven that the dead never truly leave us. Even if the logical side laughed at him for believing such things.

Science was great for explaining a lot of things. Ben was very well aware that it didn't explain everything, though. No matter how hard it tried.

Ben opened up the laptop again since his wife was out enjoying herself and getting needed supplies. He had already concluded that both Dr. Corbin Dallas and Dr. Elaine Cox would attend the conference, with Dr. Moore giving the keynote address.

There was no Dr. Edward Sterling, however. There was barely an Edward Sterling at all that he could find that would remotely fit into Sophie's puzzle. A dentist didn't exactly strike him as a player of the game. Then a memory floated back to him.

"My mother's name was Jess, and my dad's name was Jack,"

Sophie had said with a smile. "There was a boy named Edward. I've only seen him once, though, so I don't really know much about him."

The only thing Sophie could remember about Edward was that her father was very protective of him. Jack had asked Sophie to keep Edward safe before Sophie had turned into a mark and her parents were murdered. She had thought he was an orphan of some sort. He was smaller than most kids and came from a very poor family with an abusive foster dad.

"Great," Ben muttered.

A kid with that kind of background rarely held on to his first name, let alone his last. It was a coping mechanism for those that were continually running from a damaging past.

"Edward Sterling," he heard Jack's voice whisper in his ears once more.

"That doesn't exactly narrow it down, my friend," Ben shouted to no one. When silence remained, he sighed and closed the laptop as James came running through the door.

"Where's Sophie?" James demanded, trying to catch his breath.

"Messing with the blood hounds before heading back, I imagine," Ben said, turning to study the urgency radiating from his friend. "What's wrong?"

"Something big is coming," James wheezed as he tried to catch his breath from running all the way from the bus station.

"Yeah, we already know," Ben said, standing up and going to sit on the bed. James looked at him in confusion. "You're not the only one dead people visit," he added with a shrug. "So let's figure out how the heck we're going to sneak into this ball and corner some doctors to get some answers."

James opened his mouth to speak, but at a loss for words, he closed it again. He tossed his bag on the floor, pulled out a notebook and pen, and sat down next to his friend.

"Looks like we're breaking into the Morial Convention Center. Mom's sending us passes to get through the front," James said, as he started drawing a rough draft of the building. He had studied it all the way to the Louisiana state line before Jess made a brief appearance.

She warned James that his love for Sophie most likely will be tested, and he needed to decide immediately if he was up for defending it to keep it. James stated, without hesitation, that he was more than ready to fight for Sophie and their love. However, even James could tell the ghost was extremely rattled and scared of whatever seemed to hide behind her.

"Hey," Ben said, breaking James from his wondering thoughts. "With the dead and the living working together, the asshole won't get anywhere near her," Ben assured.

"I know," James replied, trying to regain his focus. "I'm just concerned that even death is scared," he said, truthfully.

"It's unnerving. I'll give you that," Ben said, honestly. "Nothing has had to deal with us as a team either," he winked at his friend. James chuckled lightly, although doubt filled his head and heart.

"I see three possible exits," Ben started, pointing out to get his friend refocused. He wasn't sure they would all survive, but Ben knew love and family were a power to be reckoned with. That's what he had to put his faith in front and let science back them up when needed.

Six

Sophie grabbed her bag and exited the train. She had an uneventful rest all the way to Nashville. She hoped her parents were okay. If having them talk to her signified she had completely lost her mind, then Sophie was okay being crazy if it meant she still had them with her. She tried to shake off the chill that remained under her skin.

Time was running out, and Sophie needed to make sure she got back in time to meet the others in New Orleans. She pulled back her hood before she exited, showing more of her face while keeping her vibrant red hair hidden.

The chill nipped at Sophie's cheeks. A sign that the seasons had definitely changed. Summer was long gone, and the trees were already beautiful oranges, golds, and reds. Something wasn't right. Sophie could feel a shift, but she couldn't place where it had taken place.

Thinking of Tina, she headed downtown to pretend to shop and take in the sights. Sophie knew any team would be far enough away to allow her to take a second to breathe. She also knew better than to savor the moment.

Like most downtowns, Nashville had a promise of busy life and shopping with country music humming in the background as a reminder of what the city was known for. Almost every shop had a gigantic neon sign hanging above it, begging for people to come in. From cowboys to guitars, to everything in between, each sign trying to gain your attention and desire to enter. At night, they would light this part of town up with bright lights and music blaring from within, enticing the prey to enter their establishment for a good time.

Sophie weaved in and out of stores and restaurants, giving the illusion she was on a hunt for something specific. This mouse always had to make sure she wasn't just blindly following the scent of cheese in this cat-and-mouse game.

She was sure someone smart enough would have noticed by now that Sophie was only seen when she chose to be seen, but the teams still came with the promise of catching her, blinding their ability to see the whole picture. Like so many of the people who had crossed her path.

Sophie couldn't really blame any of them. She inherited her mother's ability to have laser focus. It took her a few years to widen the picture like her father. Balance. Her mother constantly harped on her about needing to have balance.

Sophie would gladly take to hearing her mother's lectures

again in person at this moment. She kicked at the pebbles that seemed to find their way onto the sidewalk. Most likely pushed by the street cleaners.

She quietly hummed the song her father used to sing to her as she weaved in and out of the unknowing crowd. Halloween decorations were up, and costumes hung in the storefront windows, whispering urgently for the passersby to come in and purchase them. Some people already wore costumes and performed on the streets. Sophie could only imagine the chaos New Orleans would provide. Still, it was a brilliant cover for getting out and doing something normal for a change.

The watch on Sophie's wrist buzzed, reminding her to work her way to the bus station and using the shadows to her advantage. She quietly slipped into the Hard Rock Café. Aromas of greasy cheeseburgers and fried foods tickled at her nose. Unfortunately, there was no time to sit and eat. Sophie pulled the hood further over her face and headed to the lady's restroom.

Taking James' hoodie off, she placed it back into her bag and pulled out her black hooded jacket. She was going to have to invest in heavier clothes before winter.

"If you make it that long," whispered a wicked voice from inside her head.

Sophie froze and looked around her. She heard a door suddenly slam close, but she couldn't see what door had been forced shut. All the stalls were empty, and the bathroom door was a swinging door that could not be slammed. Sophie looked at her own scared reflection in the mirror.

"Go, Peanut," she heard her father's voice urge her on wearily.

Sophie quickly fastened the bag, slid it back on her back, and snuck out the bathroom window completely unnoticed.

An entire day had come and gone, and Sophie was still MIA. James had an uncomfortable feeling stirring in the pit of his stomach. Tina and Ben continued to work on their puzzle pieces while James was forced to sit and wait. It wasn't something he did well. The sun was going down quickly, and a chill whipped around the French Quarter, reminding everyone that fall had long taken over for summer.

He knew this would give his mother some peace, but the air definitely felt different, and James wasn't entirely sure it was the best idea to be so public, even with the masks on. One thing he could agree on was the mouth drooling food this town offered. Ben had collected a feast of food, guessing Sophie would be famished by the time she arrived. And he was correct.

Sophie slid into Ben and Tina's room, with her stomach growling loudly in response to the intoxicating smells that came from the small desk set up in the corner. James knew better than to stop her when hunger hit her this badly. He had stopped pacing the floor and smiled as he watched Sophie drop her bag and head straight for the food waiting for her.

"Nice to see you too," laughed Tina, as she prepared a proper plate for her friend instead of Sophie just grabbing everything with her craving fingers.

"Sorry," Sophie mumbled with cornbread falling out of her mouth. "It's been a while."

Her friends gave her a few minutes to stuff her face before asking her questions.

"So, where did you end up going?" Tina asked.

"Nashville," Sophie said, in between bites.

"Why Nashville?" Ben asked with curiosity.

Sophie giggled and blushed when she looked at James. "I had a vision of James acting like a cowboy," she said, sheepishly. "I figured it was a sign." Everyone busted out laughing. "So why are we here?" Sophie asked once her stomach was satisfied, and her friends had stopped rolling around in laughter.

"The doctor's national annual convention is here tomorrow," James said. "My dad's giving the keynote and my mother all but demanded a meeting," James said, with concern creeping into his voice.

"We need to go anyway," Ben inserted. "There's some people we need to talk to."

"Like who?" Sophie asked, intrigued.

Ben could not look Sophie in the eyes and began shuffling his feet, making the entire room uncomfortable. "Sophie," Ben said, in hesitation. "We need to talk."

Even Sophie got nervous. "What's going on?" she asked, looking nervously from face to face.

James and Tina took their usual spots next to Sophie. Although James wasn't sure where this was going, he could tell it was important to Ben. He just worried about the "why" behind it being such a struggle to get out.

Tina broke the silence to help her husband out. "Honey," she started as she pulled Sophie's hands into her own. "You know you're a very special girl, right?" Tina said, slowly.

"I mean, isn't everyone special?" Sophie replied in complete confusion about where exactly this would be going.

"True," Tina stated in her calming, motherly voice. "But you are more special than others."

"If you're talking about all the key junk," Sophie replied, "that doesn't make me more special than you. It just means I have an insane psychopath that wants it. That doesn't exactly make me special. It just means I drew the short straw in life."

Ben tried to be more specific. "Have you ever felt like you're a little more different from everyone else? Like you can hear better, run faster, jump higher, and heal faster. Things like that?" Ben asked, trying not to look at James directly.

"What's going on, Ben?" James interrupted, getting defensive that his friends seemed to know something he didn't and were purposely dragging it out.

"Sophie," Ben hesitated, looking her in the eyes with as much love as he could illuminate. "We think you have been genetically altered," he finally pushed out.

"We?" James said, looking wildly at his friend.

"What do you mean?" Sophie looked from Tina to Ben and back to Tina again.

"Just think about it for a second," Tina tried again. "You heard the vans before they ever arrived at the house."

"Yeah, but you could hear that too," Sophie insisted.

"No, Honey," Tina said, softly. "No one heard it except you."

Sophie replayed the moment in her mind, slowly realizing that she heard things before others registered it. She had originally thought that they had just blown out their hearing from listening to loud music throughout their life.

"Sophie, you may still need to heal like a normal person, but your timeline is much faster than others," Ben added in his doctorly tone. "It doesn't take a couple of days for cracked ribs to completely heal, and bruising doesn't disappear within hours."

Sophie looked at him as if she were a lost child while she replayed what memories she could pull forward of every time she had ever been hurt and healed within hours and days while other kids remained in casts for months.

"You are definitely more graceful and faster than anyone I have ever come across," Tina smiled at her.

James looked at his friends madly before settling his eyes on Sophie. His own memories of her ability to jump over the van like a cat, her rapid fighting skills, and everything else he had witnessed Sophie do unlike anyone else he had ever met before.

Sophie turned to James, obviously overwhelmed by various emotions all at once. "So, I'm a freak?" she asked him desperately, unable to find a better word. It was Tina that turned Sophie to face her and pulled Sophie into her arms.

"No, Sophie," Tina soothed as she ran her fingers lightly through the back of Sophie's hair as she calmed her. "You are NOT a freak," Tina emphasized.

She let Sophie have a couple of sobs from the realization that she was more special than even she knew. Tina pulled Sophie back and put her finger under her chin to make Sophie's eyes meet her own.

"You're the protector," Tina stated matter-of-factly. "Somehow you were altered," Tina rushed on before her friend could get lost in the negative. "And your parents turned your alterations into strengths and incredible assets. I don't think you were just designed to keep the key safe," Tina stated honestly.

"What do you mean?" Sophie asked as she stared at Tina, desperate for answers to a puzzle she didn't even know existed.

"I am not a hundred percent sure," Tina answered truthfully. "But the key is only a small part of the puzzle, Soph," Tina continued. "Something bigger is coming, and only you will be able to keep everyone safe from it," she finished, looking at her friend firmly.

"What are you talking about?" Sophie asked, feeling sick to her stomach. Wasn't the key enough? Wasn't the man with the cane enough? She felt James put his arms around her waist and pull her against him.

"Your parents have visited us all," he whispered softly in Sophie's ear. "They don't seem to know what's coming either, but they want us to be prepared."

"Which includes getting more information on what shots you received, and just exactly how badass you truly are," Ben said, forcing an encouraging smile on his face while he winked at Sophie. "Your dad gave me two names, and both Dr. Cox and Dr. Dallas will be at the convention. We just need to figure out the safest way to get them alone and find out what they know."

The room spun as Sophie's brain tried to absorb all the information she had just received in the last couple of minutes. She laid her head against James' shoulder and tried to get the terrible chill that consumed her body to thaw out.

"You ARE the protector, Peanut," she heard her mother's voice whisper in her ears for the first time in what had seemed like forever. The reminder she needed to find the floor again.

Sophie lifted her head, opened her eyes, and looked each friend in the face with determination and confidence. She put on her Cheshire smile before asking, "So, what's the plan?"

Halloween had finally arrived, and a solid plan was in place. Horror movies had played on every channel throughout the night and day, with the occasional news announcement of all the parties taking place in the French Quarter. Kids grew eager to get their costumes on and go trick-or-treating, and the atmosphere shifted with the promise of the dead coming to play with the living for one night only.

The group of friends stayed silent for most of the day, going over their portion of the plan a thousand times inside their head. Although they would be in masks, they would still be out in public, where anything could happen.

Sophie was sure she had left a distinct trail that ended in Nashville, Tennessee, with no future location to be found. She was taught by the best for being seen and not being seen. It didn't seem to keep the chill off her back, though, despite being indoors all day.

Her dreams had been peaceful enough the night before. Sophie's memories had played out like a rapid movie as she came to realize how different she actually was. It was a feeling she had always had, but nothing that she had taken the time to consider.

Sophie had simply accepted that she was weird and would never fit in anywhere. Well, until she met James and his friends. Sophie realized the strength of their love for her.

Even after finding out that someone was trying to get her, and would do anything to have Sophie, including killing anyone that got in the way, they stayed. They gave up their lives to live on the run until whatever this was had been finished. They knew before Sophie did she was weird and not normal, and they had accepted her and loved her, anyway.

Sophie spent a lot of her time wondering if she was being selfish about keeping them, and if she was ruining their lives instead of saving them. Finding out that they accepted her this much no matter what made Sophie realize it wasn't being selfish if you were protecting the people that refused to leave you. It had given her some peace in knowing she was doing the right thing after all.

However, too many questions remained. Sophie agreed that this was their best option, because she had questions of her own that needed to be answered. Like why she had been altered, and by whom? The room grew darker as the sun hid behind the horizon, along with Sophie's concerns about herself. She needed to remain focused to keep everyone safe.

"It's time to get ready!" Tina whispered with excitement in Sophie's ear.

"You're enjoying this way too much," Sophie chuckled and shook her head at her friend as she got off the bed.

"We never get to dress up," Tina whined. "And I can't WAIT to see my final masterpiece!" Tina exclaimed; way too excited to use Sophie as a barbie doll for the night.

"You are drop dead gorgeous regardless," James said, as he came over with his boyish grin and kissed Sophie on the cheek before Tina dragged her into the bathroom and slammed the door.

"I love my wife," Ben said, with a chuckle, "but poor Sophie."

The boys gave a light laugh and clinked their beers, trying desperately to settle their own nerves.

"What if we find out something terrible?" James finally breathed out his worries to his friend.

Ben put his hand on James' shoulder.

"There is absolutely nothing I have witnessed that points anywhere in that direction," he assured James. "I honestly think it's about unlocking the actual key. We just didn't know it would be Sophie instead of the necklace," Ben shrugged as he took a sip of his beer.

"You don't think it will shorten her life or anything crazy like that?" James asked Ben out of nowhere.

Ben thought about it and then laughed. "My friend, I'm pretty sure that girl's going to outlive us all."

James processed his friend's remark while he took a sip of his beer. He had never thought of Sophie outliving him, although that made much more sense with all she could do. James was still a little mad at himself for not seeing it first, but Ben made a good point.

He was too busy falling in love with all of Sophie, badass skills or not. She was the light and force that woke up his own deadened heart and kept it beating. James knew all too well that love was blinding. He tried not to be too angry at his friends for not letting him in on their suspicions. James understood they had to have all the puzzle pieces before making such a claim.

The boys got dressed in their tuxes and watched numbly as Freddy chased down some teenagers that had made the mistake of falling asleep so he could kill them.

"Why do they always go up when someone is chasing them?" Ben asked out loud.

"Right? Like they suddenly can fly once they get to the roof?"

James agreed. "Then again, they always go towards the noise instead of going the opposite direction, too," he muttered in annoyance.

"I never understood that," Ben said, shaking his head. After a second, he turned to James in urgency. "Let's make a pack!" he said in excitement. James looked at him cautiously and wondered where this was heading.

"We will never follow creepy sounds, and we will never run in stupid directions that will get us killed," Ben said, proudly holding out his hand to James.

"What?" James laughed.

"Seriously," Ben urged. "We've seen enough of these horror films to know what NOT to do in order to survive," he rushed on in excitement. "We do not know what's going to happen. Maybe if we don't do what all the stupid kids that deserve to get killed do, then we can beat that douche bag and live to tell the tale!" Ben exclaimed as he thrust his hand out at his friend again.

"You're a dork," James said, shaking his head, but took his friend's hand and shook on it.

Ben had a point. They had watched enough horror films to know certain things you just don't do if you wanted to survive.

The boys heard the door open, and Tina cleared her throat. They turned eagerly to see their girls all dressed up, and their jaws dropped open immediately.

Tina stood in the doorway with a sleek, shiny, emerald green spaghetti strapped dress with a slit up the side nearly to her hip. Her mask covered the top portion of her face and cheeks with matching emerald green material and feathers with rhinestones, shining to capture the light just right.

Tina's killer blue eyes glowed through the eyeholes, and the color complemented her shorter brown hair with blonde streaks that were curled to perfection to frame her face. Her ruby red lips and gold dangling earrings made the complete package.

"Whoa," James breathed out.

"She's mine," Ben said, distracted.

His mouth had stopped producing the saliva it required to function properly, and he crossed his legs to hide his immediate excitement from James' view. Ben knew with as tight as that dress was, there would be no underwear worn underneath.

Tina chuckled, glad to turn her husband on so immediately. She let him stay seated until the blood dispersed back to where it belonged for the party. Tina sauntered over and sat on his lap, wrapping her arms around his neck.

"I don't think that's going to help," Ben whispered dryly into her ear.

"Who says I came to help?" Tina taunted as she kissed her husband's check gently.

"I don't see how you think I can do any kind of protecting if something goes wrong in this massive thing," they heard Sophie grumble from the bathroom.

"Stop fussing," Tina warned. "It's a BALL," she emphasized. "And every princess needs to wear a Cinderella dress once in their lifetime."

"You're not wearing one!" Sophie retorted back from behind the wall.

"Well, there's no time to go shopping, so stop complaining and get out here," Tina ordered. "Wait until you see this," she whispered into her husband's ear.

"I don't think it's very practical," Sophie mumbled, fussing with the large skirt as she barely made it through the bathroom door opening. James' heart stopped beating.

Sophie was wearing a strapless black corset ball gown that was covered in sequins and feathers. Despite her efforts, the bottom flowed out from her tiny waistline into a giant hoop around her feet. Her mask was a copy of Tina's, only with black material, feathers, and rhinestones to match her gorgeous black dress.

Her breasts were held tightly and pushed together to show a distinct crease down the middle. A touch of white glitter sparkled off her shoulders, while her dark wine lips matched her very vibrant dark red-wine hair that was pulled back with strangling pieces framing her face. Silver, simple dangling earrings hung from her ears. Her deep crystal blue eyes were undeniable when she looked up and saw the open mouths of the boys staring back at her.

"What?" Sophie asked in panic, completely self-conscious.

Tina grinned from ear to ear. No one else responded.

"I told you it's too much!" Sophie mumbled to Tina.

"It's just the right amount, Babe," James whispered as he fought to get his heart going and find his voice.

"I'm not sure you girls are going to be doing much blending in," Ben said in his own whisper. "We won't be able to do the plan, because we will be too busy fighting the guys off you two."

Tina kissed her husband on the cheek again and smiled.

"I'm still wearing my tennis shoes," Sophie declared.

"You will not!" demanded Tina immediately.

Ben held onto Tina and James jumped up between them. "No one's going to see her feet," James assured Tina, who was frowning immensely.

"Let her be comfortable in something," Ben whispered quietly. "She's still a breath taking masterpiece, and no one will be the wiser," he added quickly.

"Fine," Tina said, rolling her eyes and standing up to cross her arms in defeat.

"I can't even bend down to put them on!" Sophie whined.

"Let me," James said, getting down on one knee.

Tina and James held their breath, but James reached over to pick up her black tennis shoes and put them gently on her feet. Completely oblivious to his friends' reaction. Ben looked at Tina, realizing she knew about the ring too, and finally shrugged.

"Should be an interesting night," he said, smiling at his bombshell of a wife.

"That it shall," Tina said in response. Then the boys escorted the girls like gentlemen to the Uber, waiting for them outside.

The Morial Convention Center laid upriver from Canal Street along the Mississippi River. Black bats and masks decorated the large glass windows that stood as a welcome mat around the front of the building. A large red carpet led the way inside, much like the red carpet of the Hollywood award shows Sophie had seen on tv.

They decorated the inside in shiny cobwebs, with various

masks hanging on the wall. They stationed pop-up bars along the vastly wide walls along the sides, along with scattered mini tables covered with black floor length table clothes and various glittery Halloween decorations that represented center pieces.

"How are we going to find anyone in here?" Sophie whispered to James once they entered.

"It will be easier than you think," James whispered back. "I let dad know what we needed before we left."

A large bodyguard dressed in black held out his hand for their invitations. James held out the burner phone so the guard could scan the barcode.

"Right this way," the bodyguard said flatly as he held open the door for them.

"Well, at least that was easy," Tina said, taking in the sight before her.

"We're going to have to divide and conquer," James mumbled. "Mom should be collecting Dr. Cox outside the theater. Sophie and I are going to meet dad and see if we can't find Dr. Dallas."

"We'll hear everything with these coms no matter how far away you are," Tina assured as Sophie scanned the crowd before her. They smiled, nodded, and split in opposite directions.

The place was much more massive than Sophie had originally thought. She scanned each person they passed carefully while James searched for the familiar figure of his father.

"Hello Dr. Samuel," James heard his mother's voice ring in his ear. She didn't miss a beat in getting Ben and Tina's attention. "Mrs. Samuel, you are absolutely breathtaking!" Sally exclaimed.

"Thank you, Mrs. Moore," Tina said, grinning from ear to ear.

"It's been a long time."

"Too long, Dear," Sally said, with a hint of frustration. "I think Dr. Cox is around the corner. He had mentioned he wanted to speak to the two of you," she said, smiling sweetly again. "Let's go see if we can find her."

"I think you dropped your earring," Tina said slyly. "Is this yours?"

Tina handed her the ear com discretely as Sally took it from her hand and slid it into her ear while pretending to put her earring back on.

"Most of the time I find these things to be quite boring," Sally rambled as she pushed the ear com into her ear. "However, I think this will be my favorite one yet!"

"Missed you too, Mom," James whispered with a smile.

Tina and Ben watched as Sally's face faltered for a second and she blinked wildly at the tears that suddenly filled her eyes, but within seconds she was back to smiling and chatting about the places they had traveled to while being on the run.

Sophie squeezed James' arm, and he turned to look in the direction that locked her gaze. Roger stood talking to a tall blonde man with broad shoulders that made his tux look like it was too tight. James nodded, and they headed in Roger's direction as casually as possible.

"Wow," Roger said, the second he saw Sophie. Her cheeks blushed a rosy pink. "So nice to see you again, Dr. Hughes," he said, keeping his eyes on Sophie, and extending his hand to his son.

"Absolutely stunning, isn't she?" James said, smiling at Sophie, as he took his father's hand to shake it.

"I'll say!" said the blonde man beside Roger.

Sophie recognized him to be Dr. Dallas immediately. "This dress is over the top, I'm afraid. It's nice to finally put a face to a name Dr. Dallas," Sophie said, smoothly while holding out her hand to shake his.

"Please, call me Corbin," he beamed his wide smile and emerald green eyes at Sophie while taking her hand and bringing the back of it to his lips for a kiss.

Sophie felt James tense up immediately at the gesture and couldn't help but smile at his jealousy.

"How very nice to meet you," Sophie said, sweetly, and quickly pulled her hand out of his grasp to wrap it around James' arm instead. James smiled a triumphant smile.

"I'm due to speak in the next twenty minutes. Perhaps we could all meet backstage so that we can discuss important matters," Roger said, holding his arm out for Sophie to take. She giggled and switched her hold from James to Roger as he led the way backstage.

"I hear you study the ability to control dreams," James said casually as he put his hands in his pockets and strolled behind Sophie and his father to the green room.

"It's a little more than that," Corbin chuckled as he stole every chance he had to stare at Sophie's backside.

"Some people believe that it's a way for the dead to reach out to the living after they have passed," James said, fighting to control the irritation in his voice.

"Everyone has the ability to control their surroundings in a lucid state of mind." Corbin shrugged. "Some are more willing than others."

"Do you teach such individuals?" James asked as they

continued to follow his father down dark skinny hallways, obviously used by staff instead of guests.

"I'm more into studying than teaching," Corbin chuckled.

"The greenroom should do," his father called over his shoulder before holding the door open for Sophie to shove the base of her dress through.

"Hello, Love," Sally said, grinning from ear to ear taking Sophie in. "You are absolutely STUNNING tonight!"

"This dress is ridiculous," Sophie mumbled back.

"Stop whining," Tina threatened. "Everyone's getting whiplash from looking at you."

"You're breaking necks too, Tin," Ben smiled down at his wife with love and admiration.

"I'm sorry," Corbin interrupted. "What is this about?"

"Take a seat, everyone," Roger offered to those who remained standing. The room was small, and Sophie's dress took up a good portion of it, but there was still a small sofa and some chairs for guests to relax in before having to perform a show.

"Yes," Elaine added. "I'm very curious myself."

"Sorry for the intrusion of your night," Roger started. "However, we have some questions that I'm afraid only the two of you can answer," he finished with a polite smile. Elaine looked around the room nervously.

"Whatever answers you are looking for, you are welcome to get from my research," she said, as she picked up the base of her own sparkling royal blue spaghetti strapped dress to leave.

Her long brunette hair was also curled to perfection to frame her thin and paler face. Her mask was black, much similar to Sophie's, but it was a paler blue in her eyes that couldn't hide the fear she was feeling.

"Please," Sophie said, softly. "I need your help," she said, as she put her hands up before Elaine. "Do you both remember coming across a Jack or a Jessica Harris?" Sophie asked eagerly. Both froze at the names.

"I have never heard such names," Corbin said, standing up to leave.

"Jack says otherwise," James said, sweetly.

Corbin froze at the name and sat back down slowly. "Jack is dead."

"We are well aware," Tina said, crossing her arms.

"They had a daughter," Sophie continued on with her eyes locked on Elaine's. "Sophie," she stated, coming closer to Elaine and urging for her to speak up.

"I don't know where she is," Elaine said, shaking her head frantically.

"I know you don't," Sophie said calmly. "We just need to know what your shots were for."

"I didn't give her shots!" Elaine hollered in confusion.

"Yes, you did," Sophie pressed.

"No, I didn't," Elaine responded firmly. "I only took specimens to study," she said, more confidently.

"Specimens?" Ben asked. "What were you studying?"

Elaine shook her head frantically. "It was just a baseline," she said, looking for a way to get to the door. "It wasn't important."

"It is to me," Sophie said, catching Elaine's eyes. Elaine froze and finally studied the girl before her.

"You?" Elaine whispered.

"Yes," Sophie said, softly. "And I need to know what you found."

Elaine shook her head slowly in disbelief.

"Please," Sophie pleaded.

Elaine allowed her mind to focus. "Your mother brought you to me," she said, slowly, bringing a forgotten past back into the present.

"No one was supposed to know," she whispered in sudden panic.

"No one does," Sophie assured. "I remembered you," she murmured gently, nodding at Elaine. "And I REALLY need to know what you found."

"You are like nothing I have ever seen," Elaine breathed out.

"What does that mean?" James asked in panic. Sally placed his hands in hers and squeezed tightly.

"So many genes, split to perfection," Elaine said, softly soaking Sophie in from head to toe. "Your mother knew you were special. She just wasn't sure how much. So, she brought you to me," Elaine continued, staring at Sophie from head to toe. "She said she had noticed since birth, but never said how it had happened," she continued.

"What exactly did you find?" Roger encouraged. Elaine shook her head to get it to clear from her wonder.

"They have sliced your DNA like nothing I had ever seen. Someone was able to add animalistic DNA and merged it perfectly with your own human DNA. It's true CRISPR perfection. Like nothing I had ever seen before," Elaine stated in her doctorly voice.

"What kind of animals?" Tina pushed.

"If I remember correctly, I think I identified chetah, bat, eagle, grizzly bear, and a mixture of others," Elaine stated firmly.

"Why?" Sophie asked louder than intended.

"Your mother never said," Elaine stated, suddenly feeling sympathy for the girl before her. "She was as surprised as I was," she added, taking Sophie's hands into hers.

"You gave me shots?" Sophie turned to look at Roger with pleading eyes.

"I did," Roger confirmed. "You will never get sick," he answered with great pride. "James will never get sick, either. It was Jack's instructions, but that is all I know of my part," he assured.

"You don't get your DNA from shots," Elaine said softly, drawing Sophie's gaze back at her. "Something was done to your mother. She didn't say when. However, giving birth to you obviously passed everything to you."

"My mother didn't seem as different as me," Sophie said, more to herself than anyone, as she tried to recollect the mannerisms of her mother.

"What if it was, but it was dormant?" Ben suggested, breaking the silence. "If she was unaware of what had happened, that would be a possible explanation," he offered, looking into Sophie's wild eyes.

"Time is running out," Tina whispered.

"Jack came to see me," Corbin said, with his eyes closed. When he opened them, his eyes were heavily dilated and in some sort of trance.

"Dr. Dallas?" Roger said, with a bit of concern.

"He wanted to know what I knew about the oneironaut," Corbin continued, without recognizing Roger. Roger stepped forward, but Sophie grabbed his arm to stop him, nodding at Corbin's swaying body. She shook her head no.

"He brought his wife to me," Corbin continued. "I taught them everything I knew. We met almost daily for a year."

"What did Jack want to know?" James asked.

Corbin turned to James with his almost completely blackened eyes. James was locked into his stare, unable to shake the chill that suddenly rolled down his back.

"He's coming for her. They had to protect her," Corbin stated flatly. "They remain in the in between to help keep her safe."

The room was deathly silent as they watched the doctor sway back and forth with black eyes as his face grew paler by the second.

"He will come," Corbin finally chanted. "If you can't stop him, then the dead and the living will all be sacrificed to the whims of evil."

"How do we stop him?" James asked, swallowing the lump in his throat.

"Who is he?" Ben asked.

"What are we supposed to do with the key?" Tina begged.

"Keep it safe," Corbin stated, turning his black eyes to Tina. "She will save us all." And with that, Corbin shook his head and wiped his forehead. "So, why are we here again?" he asked, full of confusion and looking around the room.

"What the hell?" Ben asked. Sophie's stare made him quiet.

"We were just going to discuss your impressive studies, but it seems we have run out of time," Sophie said, as if nothing had just happened. The room looked at her in complete disbelief. "Sorry to keep you, Dr. Moore," Sophie said, as she leaned over and kissed him on his cheek. It was his turn to have his cheeks turn a rosy pink.

"It's time to go," Sophie announced to the room and reached

over to try to hug Sally through the enormous black dress.

"Stay safe," Sally whispered in her ear. "I look forward to seeing you again soon."

"Of course," Sophie smiled. "Thank you so much for sharing your findings with us," she said, taking Elaine's hands in her own to squeeze them.

"You must remain calm," Elaine warned. "Sometimes when things have been that altered if they get overheated, the brain will shut down as a safety mechanism," she added with a weary smile.

"Thank you," Sophie said, squeezing her hands once more and waddling to the door.

"Don't wait too long," Sally whispered into James' ear. "Time is a finicky creature," she warned, before kissing him on the cheek.

"I hear you," James assured before kissing her back.

Tina and Ben said their goodbye's, and a very confused and hungry Corbin stumbled out of the room in search of food with Elaine holding him up.

"I'm proud of you," Roger whispered as he pulled James into a hug.

"I miss you too, Dad," James whispered back.

"Help keep her safe," Roger winked.

"Always am," James winked back, and everyone exited quickly while a staff member pulled Roger to the back of the stage.

"I'm sorry, but what the hell was that?" Ben asked as they made their way back to the party.

"A trance," Sophie responded quietly. "I've seen it before. Dr. Dallas has made sure that he doesn't hold on to the information of meeting my father for safety reasons."

"So why did he tell us then?" James asked.

"The code word was said," Sophie said flatly. "Whatever safe word he was given to be able to share the information with only those that needed to have it."

"Will it really keep him safe?" Tina asked.

"We'll find out," Sophie replied, trying not to think about what the man with the cane would ever do if he found out about Corbin Dallas.

James stopped abruptly, forcing everyone to run into his back.

"What gives, Bro?" Ben asked in confusion.

"I have to find another way out," James said, not moving his eyes from the blonde-haired woman in a red dress on the other side of the room.

"What? Why?" Sophie asked him in sudden alarm.

Tina followed James' glance to see a ghost from their past. "You have got to be kidding me!" Tina huffed louder than she had intended and got a few stares in their direction.

James turned his back to the girl and took Sophie's hands into his own and squeezed them. He stared at Sophie. "I can't go out with you. I will have to meet you back at the hotel," James said softly.

"What..." was all Sophie got out of her mouth.

"Because someone who could possibly spot me out in any crowd is here, and we can't afford to be recognized," James said firmly. "It is the ONLY reason that I am forcing myself to leave your side at this moment," he said, as he wrapped his arms around her and pulled Sophie against him, puffy dress and all.

"What's going on?" Ben asked. The look on his wife's face silenced him, even through the mask.

"I WILL never leave you," James emphasized. "You are the only one that I love with all my heart," he said, guiding her to him and pulling Sophie into the most passionate kiss they had ever had.

"James," Tina warned when more people turned to see the show, including the blonde-headed girl in the red dress and mask.

"See you on the other side," James smiled at her before he let her go and disappeared into the crowd.

It took a second for Sophie's head to stop floating on cloud nine. "We have to go," she heard Tina say before she grabbed Ben's hand and dragged him into the crowd.

When Sophie's head cleared and her eyes refocused, her friends were completely gone, and the blonde-haired girl in the red dress was staring at Sophie with her head tilted to the side. She was about Sophie's height, and her hazel eyes shined with curiosity through her red mask. She, too, had a ball gown on, and she floated across the floor towards Sophie.

The crowds squeezed in as people headed toward the theater, blocking Sophie's escape from this strange woman that took too much interest in Sophie. She looked around to see the nearest exit.

"Hello," the woman said, sweetly, with much sarcasm. "I haven't seen you at one of these events before."

"My first one," Sophie said politely as she looked around her. The people were closing in like a herd of cattle being driven by expert drovers.

"Who was that handsome man that was kissing you?" she asked with way too much interest.

"No one that concerns you," Sophie said sweetly and went to walk around the woman.

"I'm sorry. Where are my manners?" the woman said, raising her voice to draw attention to them. "My name is Helen. Helen Wood."

Sophie looked at the woman. She vaguely remembered hearing the name once before, but she couldn't think of where.

"And yours?" Helen pushed.

"Jessica," Sophie said, hoping her mother wouldn't mind if she borrowed her name momentarily.

"What a pretty name!" shrieked Helen. "I don't mean to be pushy about your friend. He just reminds me of an old friend that I haven't seen in forever. I was hoping to catch up with him if it was my friend," Helen cooed as she looked around Sophie. "Did he say where he was going?"

"What's your friend's name?" Sophie inquired casually.

"Oh, James Moore," Helen said, taking Sophie in. "I'm sure that was him. I could spot him a mile away!"

Sophie remembered where she had heard the name. It came from Tina when they were in the hotel waiting for Ben to come back after he had stormed off back in Maine. This was the woman that had left James at the altar.

"I'm afraid you have the wrong person. That was my husband, Dr. Jack Hughes," Sophie said, not skipping a beat.

James paused for a moment, hearing the word "husband" come from Sophie's mouth like it was second nature. He liked the sound of it. His grin grew from ear to ear as he desperately looked for the third exit option he had located when looking at the plans.

"Hmmm," Helen said, completely not convinced. "Well, he seemed quite dashing. How long have you been married?" Helen pressed, examining Sophie from head to toe as she spoke.

"Hard to say," Sophie shrugged. "When you find your soulmate, years don't really get counted when you're going to be together for life."

"Damn!" she heard Ben laugh in her ear. She had forgotten about the coms.

"So very true," Helen said, taking a sip of her drink and studying Sophie like she was a specimen under a microscope.

"Are you married?" Sophie asked, not caring at all.

"Not at the moment," Helen smiled and winked at Sophie.

"I'm sure the right one will come along," Sophie said, picking up her skirt and getting ready to go around Helen and move on.

"Unfortunately, I think he already did," Helen sighed.

Sophie knew her kind and knew where this was going. She also knew Helen wouldn't let her pass until she was done trying to humiliate Sophie one way or another.

"Sorry to hear that," Sophie said, pushing around Helen and moving on, but Helen was quick on her heels despite the massive skirts colliding constantly with every step.

"That's why I hoped that was my friend, James," Helen continued, not skipping a beat.

"Sorry to disappoint you," Sophie said, as she pushed her way through the opposite moving traffic in front of her.

"James was the one that got away," Helen said, scrutinizing Sophie suspiciously as she chased after her. "And sometimes people think they're soulmates when their partner is meant to be with someone else entirely."

"Well, then I guess you shouldn't have let him get away," Sophie responded flatly.

Helen smiled and batted her lashes as she pursued Sophie.

"It's true. It was completely my fault," Helen continued, despite Sophie's lack of interest. "I wasn't ready for marriage, so I got cold feet. I made a silly mistake and now I would like to make amends."

Sophie stopped trying to push through the crowds and turned to face Helen head on. It was time to change tactics. "Then you should probably find him," Sophie said, as if she were providing sisterly advice.

"Whoa, what?" she heard James's panic in her ear.

"Well, that's the thing," Helen frowned. "No one can find him."

"That usually means the person doesn't want to be found," Sophie said, patting Helen on the shoulder lightly. "Sometimes, our mistakes are too big, and we have to pay the price. Sometimes..." Sophie said, smiling sweetly, "sometimes people realize they deserve better and go find it."

Helen glared at Sophie and shrugged her hand off her shoulder.

"Sometimes," Helen said, shaking her head and shoving her chin to the ceiling. "Sometimes, that person will realize that he already had the best thing he's ever going to find and comes crawling back. Mostly because the other person can never give him the life HE deserves."

"This is true," Sophie said, as if she was taking Helen's words into consideration. "I'm sure that if it's meant to be, he will come back," Sophie said with a smile and a shrug. "No harm in looking around until he does," she winked. Helen was thrown off and not sure what to take of Sophie's manner.

"Right now," Sophie continued. "This corset has squeezed all the life out of me, and I have to get these horrid heels off my feet," she lied. Helen tilted her head and eyed Sophie with full suspicion.

"What about your husband?" Helen pried.

"He will find his own way. He always does," Sophie said, with a smile. "Enjoy the evening, Dear!" she shouted over her shoulder as she continued to push through the remaining crowd.

"Remind me to kiss you when I see you," James chuckled in her ear.

"You can kiss me after you get this damn dress off," Sophie gasped, trying to get her ribs to accept air back into her lungs. A distant sound stopped her dead in her tracks as people continued to push past her.

"Honey, what's wrong?" Tina asked her, noticing Sophie had stopped pushing her way through as Tina and Ben watched her from a distance.

Tina knew Helen would identify them as well, which is why she dragged Ben and herself out of Helen's eyesight. However, the color Sophie contained in her cheeks was quickly depleting.

"Sophie..." Tina repeated more firmly, watching her friend become suddenly in distress.

James came to a halt right before opening the door to his escape. "What's wrong?" he asked in sudden panic.

"Get out, now," Sophie ordered in a gasp of panic. "Everyone!" she hissed.

"What's wrong?!" James pleaded.

"He's here," Sophie whispered in fright.

"Who?" Tina urged.

Sophie heard the tapping of metal against the floor before she could locate the face to go with it. "Get OUT!" Sophie demanded one last time. Ben grabbed Tina and dragged her out of the building. If it was enough to spook Sophie, Ben knew it could only mean one thing...the man with the cane.

"I'm not leaving you!" James hissed as people stared in his direction.

"I've got her, Dear," they all heard Sally soothe. "Go, Son," she said. They had forgotten Sally still had on an ear com.

"Get Roger and get OUT!" Sophie hissed as she looked frantically around the room for the face that matched the sound that haunted her dreams since she was a child.

"No, Peanut. Come with me," they heard Jack say as he slipped his hand into Sophie's and pulled her away dressed in a tux and feeling as real as the other bodies that pushed against her.

"Get out," they all heard Jess's voice confirm in their ears.

"Who is that?" Sally asked, confused.

"Go get dad and get out," James told his mom firmly.

"Stay safe, children," Sally whispered as she rushed to collect her husband before it was too late.

Sophie couldn't believe the figure before her that was pulling her safely through the crowd. It was only the sound of the cane hitting the floor again that broke the spell. Sophie stopped suddenly and whipped her head in the direction of the haunting familiar sound.

"Not today," Jack said, as he tugged on her hand and dragged her out to safety.

Seven

He looked around the room gradually, taking in the herding mass headed towards the theater. It was supposed to be the best of the best in the medical world attending. What devastation would be caused if he wiped them all out, right here and right now. However, he needed one of these ants to do his bidding. Besides, this was his favorite holiday, and he needed to stretch his legs, anyway.

A sparkling cream spaghetti strap fitted dress with a slit almost up to the hips and strappy heeled shoes to match caught his eye. It was a figure that haunted his dreams. He would know it from anywhere.

The dress hung nicely over her athletic curves, as her red chin length curly hair framed her face covered lightly by freckles. Her eyes were as blue as the sea. She waited patiently for him across the room with her arms crossed in front of her chest. His cane echoed across the floor as he sauntered his way towards her amidst the crowd.

He took in every inch of her standing before him and smiled the most disturbing grin ever seen. Although it would have sent chills down people's body, the woman stood unfazed. "Hello, Jessica," he snarled at her.

"Algos," Jess greeted him coldly.

The man with the cane threw his head back and laughed wildly. "So that's what you're calling me these days," he said in a wicked voice.

"It is your name," Jess responded dryly.

"Not my only one, now is it?" he said, walking around her as if she was his prey. Jess remained unimpressed.

"Looking good for being a dead woman," Algos chuckled.

"No thanks to you," Jess retorted with little emotion.

"Well, you were the one that chose to be difficult," Algos shrugged.

"What are you doing here?" Jess asked flatly.

"Oh, I believe you already know, my dear sweet girl," Algos hissed. "You always underestimate me child."

"Not nearly as you always underestimate me," Jess said, letting the ends of her lips curl up in an admitting smile.

"Did you really think I wouldn't figure out what you and your sorry excuse for a husband were up to?" Algos said, with more frustration than he intended to share.

"No, but it took you over ten years," Jess said, with her own wicked smile. The man's half scarred face reddened, and Jess knew she had pushed a button.

"Well, I'm sure Dr. Dallas can assist me in leveling the playing field," Algos said sweetly.

Jess didn't falter. They had warned Corbin upfront what the price would be if Algos ever found him out. Corbin had made his own decision to help them, and told them it would be nothing he would regret once death greeted him. The three had sat down and had several discussions over the matter. Corbin had insisted and sealed his fate.

"See you on the other side," Corbin had always smiled and said when they left each of their sessions. Jess knew there would be no way to save him. Sophie was the one they all agreed needed to survive. It still saddened her to her core.

"Where is the young lad?" Algos asked, looking around the emptying room.

"Wouldn't know," Jess shrugged as she looked at her nails painted such a pretty red. It would be a shame to destroy them in a fight.

However, a thought crossed his mind, and his demeanor changed immediately. "Your presence must mean our dear Sophie is also present," Algos said, in realization, as he whipped his head to search the surrounding crowd.

Jess knew better than to falter at the mention of her daughter's name. She was the distraction to allow Jack to get Sophie to safety without either crossing paths.

"It is my day to play," Jess said, smiling her wicked smile. "Something told me you would visit this lovely party," she shrugged as she walked around him. Stalking him like prey. Her powers were limited on this night. Being a human again didn't bode her daughter much protection if something went wrong, but she had to at least try.

The old man drew his attention back to his protégé. "And where is dear Jack?" Algos asked, curious what she thought her plan was going to be.

"He had someone to visit," Jess shrugged and took a drink from the server as he walked by. "Thank you," she said politely to the very confused server as she waved him off to safety.

"Did he, now?" Algos asked, with intrigue.

"So, what are your plans for the evening?" Jess asked, quickly changing the subject.

Algos eyed Jess suspiciously, but he decided to play along.

"Well," he stalled. "Thought I would visit dear Dr. Dallas to either add to my team, or simply take out," the old man stated as if he were simply marking off his To-Do list. "I figure with good old Dr. Moore speaking, the obnoxious four would be close by," he said, giving a quick look around. "It was such a chore to get him to be the keynote speaker."

"You play such boring games in your old age," Jess said, before taking a sip of the champaign she held. She knew better than to take her eyes off the man before her.

Algos chuckled, a deep, throaty chuckle. "Well, some surprises take more planning than others," he replied wickedly.

"How's your face doing?" Jess nodded at his disfigured half.

Algos stopped smiling, and Jess knew she had his attention. It was a sore spot for him, and she had been the one to give it to him. That pleased her and gave her some courage to continue to poke at him despite the crowd becoming absent, leaving just the two of them with no witnesses.

"Your cane looks new," Jess poked again. The limp was also her doing. His amusement left his eyes, and he no longer was in the mood to play her games.

"Don't think I won't take you right here, Dear," he scowled. "Then what would Sophie do with her dear mother dying by my hands twice?"

"Won't do well for her joining your team," Jess shrugged as she walked past him to add distance all the same.

He paused for a moment, knowing she was right. Until he achieved what he came here to do, then he couldn't touch Jess. Dead or even temporarily alive. No matter how easy it would be. Dead would be much more satisfying.

"Hey Jess!" They both turned to see Corbin keeping his distance. He was leaning up against one of the side bars with a drink in hand. "Jack said you would visit," he beamed at her. He kept his eyes on the disfigured man before her.

"Oh, did he?" Jess said, with a hint of nerves coming through her voice.

"Oh, yeah!" Corbin shouted. "Said some asshole would try to come kill me too," he said, winking momentarily before looking back at the man with the cane who didn't look pleased at all.

"Funny thing is," Corbin continued, taking a sip of his drink, "that asshole has no clue how to succeed, and I don't intend on teaching him."

Jess quietly slipped off her shoes, preparing herself to fight while Algos was distracted. She wasn't exactly sure what Corbin was up to, but she would take what she could get and do her best to keep him safe in the process.

"I can be very persuasive," sneered the man with the cane as he contemplated a fitting punishment for the good doctor that continued to poke at him dangerously.

"The problem is that I already made my choice long ago," Corbin said, looking at Jess passionately as he gulped the rest of his drink down. "And I don't regret a damn thing," he said as he winked at her. "Would do it again even!" he shouted across the room. "So, I guess I'll see you on the other side," Corbin said weakly, before foam exploded from his mouth and his body convulsed.

Jess only hesitated for a split second as Algos' scream was heard around the world. She looked down at the man that wisely took his own life before Algos could torture him, and she took off running as fast as she could down the hallway to look for a way out.

Algos cried out and limped as quickly as he could to the doctor. "Get help NOW!" he yelled at the horrified bartender that had just served the dying man before him.

The bartender ran off as fast as he could. Algos looked down at the man that was going to finally even the playing field for him. Anger boiling in his blood. He looked behind him to see the heels Jess had taken off in the place she once stood, and just a flicker of her dress as she turned the corner.

"You will not win!" Algos screamed after her, spitting while he yelled like a rabid dog. Jess didn't stop for one second. Sophie's life depended on it, including her own. She took off running barefoot into the night.

"Where's mom?" Sophie asked in confusion as her father continued to drag her down Canal Street.

"She'll meet us," Jack said, over his shoulder as he looked around eagerly for a mode of transportation to get them much further away.

"How are you here?" Sophie uttered in a dry voice.

Jack pulled his daughter gently onto the passing streetcar. Despite her massive dress, he held her tightly against him and smiled. "It's Halloween, Peanut. It's the one day the dead are allowed to be amongst the living," he smiled a Cheshire grin at her.

"You never have before," Sophie murmured in a hoarse voice.

"We have, Peanut," Jack assured. "You just never get to remember," he added sadly.

"He was there," Sophie whispered, looking her father directly in his matching blue eyes.

"He was," Jack said, breaking the stare to watch the kids race up and down the street to collect their candy. "We only have an hour left," he said, watching parents hold their children by the hand as they walked. He pulled Sophie closer to him. "Let's not waste it," Jack whispered softly and kissed her on top of her head.

Remembering they weren't alone; Jack began giving orders. "James, we need to get my daughter out of this gorgeous dress so she can blend in a little better," he said, next to Sophie's ear. "That goes for all of my little helpers," he added. "Including you and your husband, Mrs. Moore."

Sophie couldn't believe how alive the figure that held onto her felt as they rode the full streetcar down Canal Street. Jack looked no older than her current self, which only reminded Sophie of how young they were when they were taken from her. Her stomach dropped and grief consumed her body.

Jack seemed to know exactly what Sophie was feeling as he studied her in his arms. His eyes cradling her soul with his gaze. "Grab your bags and meet us at Saint Louis Cemetery at 425 Basin Street. We will be protected while we are there," he said, smiling down at his daughter. "Get there when you can. I'm going to have a moment with my daughter," Jack said, softly, taking out her ear com and putting it in his pocket.

Everyone froze when Jack's voice came across the ear com. No one seemed to wrap their head around the fact that a dead man was giving them orders. "See you soon, children," Sally's motherly voice broke the silence, giving everyone the hint to do as the dead man requested.

Jack helped Sophie jump off the streetcar. He held her hand in his as they walked towards their destination. He couldn't believe how nervous he was to be with her in person, but every year started off the same way. Only this one had the man with the cane too close for comfort.

"You look absolutely stunning," Jack whispered to Sophie. "A spitting image of your mother," he added softly.

"Oh, I don't know," Jess added, a bit out of breath, grabbing Sophie's free hand. "She's got your ornery Cheshire smile for starters," she chuckled lightly.

Jack looked at Jess to make sure she was still fully intact, with no battle wounds. Jess smiled weakly at her husband. It was Sophie's question that broke the silent trance between them.

"Where are your shoes?" Sophie asked numbly, staring at her

mother's bare and filthy feet. Jack looked at Jess in alarm.

"A long story that we don't have time for tonight." Jess shrugged with a weary smile. She shook her head at Jack, letting him know to drop it. She would catch him up later. "You look quite amazing in this dress! Who picked it out?" Jess asked, quickly changing the subject.

"Tina," Sophie said, finally looking up into her mother's matching blue eyes. "It's way too big," she said, frowning.

"Oh, Peanut!" her mother laughed. "It was perfect for the ball!" She reached over and slipped off Sophie's mask. "There's my little girl's pretty face," Jess said, stopping Sophie as she caressed her daughter's face in her warm hands. Jess smiled and leaned in, placing a kiss on Sophie's cheek before taking her hand again as they continued to walk towards the cemetery.

"So, tell us all about your friends," Jack said, as his family walked hand in hand.

"And James," Jess insisted.

Sophie knew she had to be in a dream, but it felt incredibly real. If she was losing her mind completely, then this was the way to go.

"You're not crazy," interjected her mother firmly, without Sophie saying a word. "I don't want to hear another word about it," Jess ordered, looking at Sophie with such authority.

"I didn't even say anything!" Sophie whined.

"You didn't have to," Jack said in a fatherly voice, also looking down at his daughter.

"It's a logical assumption!" Sophie protested.

"Sophie Lee," her mother warned.

Sophie just shook her head and dropped it. "Not like you can ground me anyway," she muttered to herself.

"Watch me," her mother threatened.

Sophie broke into a hysterical laughter just as they came to the entrance of the cemetery.

A solid white wall over six feet high surrounded the cemetery, with a black wrought-iron gate at the entrance. Jack pushed it open and ushered the girls inside. Sophie saw an enormous number of various tombs before her, each with a unique style, much like the individual bodies it contained.

Sophie knew because of the ongoing hurricanes and floods, New Orleans kept bodies mostly in tombs so that they wouldn't float away in God's wrath. Some were made of brick while others were simply straight cement, all various shapes and sizes.

"Let's find a nice place to meet your friends," Jess suggested, as if there was a nice place for everyone to meet her dead parents in person. Sophie shook her head at the absurdity as she followed her parents around the cemetery as they discussed the best location.

"Are Sally and Roger nice?" Jess asked Sophie, suddenly fussing over her red chin length curly locks.

"Very," Sophie answered honestly. "Tina and Ben are like having a brother and sister."

"And James?" Jack asked, raising an eyebrow at his daughter.

Realizing that her parents could apparently read her mind in their current state, she tried desperately to push the thought of having amazing sex with the boy she loved as far out of her mind as possible.

"A perfect gentleman," Sophie added sheepishly. "Although, sometimes too stubborn for his own good," she added, frowning at his only flaw.

"So, he's just like your father," Jess stated with her wicked smile and her hands on her hips.

"More like your mother," Jack retorted back, mimicking his wife's stance.

"Good to see you still getting along after all these years," Sophie giggled at the both of them.

"Eternity is a long time to be stuck with someone you despise," her mother warned. "He's lucky I like him," Jess added, winking at Jack, who looked at his wife with as much love and admiration as Sophie had always remembered.

"Just don't nag him to death," Jack chuckled. "Because it doesn't stop there, and there's no escape from it." Jess stuck her tongue out at Jack, and he laughed and shook his head.

"So, we're not going to talk about what's going on, or what I'm supposed to do with the key, huh?" Sophie asked sarcastically, already knowing the answer.

"You have the key," Jack shrugged. "You will know what to do with it when the time comes."

"Very insightful, Father," Sophie said, rolling her eyes.

"Do your best to keep those deserving safe," Jess stated matter-of-factly, as if it was just a simple request, but that just stirred an unexpected anger from deep within.

"What did you do to me?" Sophie asked, overwhelmed with emotion.

Jack looked at her, confused. However, Jess knew exactly what she meant.

"WE did nothing to you," her mother said, firmly. "What we DID do was make sure that we gave you the most tools and the best possibility to outlive us all," Jess said, as tears filled her own eyes. "Do you think it was easy to find out that not only had I been altered against my knowledge, but I had passed those alterations onto MY OWN DAUGHTER?" Jess said, as she turned her back to her daughter to wipe away the tears that were escaping down her cheeks.

Jack immediately pulled his wife into his arms. Sophie felt an immense wave of guilt squash her anger immediately. She had always assumed it was her parent's choosing to make her different. Not that it was forced.

"Mom, I'm sorry," Sophie said, going to her mother. She threw her arms around both her parents. "I didn't know," she whispered as she breathed them in. A gust of wind blew past them, and Jess pushed away from them both as she quickly wiped her tears.

"We're running out of time," Jess said, as she cleared her throat. "And I look like a hot mess to meet your family!" she said, fussing with her human looks.

"You look amazing," Jack said, kissing his wife on the top of the head. She looked at him lovingly. Sophie heard them before she saw them.

"They're here," Sophie smiled at her parents.

"Good!" Jack said, getting excited.

The living walked into the cemetery and found the dead, with Sophie in the middle of it.

"You must be Sally and Roger!" Jess exclaimed as she eagerly shoved her hand towards James' parents.

Sally looked at her husband in a bit of hesitation before she took Jess' hand into hers. It was shockingly warm. "Hello, Dear. I'm glad to finally meet you," Sally offered with a warm smile.

Jack held out his hand to Roger. Roger looked at it with hesitation. "It's a bit deceiving, but it's safe," Jack assured. Roger took his hand and was shocked at how real it actually felt. Jack chuckled at his response.

"I'm sorry," Roger apologized. "The doctor side of me is truly nerding out right now," he said, in pure fascination.

"Hello Mr. Harris," Tina said, breaking Roger's trance. "I'm Tina."

"Oh, call me Jack, Dear," Jack said, smiling. "I've heard a lot about you," he said, winking at Sophie.

"I hope it was all good," Tina said with a bit of anxiety.

"Only the best," Jack assured.

"This is my husband, Ben," Tina said, pulling Ben towards them.

"Hello again, Benjamin," Jack said, with a warming smile. "I'm sorry our first meet was so short."

Jess was in deep conversation with Sally off to the side. Sophie took James' arm and lead him to her father.

"Dad, this is James," Sophie said, suddenly very nervous.

"James!" Jack said with excitement. "So nice to see you again!" Jack slipped his arm around James' shoulders. "There's something I need to talk to you about, so if you all will excuse us," he said, smiling his Cheshire grin. "Jess, Dear," Jack called to his wife. "Can you please take over?"

"On it!" Jess said, escorting Sally back to the group.

Sophie nervously watched Jack drag James off to the side. It was odd to see Jack against James. Her parents were timeless and not much older than Sophie and her friends. Sophie wondered briefly if they would get to be older than her parents.

"Stop fussing," Jess demanded.

Sally put her arm around Sophie's shoulders and whispered in her ear, "Don't stress, Love. It's just some man talk. Trust me," Sally said with a wink.

"I'm sorry to be so brief, but time is running out," Jess said to the group.

"What's the man with the cane up to?" Ben asked outright.

"Who?" Roger asked, confused.

"I think that's the man after Sophie," Sally offered.

"Unfortunately, we're not exactly sure what he's up to at the moment," Jess said with a frown. "I had originally thought it was to take Jack and I away from Sophie, but I believe it to be much greater than that," she added in frustration. "Dr. Corbin Dallas sacrificed himself in order to keep his teachings safe," Jess said, looking at the floor, taking a moment to mourn the loss of their confidant. "So, we will all need to keep our guards up," Jess warned.

"How can we help Sophie?" Tina asked. She knew time was closing in and they needed to get to the point.

"Keep the key safe." Jess gave Tina a knowing smile.

"What abilities does she have?" Ben asked in his doctor's voice.

"Only Sophie will know that answer," Jess said, looking into her daughter's eyes. "I did not know of my alterations until Sophie was born. Jack and I noticed her gifts immediately," she said, giving Sophie a motherly smile. "We did our best to teach her how to use the ones we were aware of as assets to her. We just ran out of time," Jess said, with grief coming through her shaking voice.

A gust of wind circled them all with a whisper as it circled Jess.

"Jack, Dear," she called to her husband. Time had officially run out.

"Here!" Jack shouted as he escorted James back to the group. "Sorry, Dear," he said, with a weary smile. "It was so nice to get to meet you in person, even if it was for only a brief moment," Jack beamed at the group. He walked over to Sophie. "You have a good crew here," Jack said, as he reached out and kissed the top of her head.

It filled Sophie with complete distress. "Don't leave me!" she pleaded.

"We never do," Jack said with an assuring smile.

Jess stepped in and pushed Sophie's hair away from her face.

"We're very proud of you," Jess said, with her voice cracking. "You are even more amazing than any parent could ever dream off," she whispered, pulling Sophie into a hug before she could witness the tears escaping Jess' eyes. She quickly removed them behind Sophie's back before pulling away. "He will try to mess with you, both mentally and physically. We will do what we can, but you cannot let him win," Jess said in her motherly tone.

Sophie looked at her mother as tears rolled down her cheeks.

"Sophie," her mother said firmly, showing she wanted Sophie to confirm she wouldn't let him win.

"I promise," Sophie said, giving her mother a weak smile.

"Good girl," Jess whispered before gently wiping her finger across Sophie's forehead. Sophie's knees buckled as they forced her into a deep sleep. James caught her as she crumbled.

"Good luck, my dear boy," Jack whispered as he did the same to James and caught both of them before they hit the ground.

Jess was in front of Tina and Ben before they could say anything, and repeated the same gesture. Roger and Sally caught them as their knees buckled and they fell to the ground.

"They won't remember anything other than the importance of the conversation," Jess assured as she helped Sally sit Tina up against a tomb.

"Why?" Sally asked, confused.

"It's required," Jack stated flatly. "They will be perfectly fine, though," he added with a reassuring smile.

"And us?" Roger asked, curious what the children were experiencing.

"Not today," Jack said, patting Roger's arm. "They have a long journey ahead of them. The man with the cane will make it as difficult as possible."

"As a parent, it will be even harder for you," Jess warned. "You must stay out of it to keep yourselves safe," she added urgently to Sally. "We cannot keep you all safe, but we will protect the children as long as we can," Jess confirmed.

"We need you to protect yourselves." Jack nodded at Roger and stuck out his hand. Roger took it and gave it a solid shake.

"I miss you, old friend," Roger smiled weakly at Jack.

"I miss you, too," Jack smiled back. "You've done an amazing job with them both," he said, looking at Sophie and James resting against a nearby tomb. "Thank you for everything." Roger nodded as he swallowed the lump forming in his throat.

"He's a fine young man," Jess whispered to Sally. "I couldn't have chosen a better mate for her if I tried," she smiled lovingly.

"Thank you," Sally smiled with pride.

Black fog crept into the cemetery and surround them all.

"Get out immediately and don't look back," Jack warned before wrapping his arm around his wife's waist as she returned the gesture. They walked past the sleeping children, and the Moore's watched them intently, as the black fog engulfed them both before disappearing as quickly as it came.

"What a beautiful couple," Sally whispered once the fog had cleared, and it left them without the presence of Jack and Jess.

"You have no idea," Roger whispered back.

Eight

Suddenly, the children all stirred at once. "What the heck?" asked Ben, rubbing his head.

"Time to pack up and get going," Sally ordered, taking control of the situation.

"What are we doing in a cemetery?" Tina asked, confused.

"Don't worry about that, Dear," Sally stated firmly. "We have the man after Sophie a little too close for comfort, so let's get going before he catches up."

"Where are we headed, Boss?" Ben asked Sophie as he tried to rub the sleep out of his eyes.

Just then, the phone in Tina's bag went off. They all looked at each other, knowing no one else had their numbers. Tina dug for the phone and pulled it out suspiciously.

"Don't open it," James warned. "It's most likely a trap."

"Which is WHY we need to open it," Tina said, frowning at the phone in her hand. She flipped the front open. "We need to meet. See you in KC, Kid. -M" Tina read out loud.

"Who's 'M'?" asked Roger anxiously.

"Mario," Sophie stated.

"How did he get Tina's number?" Ben asked cautiously.

"Not sure, but if there's an emergency, he would be the person to find a way," Sophie replied.

"Then Kansas City it is," James said, handing Sophie her bag. "Indirectly, of course," he smiled as he kissed her on the cheek. Sophie's hesitation was caught immediately. "What is it?" James asked her.

"I just never go home," Sophie said, in a light whisper.

"You're from Kansas City?" Tina asked in a bit of surprise. Sophie had never mentioned where her home was. They figured she didn't remember.

"Maybe you and I should travel together this time," James offered as he gently put his hand around Sophie's waist and pulled her in.

"No," Sophie said, after a second or two. "Spread out and meet at the Extended Stay America in Overland Park on 106th Street by November 18th," Sophie stated. "Take your time and leave a mark. This is the second time he's gotten too close for comfort. Let's give him the chase of a lifetime," she said with determination.

"On it!" replied Tina in a salute as she pulled out the phone to look for the nearest and fastest exits out of town.

"You sure you're okay?" James asked Sophie with concern.

"Everyone has to go home sometime," Sophie shrugged and gave him her best smile.

Roger helped Tina get some tickets ordered while Sally walked over to her son.

"Don't worry about us," Sally said. "I've been nagging your father to take me to London for a while now," she chuckled. "That Michael McIntyre is so yummy! I would love to see him in person," she said, almost swooning.

James looked at his mother in awe. Leave it to his mother to distract them all. He shook his head, but the giggle that escaped Sophie's mouth made him feel better. James stepped in front of Sophie and pulled her into his arms as their noses touched.

"I love you," he said, firmly, before kissing her as if it might be their last.

Sally looked at her husband and winked before stating, "As sweet as that is, Dear, you both need to get going."

Sally pulled Sophie into an enormous bear hug and Sophie accepted it graciously. Then Sally turned to James. "Don't take too much time," she warned her son.

He knew she meant about asking Sophie to marry him. Now was not the time. Although he couldn't trace his steps from the moment Sophie encountered Helen to the time they randomly ended up in the cemetery, he sensed it had been enough for one day.

"Yes, Mother," James muttered as he hugged Sally and kissed her on the cheek.

They said their goodbyes, and all headed in opposite directions. Sally squeezed Sophie's hand as everyone left one-by-one.

"You've got this," Sally whispered to her. "Your parents did an amazing job with you," she said, looking down at Sophie. "So, make sure you keep making them proud, because they are Sophie. So proud."

Sophie fought the need to sob as she squeezed Sally's hand. "Now let's go kick some ass. What do you say?" Sally asked, and Sophie let out a laugh.

"Yes, Ma'am," Sophie responded with a loving smile.

"Oh, call me Mom, Love," she winked and took Roger's arm to follow him to get to the airport. The wind whipped around Sophie, forcing her hair to fly chaotically around her face. She breathed in the crisp fall air.

"You're gorgeous, but it's time to get you out of that dress," said James once Sophie exited the cemetery. He had waited for her just on the other side of the wall.

"You're supposed to be getting out of here," Sophie said, staring at James in disbelief.

"Like I was going to let anyone else besides me help you get out of that dress," James said with his boyish grin. "Come on," he said, holding out his hand to her. "I have just the place."

Sophie took it without hesitation and walked with the man she loved down the empty streets of New Orleans.

"What is this place?" Sophie asked as she entered the abandoned apartment. It was bland and covered in simple furniture with white, beige, and wood providing the only color.

"An old CIA safe house," James said with a shrug as he pulled their bags inside. He walked up behind her, moved her vibrant, dark red-wine hair off to the side, and gently traced the back of her neck and shoulders with his fingertips.

"We don't have time for this," Sophie whispered, letting her head fall back as she enjoyed his touch.

"I'm just helping you get out of your dress for safety precautions," James whispered in her ear before nibbling on it. Sophie groaned in pleasure. "You didn't say HOW I had to take it off," he murmured against her neck as he worked his way down it with kisses and nibbles. Sophie gasped and bit her bottom lip in anticipation.

James's fingers worked efficiently at the ties that kept her body trapped within the corset. Sophie held up her now fallen hair and looked over her shoulder as he loosened the laces. She could finally breathe again! She heard the zipper move down and she released her hair to fall gracefully onto her shoulders. James slipped his hands gently down the front of her and cupped both her breasts.

"I spent all night thinking about how much fun it was going to be to take this off you," James whispered in her ear with heat and need.

"That's good," Sophie moaned. "I've been waiting for you to take this damn thing off me all night," she said, as her Cheshire grin made an appearance.

James gently pushed the dress down her body and held her hand for balance as she gracefully stepped out of it.

"The tennis shoes are a nice touch, but God, would I love to see those legs in some heels," he said, taking her in.

Her breasts were bare, and she wore black lace underwear to match her dress. Her legs were lean, with athletic curves from her hips to her calves. The black tennis shoes gave him a chuckle.

Sophie pressed her naked breasts against his body as she threw her arms around his neck. "I suppose we have a few minutes," she breathed, with need and desire oozing in her voice.

"Yes, Ma'am," James smiled back as he crushed his mouth against hers and carried her to the bed.

He needed her like never before. He needed her to know how much he loved her, and he didn't care if it took all night to do so. James looked down at Sophie, with her dark red-wine hair spread like a sun around her face. "You're keeping the red," he ordered before he bent down to fill her with all the love he had to give.

After an amazing night full of more love than Sophie could physically handle, it was Helen that invaded her dreams that night. Not that she thought James would go back to her, or that Helen ever had a chance at changing James' mind. It was the reminder of James having a normal life that haunted her as she tossed and turned that night.

He loved her. Sophie couldn't deny it. James had spent all night proving such to her. His gentleness and his desire and passion that made her explode repeatedly throughout the night were enough to make any girl go mad. Sophie worried if it would be enough for him.

She dreamt of a future. Walking down the aisle in a gorgeous white dress, to the man that would forever hold her heart from the first day they met. However, a future would never exist as long as the man with the cane hunted Sophie, and those she loved dearly.

Would setting James free keep him safe? Or would he simply become a bargaining chip after they had parted ways, and he found someone safer to be with? Sophie knew she would love no one else.

Even if the man with the cane allowed her to be free. No one would touch her heart as deeply as James did.

Sophie slid out of his arms and stared at the beautifully naked man lying under the sheets. She only wanted the best for him. She just didn't know if staying or leaving was best. It would kill her, literally, to ever walk away. Sophie honestly didn't know if she even could at this moment. Only death could help her do so. She studied his face in the dawn's early light seeping in from the crack of the curtains. Then the alarm on her watch went off, yanking her back to reality.

"James!" Sophie called over her shoulder as she rushed to get dressed. "We need to get out of here!" She heard his mutter of protest. "Seriously!" she begged.

"Can't we just stay here forever?" James muttered, pulling the covers over his head. Sophie yanked them off the bed, leaving his beautiful muscular body to feel the cold air around it. "Hey!" he shouted, but he had his boyish grin on. "If you want more, all you have to do is ask," James chuckled as he sat up to rub his eyes. Sophie threw his clothes at him.

"We don't have time!" Sophie shook her head and laughed. "And unless you want to die in this bed, we HAVE to get moving!"

"As long as I am with you, I'm good," James said, with a smile and sleep still in his eyes, but he knew she was right. "We should do that more often," James said, sheepishly as he forced his body to get dressed.

"Do you ever think of anything else?" Sophie laughed as she tossed his bag at him.

James thought of the ring burning a hole in his bag. "Just you,

Babe," he said, with a shrug. They grabbed their things and James grabbed Sophie's hand to pull her into his arms for one last passionate kiss. "See you on the other side," he breathed once they parted.

"See you on the other side," she breathed back.

God, she loved him. They exited the apartment and walked in opposite directions. Both determined to send the man with the cane on the wildest goose chase they could think of.

Sophie sat on a bus bound for Utah. She looked out the window and watched the colorful leaves fall quickly towards the ground as the bus whizzed by. Her thoughts kept drifting back to the man she loved and the amazing night they just shared.

James had such a need to prove his love to her last night, and she had accepted it willingly. However, the thought of him having a normal life if she wasn't with him still tugged at her heart.

"Sleep, Peanut," her mother whispered lightly in her ear. Sophie didn't have the energy to argue and closed her eyes eagerly for some rest. The wooden door appeared before her, and Sophie's shoulders slumped over automatically.

"I thought you wanted me to sleep," she whined to no one.

"Open it," her mother said, with a warning tone.

Sophie rolled her eyes as she pushed open the door. Before her laid a younger teenage version of her mother sleeping in a bunk of some sort. Gas seeped through the vent.

"Mom!" Sophie yelled. The girl remained asleep. Sophie stepped forward to go to the girl, but a hand on her shoulder made her stop.

"Just watch, Peanut," her mother whispered with sadness in her voice.

A team came and collected the girl's body and placed it on a gurney. They wheeled the unconscious girl out the door. Sophie found herself following them. "Where are they taking you?" she asked in a whisper.

"Just watch," was her mother's only response.

They placed the girl on a metal table. A younger man in a dark brown suit entered with a mask on his face. "Do it again," he ordered in a growl.

"Sir…" hesitated a female black-headed nurse. "I'm not sure this is safe. If she's not showing signs of advancement, then she most likely never will," she responded nervously.

"Do. It. Again," the man stressed, with much warning in his tone.

"Is that…," Sophie whispered.

"Yes," Jess confirmed.

They put an IV into the girl's arm, and gold liquid dripped from the bag into her body.

"Cut her open if you have to," the man offered eagerly as he watched with excitement.

"It's unnecessary," the nurse replied. "She has already had dialysis, and we replaced her blood with the synthetic. This is just an added supplement to charge the DNA already placed within her body."

"Cut her if it's needed," the man said, again not lifting his eyes from the sleeping girl. He paced the floor with much anticipation. "How long before I will know?" he asked, brushing the girl's hair from her face.

"This is entirely experimental," the nurse responded with fear in her voice. "It's hard to tell. She is the first."

The man's dark eyes glared at the nurse before he turned to kiss the girl on her head. "Keep me posted!" he barked as he left the room. The girl and everything before Sophie disappeared into smoke. They were replaced by the same man and the same nurse in an office with a large red chair behind a huge wooden desk.

"NOTHING!" he shouted as he slammed his fist on the desk.

He had a short military haircut, but you could see the dark brown roots of what remained. His eyes were dilated in his fury. There was a hint of a chocolate brown around the widened pupils. He stood about 6'5" with broad shoulders and very distinguished facial features. His brown suit matched his eyes, and he had obviously not yet gained the need for a cane yet.

"We told you it was experimental," stammered the nurse, clearly fearing for her life. "There were NO guarantees," she tried to emphasize.

"Leave," the man ordered. "Before I change my mind," he barked as he spun his back to her in the red chair. The girl didn't hesitate to follow her orders and raced out of the office. The scene before Sophie quickly turned into smoke.

"Why are these different?" Sophie asked with curiosity.

"Because they're my memories," Jess stated flatly.

"You witnessed that last one?" Sophie asked, confused.

"From the vent in the wall. He never knew," Jess said, walking away.

"What did he do?" Sophie asked as she tried to swallow the

lump in her throat and raced after her mother.

"I honestly don't know," Jess said, continuing to walk away from her daughter. "I only wanted to show you what I knew, so you understood it was not my choice."

"Mom," Sophie said, pausing. "I'm sorry for thinking otherwise. I didn't know," she said, staring down at her feet.

Jess quickly swatted at the tears that threatened to escape her eyes before she faced her daughter.

"I did my best to make your gifts your assets. Never think of them as anything other than that," Jess said in her motherly voice.

"Yes, Mother," Sophie said, giving her a smile.

Jess walked up to Sophie. "Now sleep, Peanut," she whispered before touching her forehead and forcing Sophie into a deep, restful sleep.

"Hey," Jack said, wrapping his arms around Jess' waist as she stared at the wooden door that had closed once Sophie was through. "She's going to be fine," he assured in her ear.

"We don't really know that, though, do we?" Jess stated, not moving her eyes.

Jack stepped in front of his wife and caressed her face with his hands.

"Actually, we do. We have done our best to give her the tools she needs to survive, and she excels beyond our dreams with every task. You should have more faith in her." He caught her as she crumbled before him and held her as she cried all of her guilt and frustration away.

"Do we have any clue where they are today?" Clarice sighed dramatically. It didn't matter where they were now. She knew where they were headed, and she would beat them there.

"I'm afraid not, Ma'am," the eager blonde tech replied sulkily.

Eddie waited patiently for Clarice to explode like she always did when they didn't have answers, but Clarice remained impassive. Eddie watched her intently. Everyone had a pattern, and Clarice's was off.

"I'm going to prep the team," Clarice shrugged. Realizing Eddie was watching her, she changed tactics. "If you don't find her in the next 48 hours, you'll be used as bait," she barked at the lab rat. "And your boss will be joining you," Clarice added sweetly, before she headed back to the training room.

There would be no team going with her on this trip. Clarice had left enough breadcrumbs and given Eddie the idea to reach out to Sophie's friends and Mario both, and he had gobbled it all. You would think he would be smarter by now, but Eddie wasn't as bright as he claimed to be. Her father might think highly of him; however, Eddie did not differ from any other human being. Easy to manipulate if given the proper material.

Clarice whistled as she headed down the hall. Unfortunately, Eddie heard her as she did.

Patterns never lie, and Clarice's had changed drastically over the last couple of days. Eddie tried to replay all the conversations that had taken place before he sent those coded messages.

It wasn't until recently that Eddie himself realized Mario was an old friend of Mrs. Harris. Eddie had never met him in person, or seen pictures of him, but it would only make sense for Mrs. Harris to trust Mario with Sophie when all was said and done.

Although Mario's records were scarce and mostly blacked out, Eddie had still put two and two together, regardless of the fragmented trail left behind. They had always suspected that someone came and saved Sophie, or she was already with them when Mr. and Mrs. Harris were taken out. There were just no clues that pieced together who that person was. It was the patterns that led Eddie to Mario. But did Clarice already know?

The old man had also changed his patterns, showing that he believed to be gaining the upper hand. Despite all of Eddie's attempts, he hadn't been able to find out what the old man was up to just yet.

It didn't help that Eddie had to be extremely careful when he did his digging. Mr. Eager Beaver, aka Clark, wasn't helping matters either. The kid was good. Eddie was better. However, Clark's constant nosing around made it almost impossible for Eddie to do the same for himself.

The combined shifted patterns put Eddie on edge, and not feeling great for Sophie and her friends. Clarice was getting closer to Mario, and without knowing what the old man was up to, Eddie realized he couldn't stand by waiting for Sophie to come save him anymore. Maybe he could still help her, within reason, of course. It didn't help that Mr. Harris haunted Eddie's dreams, either.

"Hello Edward," Jack had said, smiling once he convinced Eddie to open some random wooden door.

"Mr. Harris?" Eddie had asked.

"Yes, my son," Mr. Harris had said, suddenly tossing a football at Eddie. It brushed off him and fell to the ground. Eddie had stared at it. "You can't catch it if you don't even try," Mr. Harris had chuckled.

"I don't understand what's happening," Eddie had said, looking up at Mr. Harris in a fit of confusion.

"You're having a dream," shrugged Mr. Harris. "How about we play your favorite game?" he smiled as he stepped aside and a giant chess board appeared. "I'm just here to talk," Mr. Harris had assured as he sat down and waited patiently for Eddie to come join him.

After much hesitation, Eddie had taken the seat across from Mr. Harris. Mr. Harris studied the board carefully before moving a black piece forward a square. Eddie had stared at him.

"Seriously?" Eddie had asked.

"Yes, Edward," Mr. Harris had laughed at him.

"It's Eddie," Eddie had mumbled.

"Ok, Eddie," Mr. Harris smiled warmly at him. "Then I'm just Jack," he said, winking. "Your move."

Eddie stared at Jack for a bit before shaking his head and staring at the board. He finally took a turn, then Jack had whispered, "It wasn't our choice to leave you."

Eddie jerked his head up to stare at the man before him, but Jack kept his eyes on the board as if contemplating his next move.

"I guess not," Eddie had finally mumbled after Jack had made his move.

"It was not ideal to die and leave you two abandoned," Jack had said, a bit more firmly than he had intended before studying the board again.

"I didn't know he killed you," Eddie had offered while Jack

looked for his next move.

"I know, Son," Jack had said, while he waited for Eddie to make the next move.

"And now I can't leave," Eddie had said, still staring at Jack.

"I know, Son," Jack said, in a softer tone, looking back at Eddie. "No one is mad at you," he assured. "Not even Jess," he added.

Eddie smiled and looked down to make his next move.

"Eddie, there's a much bigger chess game happening on the other side of that wooden door," Jack had said in warning. "And I need my best player on board to help me win."

Eddie didn't move his eyes off the board. He knew exactly what Jack was asking him to do. He tilted his head as he weighed his options.

"She didn't knowingly leave you behind, either," Jack had stated while he stared at the board with Eddie.

"She hasn't exactly come looking either," Eddie had said, with more anger than intended before moving his piece to take over one of Jack's on the board.

"It's hard to come looking when you're constantly running," Jack had said as he stared at the board before him. "But getting amnesia doesn't exactly help either," he shrugged, speaking in his fatherly tone.

Of course! The van had done the damage that Eddie feared. That's why Sophie's pattern altered for so long.

"How much is still lost?" Eddie had asked, trying to sound casual.

"Enough to be in more danger than usual," Jack had stated once he made his move. "It's coming back, but it's a slow process."

"So, she doesn't remember me," Eddie said flatly as he

attempted to take over Jack's pawn.

"More than you would think," Jack had said with a Cheshire grin as he moved his pawn to safety. "Everyone wants to win the game," Jack had said, looking up at Eddie. "Some games require assistance, and this is one of them."

"He'll kill me, you know," Eddie had said, staring back at Jack.

Jack's face had fallen. "Yes, it's a possibility," he had said, with sorrow in his voice. "Stopping him is worth the price, don't you think?"

Eddie stared at Jack.

"Letting Sophie be free for the first time in her life would be worth bending the rules a time or two, wouldn't it?" Eddie didn't answer. "Knowing she was finally safe would be worth everything, wouldn't it?" Jack had pushed.

Eddie's eyes grew misty. Jack had stood up and come to pull Eddie into his arms and rock with him like Mrs. Harris used to.

"The choice is yours, Son," Jack had continued on. "But right now, you need to get some sleep," he had said, pulling back and touching Eddie lightly on his forehead.

Eddie didn't wake until the next morning, feeling fully rested, and his heart full once more. Eddie knew exactly what he had to do. Help Sophie reach safety.

So, when he had learned of Clarice's plan to attack Mario in Maine, Eddie had sent everyone home. He had carefully hacked Tina's burner phone to send a message from Mario so they would surely go, and one for Mario from Tina to come. He had erased his tracks and prayed that it had worked.

Eddie knew Clarice was excited to take out Mario. It would be an extensive blow to Sophie. Even Eddie knew that much. So, he had done everything in his power to spare her. They had pulled the teams long ago from Sophie's house. Only one agent remained to watch it.

Sophie could take them out in a heartbeat. And maybe going home would help her with her memory loss. Maybe going home would help her remember him. Eddie knew better than to get his hopes up, but it didn't hurt to try. However, Clarice's pattern remained off. Something still wasn't right...

Everyone had been traveling to various places across the United States, being caught occasionally on camera and enjoying the fact that they were taunting the man with the cane to find them. It was almost time to head to Kansas City and meet up, but Sophie's head had been spinning since Halloween.

She had always known she differed from everyone else. It never dawned on her it was more than just weirdness that kept her different from the rest of the human population. Was she even actually human after everything the man with the cane did to her mother? This was a very unsettling thought.

Her mother and Tina had called her "the protector." The protector of what? The key had led to a dead end, and although it was a powerful weapon for the man with the cane, it was purposely incomplete. It made no sense to hold on to it for Sophie's whole life when it was useless without the code to the satellite her father had altered. Nothing made sense.

Why did Mario ask them to go home? He had never done that before. He knew how painful it was for her, so they had avoided it at all costs. So, why go back now?

Her mother had so much experimenting done to her by that horrible man, and yet Jess had survived with none of it surfacing. Sophie was mostly glad for that. Her mother had been through enough.

She shuddered at the thought of the man with the cane finding out that everything had been a success. The things he would have forced her mother to do...Sophie shook her head to clear it and looked out the window at the droplets that chased each other down the pane before her eyes. Did he know about her? Was that the "test" at the pool that her mini me had referred to?

Sophie thought about how her dad had taught her to close her eyes and focus on the sounds she heard, no matter the distance. From the leaves brushing against the sidewalk as they danced with the wind to their next destination, to the clicking of her mother preparing a gun for firing and guessing how far away she was hiding.

She thought about how her mother trained her. Sophie realized her mother was teaching her to control her strength and speed, along with other "assets" with fighting. She wondered if that's why her mother got so mad when she found out Sophie had been fighting the bullies at school in a physical fight instead of a mental one and remaining unnoticed.

She tried to remember when she, herself, noticed her "talents". However, it was a blank slate. Probably because her parents had always made it like Sophie did not differ from any other kid, despite knowing the truth.

Her dad always gave her books to ease her racing mind as a child. Her mother and Eddie had always taken her outside to burn off the extra energy that consumed her, and she had always beaten them by miles when they raced.

Eddie…the boy Sophie was always meant to protect but left behind when her life was shattered within seconds one sunny afternoon. The day she lost everything.

He had been annoying. That was mostly because he had no patience unless he was studying people. It was the only time Sophie could get him to sit still. Eddie hated books. Yet, he loved it when Sophie shared what she was reading by retelling it in story form. He had struggled in school. Eddie wasn't book smart, but he was plenty life smart. He loved gadgets and people watching the most.

Sophie was still piecing together her fractured memories, nevertheless she had always had a soft spot for Eddie even though she never showed it. He was already following her around like a lovesick puppy, and Sophie didn't want to hurt his feelings. Eddie would always be special to her. In a brotherly way. Not the way he wanted.

She wondered if he was safe. If he had escaped his family and went off to do the great things he always talked about doing with her when they were kids. Surely, Eddie was in a much better place without her putting him in danger. Sophie watched the rain race against itself down the pane, closed her eyes, and drifted off to sleep.

Nine

The wooden door awaited her once she opened her eyes. Sophie hesitated to open it. Her mind was already swimming. She wasn't sure she could add any more to it, quite honestly.

"It's time to remember, Peanut," her father said, softly. "Go on," he urged.

Sophie sighed. She knew her father only meant well, and it was time that she remembered. She turned the doorknob and pushed open the door. Light consumed her immediately, and it took a while for her eyes to adjust. She heard the kids laughing and running behind her and she froze. How many times did she have to keep drowning to move on?

"If you want answers, you have to open your eyes, Peanut," her father pressed.

Sophie reluctantly turned around to see a younger version of herself in a birthday girl hat and dress. She was once again talking to another young girl by the pool. Promptly, a young woman, who looked similar to her mother, approached her with a much older man walking with a cane. Sophie saw his face this time.

It was an older version of the man that had been in the operating room with her teenage mother. She couldn't hear what they said to her younger self, but within seconds, the woman pushed her into the pool and held her head under the water.

Her mother flung open the back door, kicked her shoes off immediately, and ran like a bullet towards the pool. She dived in immediately and pulled Sophie from the woman's grasp before swimming them both to the opposite side of the pool.

"Have you lost your damn mind?" hissed Jess, glaring at the woman and man standing calmly on the edge of the pool opposite of her as she pulled Sophie out of the water.

"Just testing a theory," the woman replied with a simple shrug, as if drowning a child was no big deal.

"She is not a specimen for you to test," ridiculed Jess as she handed Sophie to her father.

"Says you," said the woman, looking bored by the whole situation.

Jess pulled herself out of the pool and turned to the man and woman.

"Stay. Away. From. My. Daughter," she emphasized to the couple. "Or that limp won't be the only thing you receive from me," Jess stated firmly at the man watching her intently from the edge of the pool.

He flinched at her statement but made no comment. He continued to study Sophie, coughing up water in her drenched party dress.

The woman looked at the man with the cane for orders. Everyone stood awkwardly, staring each other down. Jack picked up Sophie and carried her away while Jess remained ready for a fight. Finally, the man tapped his cane and walked away with the woman close on his heels.

Jess waited for them to leave their property before she went inside to her family. "He suspects," she said, full of concern.

"What do you want to do?" Jack asked her before instructing the soaked Sophie to go change her clothes.

"I don't know what to do," Jess said, with her voice cracking. "If he already suspects, he will never stop," she said, as panic gripped her heart.

Jack pulled his grieving wife into his arms. "Then it's time to prepare her to fight," he said firmly.

"We can't do that to her," Jess said, in alarm, pulling away from her husband.

"It's already done," Jack said, grimly. "But if we prepare her, then she will have a chance to actually win. Don't you want that for her?" he asked softly. "Shouldn't we give her every chance to be free?"

"It's not like he's just going to give up one day and call it quits," Jess snapped, walking away from her husband. "He never stops," she said, with anger oozing from her voice.

"Then we might as well hand her over now," Jack said,

frustrated. "She'll never be able to fight if you won't fight for her."

Jess turned to glare at her husband. Jack didn't care. He knew the control the man with the cane held over his wife since she first encountered him. He had groomed and brainwashed Jess to be the best assassin in the world. Only Jack could wake her up when she needed it most. They both knew it, but Jess still fought Jack, mostly when he pointed out the obvious.

"Who said I don't fight for her?" exclaimed Jess.

Jack sighed. "I don't know about you, but I'm not willing to give him our daughter to do the same to her he did to you," he said softly. She flinched at the reality. "So, how can we help her win?" Jack asked, waiting for his wife to see the whole picture with him.

Jess stared at the floor for a couple of seconds before lifting her head to stare at her husband with confidence and determination.

"We beat him at his own game," she said, showing her wicked smile.

"That's my girl," Jack said, sharing his Cheshire smile. The scene before Sophie disappeared. "We did our best," she heard her father's weary voice speak behind her. She turned around to see a very exhausted version of her father before her.

"Does he know?" Sophie whispered, unable to speak.

"No one knows everything, Peanut," Jack offered honestly.

"He really messed with mom, didn't he?" Sophie asked, looking at the ground with a loss of what more to say.

"That he did," Jack answered angrily. "He made her into the very thing he wanted most," he said, bringing his hands into tight fists.

So many questions came to mind. "So, what changed?" Sophie asked, looking at her father, who was clearly in pain.

Jack chuckled, changing his mood immediately. "She blames me," he said with a slight smile.

"I can see that," Sophie said, smiling at her father.

"Yeah, well, you changed her even more," Jack added, winking at his daughter.

"How did he find her?" Sophie asked with curiosity.

"That is not my story to tell," Jack said, more sternly. "She will share it when she's ready," he added, knowing his daughter's curiosity well.

Sophie knew that meant she was to drop it, but she wondered if knowing the whole story would give her what she needed to be free once and for all.

"Mario wants me to go home," she said, slowly changing the subject.

"Does he know?" Jack said with interest.

"He sent Tina a message," Sophie informed him.

"How do you feel about that?" Jack asked cautiously.

"I've never been back," Sophie said, looking at the floor uncomfortably.

"That's understandable," Jack said, walking towards his daughter and putting his hand on her shoulder. "Home is never the structure that takes up space," he offered.

Sophie distractedly rubbed the necklace. "It's where the heart is," she said, softly.

"That is true," Jack said, lifting his daughter's chin to look into her eyes. "Don't let the past haunt you, Peanut," he said, softly. "Our journeys don't define us. They're simply a part of who we are."

"You make everything sound like a Hallmark card," Sophie

retorted.

Jack chuckled. "Maybe they'll hire me in my next life," he said, winking. Sophie stared at her father before shaking her head and rolling her eyes.

"You take being dead lightly," Sophie said flatly.

"Eternity will do that to you," Jack shrugged. "But for now, you need your rest."

Sophie sighed and prepared to be pushed through the door, but then her father hesitated.

"What?" Sophie asked.

"Just keep your guard up," Jack added with concern.

"What's wrong?" Sophie asked, knowing her father's instincts well.

"Going home shouldn't be bothersome," Jack said, slowly, as if he was trying to find the right words. "Never underestimate the enemy. They may be closer than you think," he added, deep in thought.

"Do you think it's a trap?" Sophie asked, suddenly in alarm.

"I'm not sure," Jack added honestly. "However, luck will not always be on your side. Don't be overly confident, because things have been going your way thus far," he added with concern.

"Is Mario in trouble?" Sophie asked in alarm.

"Looks like you're about to find out," Jack said, with a frown, and before Sophie could say anything else, he touched her on her forehead and put her in a deep dreamless sleep.

The leaves were holding on for dear life to the dormant trees they called home. The wind smelled of autumn, and people were enjoying the sweater weather while it lasted.

Christmas lights were making their appearance, and the cheerful sounds of Christmas played throughout the bus station as Sophie stepped off. Christmas always came sooner and sooner with each passing year. Before too long, it was going to appear before summer had actually said goodbye.

However, it still remained Sophie's favorite time of the year. Not for the commercial aspects, but because the songs and decorations always brought out the kid in her. Her Cheshire grin shined as she recalled the memories of her past.

Sophie remembered smashing her nose against the cold window as her parents drove her around to look at the lights. Decorating the tree with her mother. Watching Christmas movies as a family. *White Christmas* was always a must for her mother. Sophie also baked goodies with Jess to hand out to friends, family, and workers in their neighborhood.

Then her dad would tuck her into bed, before reading "The Night Before Christmas" to her as she drifted off to sleep. Christmas morning was full of presents and eating cinnamon rolls for breakfast and a Christmas feast for a late lunch/early dinner, followed by laughs and quality family time.

Sophie sighed as she made her way through the station unseen. Kansas City was a lot of things, but it was definitely a city that did Christmas right.

Mario had done his best to keep many of those traditions alive as she grew older, and only the two of them remained. Even though Sophie's anger and frustration at her parent's murder ruined the holidays more often than not, Mario had always been patient with her. Understanding her pain and even suffering with her.

However, her dad's warning kept circling in her mind. "Just keep your guard up," Jack had said. He seemed just as bothered by this trip as she was. Something wasn't right. Sophie would check in with Tina to see if any more messages had arrived in her absence once they all got to the hotel.

She called for an Uber and waited patiently at the bus station entrance for the driver to arrive. A blue Honda Civic pulled up to the curb, and Sophie quickly hopped in.

"Good afternoon, Ma'am," the boy, who didn't look much older than Sophie, greeted her. He had messy jet-black hair, and a tan complexion despite the lack of sun hiding behind the winter grey clouds in the sky.

"Hello," Sophie replied politely as she looked out the window while he started their journey.

"First time in KC?" he asked, insisting on small talk.

"No," Sophie answered politely as she continued to stare out the window. He gained no insight from her body language that she wanted to be left with her thoughts. Christmas music blared from his radio.

"Some people say it's too early," he babbled on. "But it's never too early to get into the cherry spirit," he said merrily. Sophie didn't respond. "I absolutely love this time of the year!" he continued. "What about you?"

Taking note that small talk was going to be her only option, whether she liked it or not, Sophie entertained the driver all the way to her destination. She had forgotten just how friendly the Midwest could actually be. It was an aspect she had missed in most locations she traveled to. He wasn't doing it to be annoying. He was just naturally overly friendly. Sophie wondered if she would be the same if she had gotten to stay.

"Thank you," she said sweetly, giving him a smile as she climbed out of the seat. He eagerly helped her with her bags to the door.

"No problem!" he said with a smile from ear to ear. "Welcome back! And may your stay be half as amazing as you are," he bowed. Sophie giggled, making a mental note to give him a good tip and rating once she was inside and out of the cold.

"I thought you only giggled for me," said, a familiar voice behind her.

Sophie turned slowly to see James leaning against the pillar with his arms crossed and smiling his boyish grin that made her knees go weak every time she saw it.

"You do get it out of me the most," Sophie giggled and winked as she headed inside.

He kept his distance, despite his eagerness to pull her into his arms. They avoided the security cameras and headed up the back staircase. He gave her a head start to get to their room first, before he entered and dropped his bag just in time to catch her jumping into his arms and kissing him passionately. He returned the favor feverishly.

"I hate these longer trips," James murmured against her lips. Her giggled response only made him want her more. He carried her to the bed.

"Seriously!" Sophie laughed. "Didn't you get enough on Halloween?" she tried to act put out.

"I can never get enough of you," James murmured in desire and placed her gently on the bed to prove to her just how much he had missed her.

ꝏ

"Can I ask you something?" James asked her nervously as he stroked Sophie's naked back lightly with his fingertips.

"If you're asking me if I'm ready for another round, I think I need to eat first," Sophie giggled as her naked body was tangled with his under the sheets.

"Well, that wasn't what I was going to ask, but duly noted," James said, deep in thought.

"What's up?" Sophie asked, suddenly too scared to look at him. She wondered if this was the end of them.

"I know that life is not ideal at the moment," James started with reluctance.

Sophie's stomach dropped immediately, and she battled the desire to curl up into the fetal position. She tried to wipe the tears away without him noticing.

"Do you ever think of a future?" James asked nervously.

"I kind of have to put all my energy in the now and what's our next move," Sophie replied, slowly wondering where this was going and hoping it wouldn't lead to her heart shattering forever.

"No, I meant," James tried again, "do you ever think of a future with me?" he asked with obvious panic in his voice.

"What do you mean?" Sophie asked, fighting the urge to look at him just yet.

"I guess, do you see yourself growing old with me?" James asked, trying to swallow away his anxiety and the lump that was lodged in his throat.

"Oh," Sophie said, deep in thought. She wondered how honest she should actually be, since she was still not sure where exactly this was going.

"Be honest, Peanut," her father whispered.

Sophie wasn't sure if she should be disturbed or grateful that her father was with her at this moment. "I've definitely had a couple of dreams," Sophie confessed.

She wasn't sure that she was ready to share that she had dreamt of walking down the aisle in a white wedding dress to share lifelong vows with him. Or the dream where they had their own house in the woods as they sat holding hands in rocking chairs well into their 80s.

"I worry that if I don't focus on keeping you safe, I will lose you all together," she added honestly.

"I understand that," James said, mater-of-factly. Sophie knew that he actually did. "If life was different," he tried again. "Would you be alright growing old with me?"

Sophie could feel his heart racing out of his chest against her cheek with anticipation of her answer. However, she had a question of her own first.

"Do you think you would be better off if I did not suck you into my nightmare?" Sophie asked slowly. It was a question that had haunted her from the first day they had met.

"You're avoiding the subject," James replied with a frown.

"I'm not trying to," Sophie admitted honestly.

"Is this because of Helen?" James asked, pushing Sophie up to meet his eyes. "She means nothing to me," he stated firmly. "I would never go back to that," he said decisively.

"I know that," Sophie assured. "But don't you ever wonder if your life would be better if you weren't constantly running for your life?" she asked quickly, becoming light-headed and overwhelmed with emotions.

James immediately pulled her to his chest and held her tightly.

"Just because you drew the short straw of life, and there's a psychopath after you, doesn't make you any less of a prize," he stated strongly. "I CHOOSE to be here. I CHOOSE to be with you. Mostly because I don't think my heart will ever beat again without you in my life. I love you that much," he confessed unintentionally. James held his breath, wondering what the consequence of his confession would bring.

Sophie contemplated his declaration seriously before answering, "Only if we can have matching rocking chairs on the deck." She smiled against his chest as his heart raced with joy more than anxiety.

He kissed her gently on the top of her head, finally having the answer he had hoped to get since the first day they met. He also started to plan his proposal as he stroked her hair gently with his fingers. Not knowing what life altering action would come that would prove to either destroy them or bring them closer together for life.

Ten

Sophie and James were dressed and cuddling on the bed watching tv when Ben and Tina finally arrived. Tina eyed them suspiciously, knowing that afterglow way too well. "You guys are worse than rabbits," she said, shaking her head at both of them.

"Like you aren't just as bad," Sophie retorted, smirking at her friend. She didn't have the heart to remind Tina how good her hearing actually was. Tina pretended to look shocked and overly dramatic.

"Any more messages from Mario?" Sophie asked, changing the subject.

"No," Tina replied honestly. "Is that strange?"

"Not necessarily," Sophie responded, hearing her father's

warning ring in her ear.

"Where would he meet you?" Ben asked.

"I don't know," Sophie said. "We've never come back here since we left."

"Well, what should we do while we wait?" Tina asked.

"Get supplies. I don't know how long we will need to stay here, but we have a kitchen here and should use it," Sophie shrugged.

"How does it feel being back?" James asked cautiously.

"Not as haunting as I originally thought," Sophie replied honestly, smiling at him. "I just remember all the holiday fun we used to do as a family," she shrugged.

"This is an awesome place for Christmas," Ben said, looking out the window. "Should we get a tree?" he asked absentmindedly.

"It's not even Thanksgiving!" Tina protested with her hands on her hips.

"Fine," Ben said, pouting. "What about a Thanksgiving feast, then?" he suggested.

"A family deserves a feast," James added, smiling at his friend.

"I'll start a list," Tina said, grabbing paper and pen.

"I know you haven't been here in a while," Ben said with hesitation.

"What do you want, Ben?" Sophie laughed. She'd never seen him act like such a kid before.

"Well, I think it's pretty cool that we finally get to see where you grew up," Ben started. "I'd like to look around," he shrugged.

Tina and James looked from Ben to Sophie. They weren't sure where this was going, or what Sophie was going to do. This was fragile territory, and they gawked at Ben's ability to not fully recognize that.

"Ben, Honey," Tina started immediately rushing to his side to help pull his foot out of his mouth.

"You want me to show you around?" Sophie asked, analyzing him with reservation.

"Well, yeah," Ben concluded. "Hey!" he yelled as his wife dug her nails into his arm.

Sophie looked at the family that was now before her. Tina and James looked scared to death, and Ben was still pouting from the abuse of his wife's nails. She started laughing hysterically as tears rolled down her cheeks. Everyone froze, not sure what to do.

Sophie wiped the tears from her cheeks and slowed her laughter to a chuckle. "Yes, Ben," she smiled her Cheshire grin. "I will show you Kansas City."

Ben stuck his tongue out at his wife and pulled his arm out of her grasp before she could do more harm. He rubbed it while he stood next to Sophie for safety.

"I'm not sure that's the best idea," James started.

"It's fine," Sophie assured. "The weather is finicky in the Midwest. So far, it's promising to be freezing, which means we can hide in crowds covered in scarves and other winter gear. Which reminds me," she added, turning to Tina. "We'll need to go shopping for that winter gear." Tina's face lit up at those magical words.

"We'll get it at a sporting goods store," Sophie clarified. Tina's face dropped. "But I'll take you downtown and to the Plaza," she said, winking. Tina smiled at her friend. She knew her so well. "So, let's get the food taken care of and go from there," Sophie added with authority.

Tina and James worked on the food list, while Ben and Sophie worked on the sight-seeing list. A new family meant new traditions. Sophie knew this would be their first holiday season together. She also knew her hometown would provide them with enough magic and a much-needed break from being on the run.

Sophie didn't forget her father's warning. She was just pulling from her mother's constant reminder that to succeed meant recharging your batteries. And what better way than creating new traditions with her new family. A day or two surely wouldn't hurt. After all, they had spent a couple of weeks giving the man with the cane the wild goose chase of a lifetime before arriving. They had earned a couple of days of celebration.

A gust of wind blew the window unexpectedly open. Sophie rushed to close it and lock it in place. A storm was headed their way. She just didn't see it before it was too late....

It impressed Eddie. Mario hadn't lost his touch with remaining a ghost. He'd had plenty of years of practicing by hiding in plain sight. Mario left immediately after receiving the text message from Tina (aka Eddie). Yet, Clarice didn't head off towards Mario's like she had stated previously. She had even been overly dramatic at the fact that he had left Maine. Too dramatic, even for Clarice.

Eddie's gut was alarmingly disturbed, and his gut was never wrong. It was too late to stop the chess pieces that were already in play. All Eddie could do was wait and watch. It was unclear if he had put his pawns in danger or led them to safety as he intended. It was now Clarice's move, and there was no telling what she had planned at this moment. This was the most important chess game in Eddie's life. He worried it would be one he wouldn't be able to win.

"Have more faith, Son," he heard Jack whisper in his ear, but it didn't bring any peace to Eddie.

He knew Clarice better than she even knew herself. And Clarice had a winning move hidden up her sleeve. Eddie just had to figure out what it was before she used it, and it cost him the game along with his life.

Although Eddie typically avoided Clarice at all costs, the only way to find out what she was up to was to do the opposite. He walked into the training room with a hot tea in his hand as he leaned against the door frame.

"How's training going?" Eddie asked her casually.

Clarice stopped immediately in mid jump. "Why do you care?" she asked suspiciously and analyzing him from head to toe.

"Oh, you know," Eddie shrugged. "Tis the season and all that bs."

"What do you want, Troll?" Clarice snapped, grabbing a towel to wipe the sweat from her face.

"Do you think we should get a tree to put up in the lab?" Eddie asked randomly, looking thoughtful as he watched her every move. Her left eye twitched, and he knew he had hit a nerve.

"I'm sure father would love that," Clarice said, sarcastically. "Go for it," she said. Her father might actually finally rip Eddie to shreds as he deserved.

"I'll be sure to tell him it was your idea," Eddie said with a wicked smile.

Clarice froze and gripped onto the towel until her knuckles

turned white.

"So, is that a no, then?" Eddie poked at her.

"How did you get to be so damn annoying?" Clarice hissed at him without making eye contact.

"Well, probably came with being in this dungeon with no sunlight for all those years," Eddie answered sarcastically.

"You didn't have to say yes," Clarice reminded him.

Eddie glared at her. He only really had himself to blame for being in his current situation. He didn't have to say yes. But he had already agreed when he heard Sophie's name.

"So, should I get a star or angel for the tree?" Eddie said, poking her right back. Clarice screamed and threw the towel at him.

"Get the damn tree!" she hissed. "It won't matter when I give my father the best gift ever," Clarice yelled. "You won't even be a blip on his radar!"

There she was. "Well, don't get him a tie. I already got him one," Eddie said, smiling as he sipped his tea.

"You cocky little prick," Clarice murmured under her breath. "Keep up the jokes. You'll be singing a different tune once I get back."

"Oh," Eddie said, in interest. "And where are you headed?"

"None of your concern," Clarice retorted as she grabbed her bag and stormed out of the room. "Enjoy your tea. I will tell Mario and Sophie you said hi once I get to Kansas City," she cooed as she passed him.

Eddie dropped his cup, and it shattered all over the floor at his feet.

"Check mate!" Clarice yelled over her shoulder as she grabbed her travel bag from one of the lackies and headed for their private jet.

Eddie's heart stopped beating. His brain shut down. His knees buckled under him as he hit the ground hard, jarring his knees. He had done the very thing he promised Jack he would never do. And now they were all going to die because of him. The room spun, and his face hit the ground with a solid thud. Darkness consumed him with no hope of ever breathing life again.

"Jack," he called out as life slipped away from him.

After getting proper attire to face the bitter cold, Sophie took them downtown to see what the city offered, and set Tina loose on the Plaza to get her shopping fix. Strips of stores as far as the eye could see.

She introduced them to proper BBQ, and they viewed amazing light displays once the sun went down. Sophie clung onto James as they walked the city streets. He loved seeing her so happy and relaxed again. Just like the first time they visited his hometown. James thought he might need a tranquilizer for both Sophie and Ben when it came to the Christmas lights.

"This is your fault," Tina had griped to James, but soon was laughing at her husband's excitement.

"I need your help with something," James whispered to Tina as Sophie and Ben raced from one Christmas display to the next like kids on Christmas morning.

"So, you're finally going to pull the trigger," Tina said, shaking her head at the grown children before her.

"How did you..." James started.

"Please," Tina cut him off, rolling her eyes at him. "Ben and I have known you've been carrying that ring since almost day one."

"Seriously?" James asked, dumbfounded.

"Seriously? It's me, Nerd," Tina replied sarcastically. "What do you have planned so far?"

"Getting on one knee," James said, flinching. He had too many ideas, but none of them seemed good enough.

"You know, for once it would be nice if I didn't have to do all the work," Tina said, stopping and crossing her arms. When she saw James' face fall, she started giggling. "Come on," she said, taking his arm. "You know I was going to take over anyway," Tina laughed as she started sharing some of the ideas she had already come up with since Sophie entered their lives.

Tina had taken a pouting Ben away from the displays to go get supplies while James took Sophie out for a quiet dinner. Tina had reported that Sophie was to meet Mario later that night alone, per his request. They had ventured into Olathe, Kansas, to go to Smokin' Joe's BBQ.

"You sure you don't want to go somewhere nice?" James asked, looking around the empty restaurant that was a hole in a wall that no one seemed to know about.

"As if!" Sophie declared as she gave their order to the short lady behind the counter. "Trust me," she said, giving her Cheshire grin.

Within minutes, James was laughing with Sophie as he ended up wearing just as much BBQ as he was consuming, but she was right.

Totally worth it!

Sophie shared what holiday traditions she could remember. It surprised her that James had similar ones with his family. "Who seriously opens all their presents on Christmas Eve?" Sophie protested.

"Monsters, clearly," James said, taking the last bit of meat off the ribs before him.

"We should figure out what traditions we should have," Sophie said, staring off deep in thought.

James loved hearing her talk about their future. He was never more certain that Sophie was ready for what he had to propose to her. James started trying to figure out what he was going to tell her as a proposal when something interrupted his thoughts.

"Hey," he said, gloomily.

"What?" Sophie asked, intrigued by his sudden gloom and doom face.

"Today has been amazing, don't get me wrong," James started. "But do you think we'll actually get to celebrate? I mean, it's not like we don't have things to be dealing with," he said, slowly.

"Yeah," Sophie said, understanding his hesitation. "I know," she sighed. "I guess I got caught up in the day," she said, a little depressed.

"Well," James said, with a sudden idea. "It's important to recharge your batteries and remember what you're fighting for."

"You sound just like my mother," Sophie grumbled and wrinkled up her nose.

"A wise woman," James smirked, trying not to be offended by her reaction. "Maybe let's just keep it simple and small. You know, until we're done with what needs to be done," he offered. "Then we can do all sorts of big holidays," he added quickly.

"The only problem is," Sophie responded, "I don't think we will ever truly be done," she sighed. "There's no way to guarantee we will ever be free," she sulked. "And I can't ask you to give up your lives to live like this forever. I just have to come up with a way to keep you all safe, and I just haven't been able to do that," Sophie said with a frown.

"Oh, no you don't," James declared.

"What?" Sophie asked, confused.

"You're not getting rid of us!" James said, raising his voice.

"First of all, calm down," Sophie hissed as the lady behind the counter stared at them.

"We're the only ones in here," James hissed back, trying to stifle his anger. "We CHOOSE to be here for a reason. You don't get to make those decisions for us," James said, crossing his arms in front of his chest, trying to curb his frustration.

"It's not realistic," Sophie started with her own temper rising.

"YOU don't get to decide what's best for us, Soph," James said, losing his battle with his frustration. "People don't leave loved ones behind like they're nothing," he muttered.

"My parents left without giving ME a choice," Sophie retorted back.

"Oh, they did, huh?" James said, understanding suddenly what he needed to make her see. "They don't visit you in your dreams?" he asked more softly. "They don't keep you safe at all costs?" he added. James watched as she flinched at his words.

He reached across the table to take her hands in his, despite the sticky BBQ that seemed to remain on them. "Sophie," he whispered softly. "Even in death, they haven't left you for one single second," he added calmly. "It's time you stop feeling like you deserve to be alone and accept that you are NEVER alone," James emphasized.

Sophie stared at their intertwined hands. She had never thought of it that way. James was right. She wasn't alone, by her old family or her new. Even death had kept her company when she was by herself. Sophie frowned. It wasn't fair that he could see what she couldn't, but she also knew it was good for her. Balance. Like her mother always wished for her.

Sophie took a deep sigh and released his hands to hand him a wet nap. "Wipe your face too, Nerd," she laughed lovingly. "And don't expect me to tell you you're right," she added sarcastically, although they both knew he was. James smiled his boyish grin. "Stop it!" Sophie said, pointing her finger at him.

"What?" he laughed.

"That," she said, waving her hand dramatically in front of his face. "If you think that look will keep you out of trouble, you're seriously mistaken," she said, trying not to sound flustered.

"What look?" James asked innocently, knowing exactly what she was talking about.

It was the orneriness that Sophie brought out in him, that his mother always warned would make girls go weak at their knees. However, James only wanted one girl to go weak with his charm. The one pretending to resist his charms from across the table.

"You know what?" she muttered as she fought to stifle a laugh. "Come on, Nerd," Sophie said. "We should get back."

"Okay, fine," James said, suddenly knowing exactly what he was going to tell her when he got on one knee to ask her to marry him. The exact date didn't matter. Only that he could call her his for life.

Eleven

Mario couldn't understand why Sophie wanted to meet at home. They hadn't stepped foot near Kansas City since the night he had pulled her from the closet. Quite honestly, it was too painful for them both. Tina's message had stated to clearly be here, so maybe Sophie could finally move past the pain. The thought made his heart swell like a proud father.

Mario, however, still needed work. He had accepted long ago that he lost the love of his life to Jack, but there wasn't even a chance for Mario when it came to the nerdy scientist.

Mario had resented Jack for years when Jess told him. It's easy to despise the guy that was the reason for your heart shattering into tiny pieces. However, Jess' heart was never Mario's to begin with. And

Jack was harder to hate the more Jess had forced Mario to get to know him. Jack was her perfect fit.

Although Jess had written off their affair as more of a fling because of the stress and excitement of their job, it had always meant more to Mario. Jess was a whirlwind of life that would change Mario forever. He just wasn't brave enough to ever tell her. However, they fought more than they made love. It was always over the same thing. The old man's hold over her.

Mario knew he had done things to Jess. Even brainwashed her. The older she got, the more she could break away. Nevertheless, a simple phone call would bring her back every time. Jess always said it was for Clarice, but Mario had a hard time swallowing that fact.

Clarice was a walking psychopathic basket case. He would never understand Jess' need to protect her. It wasn't totally Clarice's fault. The old man tortured her to no end mentally. He refused to give Clarice the one thing she ever wanted...love.

Jess was always determined to be the one thing Clarice would never get from her father, even if she didn't appreciate it or accept it. Mario was certain it was because Clarice wasn't capable of accepting love. Jess refused to see it that way.

Then Jack came and broke the spell the old man had over Jess. He was the one human being that could free Jess from the old man's hold, and he despised Jack for it, making Jack the biggest target of all. Until they found out they were pregnant.

Although Mario came to like Jack, it didn't make it any easier being around the super couple of love regularly. Mario continued to take jobs on the side as an excuse not to be dragged out to be a third wheel. When he had heard Jess was pregnant, it was just too much to take, so he packed his schedule full of dangerous missions, not caring if he didn't survive.

Nine months later, Jess had cornered Mario and insisted that he come to the house. She was savvy enough to know that he couldn't tell her 'no' to her face when she looked at him with her puppy dog eyes. Mario had reluctantly agreed. He showed up at the house for dinner and immediately had a red headed blue-eyed baby girl shoved into his arms despite his protest.

"Get used to her," Jess had smirked. "I refuse to have an absent godfather in her life," she had said over her shoulder as she walked away.

Mario froze and stared at the creature currently cooing in his arms. "I'm sorry, what?" he had asked, racing after her.

"Godfather," Jess repeated as she had continued making dinner. "And not the Marlon Brando kind either," Jess had emphasized, pointing the knife in her hand in his direction before she went back to cutting vegetables.

"I don't know a thing about children," Mario had protested. "I don't even know if I even like them," he had added honestly.

"Well, you'd better like this one," was all Jess had said.

"Why me?" Mario had asked, completely confused and trying to hand Sophie back to her.

Jess had put the knife down with a sigh.

"Because there's no one else I trust with my life when danger comes knocking at my door," she had said, staring at him sadly. "You're the only one I trust to always keep her safe should something happen," Jess had added, looking into Mario's eyes. "Besides," Jess had said, "it will be a wonderful challenge for you. You know if she's mine, she's going to be a handful. I need all the help I can get!" she had chuckled, not knowing how true that statement actually was. Neither of them had known then that it would be Mario raising Sophie for half her life.

Mario had stared back down at the child, whose eyes seemed to look straight into his soul. "Well, you're screwed, Kid," Mario had said to her. Sophie giggled in his arms, and his life changed forever.

He got off the bus and immediately stretched his stiff body. Man, was he getting old. He looked around the station. He didn't see any trouble waiting for him.

Mario tossed his bag on his back and headed off to catch his Uber. He was too caught up in his memories to see Clarice watching him from a distance. A shiver shot down his spine. The wind blew with a warning around his body, but he couldn't hear what it had to say. He took one look around the station before climbing into the black 2010 Lincoln MKZ, not knowing it would be his last.

The Uber stopped just down the street from the old Harris household in Blue Springs. The old man made sure it never went on the market and it remained a shrine for his most epic kill. It disgusted Mario to his core. Another reason they never returned "home".

He spotted the stakeout a mile away, sleeping in a black sedan across the street. When Mario snuck up to it, the kid inside was already dead. A wind gust circled him once more, but Mario missed the warning being sent. Instead, he blindly rushed inside to try to save Sophie, and was struck immediately from behind with a solid object that made the room spin immediately. He fell to his knees, falling forward.

"Hello, old friend," a woman's voice chuckled as he hit the ground.

"Sophie?" Mario asked, confused.

"Try again," sneered the woman.

"Clarice..." Mario breathed out as the darkness consumed him.

"You're as easily manipulated as usual," Clarice barked as she threw a bucket of water at Mario's face.

He struggled to get the room back into focus. They were in an abandoned warehouse somewhere surrounded by cement, pillars, and dust. It was obvious no one had been in there for years. Mario shook his head, trying to get his mind to work as he listened for cluing sounds outside.

"Still making Jess proud, I see," he slurred, buying himself some time.

"Poor Mario," Clarice chuckled. "Still pining over a woman who never wanted him in the first place.

Ugh, this woman was obnoxious. "Focus," he heard Jess' voice ring in his ears.

"Trying to," he said, annoyed at no one.

Clarice just rolled her eyes at the man tied to the beams above them. Topless, wet, out of shape, and aging poorly, in her opinion. He was 6'3" with a grey beard and mustache, small gold hooped earrings, and a black skull bandana wrapped around the top of his head. His black cargo pants and boots had seen better days.

At first glance, you would assume he belonged to a biker gang of some sort, but Clarice knew better. The hair on his chest had turned grey like all the others, and although his weight didn't overpower his frame, it still lacked its 20-year-old firmness. She would have to pace herself. He was much easier to kill in this state. However, it wasn't about being quick. It was about getting her ten plus years of frustration out.

"Wow," she chuckled. "Someone's really let themself go over the years."

"What do you want, Clarice?" Mario asked flatly as his head bobbed around trying to find clarity to his situation.

"Our dear Sophie, of course," Clarice shrugged as her heels clicked against the cement as she walked around her prey.

Mario laughed so hard it made his head throb. "Good luck with that," he smiled.

"Oh, she's closer than you think," Clarice smiled.

Mario's body tightened in anticipation. Clarice took pleasure in his inner torture.

"And you think killing me in front of her is going to get her to sign right up?" Mario asked, bewildered at Clarice's planning process. Had she really not thought this all the way through, even a little?

"The end result is none of your concern," Clarice shrugged as she eyed him thoroughly, wondering how she wanted to torture him first.

"Wow," Mario said, shaking his head. "Jess always said you were smart. It's a shame she can't see how wrong she actually was."

Clarice stopped and fisted her hands. "I think I will start with jumper cables," she said with a growl.

“I’m not going to tell you anything,” Mario said, sounding bored.

“I don’t need anything from you,” Clarice said, sweetly, getting the cables from the table. She clipped an end to each earring. “This is just for fun,” she smiled as she turned on the battery and Mario’s body convulsed before her.

“Mario,” Jess pleaded in his ear.

His breathing was shallow, and he tasted the blood in his mouth. He felt it running into his ears, and his eyes almost swelling shut. It had been a couple of hours; he had guessed.

From the noises outside, Mario guessed they were in the West Bottoms just immediately west of downtown Kansas City. Where no one would hear screams since the haunted houses were closed and no one would venture out at night to this side of town.

Mario knew he was no longer hanging from the rafters. Clarice was using every form of torture known to mankind on him. Now, his hands were handcuffed behind his back, and his head throbbed from all the blood and organs being electrocuted and attacked.

His options were limited. Clarice was taking her time torturing him. He figured over ten years of pent-up anger was bound to cost him something. A chuckle escaped his lips at being the cause of her suffering for so many years.

“What’s so funny?” Clarice snapped from behind him.

“You don’t want to know,” Mario answered honestly. His head hung low. The warehouse reeked of cooked skin and blood.

"You might as well share your last thoughts," Clarice said, smiling as she walked to face him.

"Fine," Mario said, pulling his overly heavy head up to meet her glance. "I was just thinking how funny it was that I was the one that kept Sophie from you all these years, and you weren't able to even come close to her," he said, smiling.

Clarice screamed out her frustration as she punched him in the face, breaking his nose. He turned his head and spat out the blood quickly filling his mouth.

"Told you that you didn't want to know," Mario shrugged.

It wasn't Clarice that held his attention anymore. It was something much more important. He had almost missed hearing her slide in carefully. He sensed her anguish immediately. His heart shattered to pieces even worse than the day Jess had told him she was in love with another man.

The West Bottoms was an odd place to meet. She was thankful it wasn't her old house. Sophie was much more willing to come to the corporate made haunted houses than the real one that rested in the heart of Blue Springs, MO. The wind gusted around her and blew a chill down her spine. "S.o.p.h.i.e," it called, but she was too focused on the past to hear it.

She reached forward to turn the knob on the metal door entrance.

"No!" Jess warned.

Sophie froze at the urgency in her mother's voice. Something wasn't right.

Sophie looked around the old, abandoned building until the skylight caught her eyes. She quietly scaled the creaking building in the pitch-black darkness and slid in quieter than a mouse. She was not prepared for the sight before her.

Mario was half naked and completely defeated, handcuffed to a chair. An ash brown haired thin woman of almost six feet towered over him dressed oddly in heels with black ops attire. Her curly chin length hair was thin. It reminded Sophie a little of her mother's. Her facial features were sharp and almost skeletal like, and the blue eyes that contained a hollowness that Sophie had never seen before. It was the woman from the pool.

Sophie's chest tightened and she could no longer breathe properly. Anxiety consumed her as she watched the sight before her. "Breathe," her mother coached in her ear, but Sophie's body refused to follow her orders.

"It's a shame," Mario called out, knowing time was limited. "Jess always thought you were better than this."

Sophie froze at her mother's name.

Clarice laughed out loud at his random statement. "Clearly she was wrong," she shrugged.

"She doesn't have to be," Mario said.

"Now, you're pleading for your life?" Clarice said, tapping her foot against the cement floor.

"No," Mario said, admittedly. "I know my time is up," he emphasized. "But it would be such a shame to break Jess' heart," he added, watching Clarice carefully.

"Yeah, well, payback's a bitch," Clarice said, clearly shaken by his statement. "I guess it doesn't pay to be daddy's favorite, after all," she shrugged, trying to regain her focus.

"That's why we're here, isn't it?" Mario asked softly.

"We're here because you've been a pain in my ass for over ten years, and I'm over it," Clarice said firmly as anger invaded her voice.

"Jess wanted her free," Mario said in his fatherly voice. "Just like she wanted the same for you."

"Yeah, well, she didn't exactly make the best choices for me to follow, now did she?" Clarice snapped back. "She buried herself," she mumbled.

"If that's what helps you sleep at night," Mario shrugged.

Clarice glared at him. "I sleep just fine," she lied.

Sophie couldn't process the information she was collecting. Panic was taking over as her body struggled between flight and fight. "Sophie, don't," her mother begged inside her swirling head, but Sophie's ears were deaf to her pleading.

"I know it's hard to see that Jess only ever had love for you, seeing that you don't know what love actually is," Mario continued, hoping that Sophie was listening to the words he was carefully sharing.

Clarice threw her head back wildly as she cackled liked a laughing hyena.

"She was just another pain in my ass," she grumbled. "Daddy's pet that went rouge," Clarice said, smiling a wicked smile as she leaned closer to Mario's face. "Love only gets people killed," she said sweetly.

The words pierced Sophie to her core as grief consumed her entire body, making it impossible to move.

"I disagree," Mario said. "Every love will make you fight harder, and every heartbreak will only make you that much stronger," he said. Sophie's ears perked up as her eyes became laser focused. "Each death will be fuel for your fire to go on," Mario stressed.

Sophie knew these words. They were words her mother spoke to her before she had fought Simon to the death. Mario seemed to know them by heart, as if he had heard them too.

Sophie pulled her hands over hear ears. This was going to be yet another sacrifice for the cause that she never signed up to fight. Anger fueled at her core.

"Each magical moment will remind you what you fight for," Mario continued, swallowing hard to push the lump lodged in his throat. "These ghosts are not to haunt you and make you weak," he said, staring at Clarice with a message meant for Sophie. "They are the silent army that carries you to victory."

"Victory?" Clarice said, in confusion.

Then her eyes quickly lit up with sickening excitement as realization took over. She grabbed the gun from the back of her pants and shoved it against Mario's head as she held him in a headlock.

Sophie's blood boiled with rage. Her cheeks reddened with the heat that radiated through her body. She only saw red when she looked at her godfather, who was telling her goodbye.

"Sophie Lee," her mother warned inside her ears, but the warning only fell on deaf ears as she jumped from the beam she had been crouched on.

Sophie landed gracefully on the balls of her feet, using her left hand to balance while holding her right arm in the air. Her vibrant, dark red wine-colored hair hid her face. Her chest exaggeratedly rose and plunged with her amplified breathing.

"Oh, look," Clarice cooed. "The prodigal child has arrived."

"SOPHIE!" her mother screamed out inside her head.

When Sophie slowly raised her head to meet Clarice, her eyes were completely dilated, and she heard nothing that was being said.

Mario shook with fear at the creature that looked back at them. He had never seen Sophie in this condition. He knew she was hurting, but if he didn't get through to her, it would be the end of them all.

"Hey, Kid," Mario whispered softly with fatherly concern oozing in his voice. "Sorry you had to come."

Sophie's head whipped in his direction and tilted at the sound of his voice.

Clarice jammed the end of the gun hard into Mario's skull. He winced at the pressure against his already swollen brain, and Sophie let out a low, gutted growl.

"Shut up!" Clarice ordered. Sophie's attention came back to Clarice.

"I don't regret a single second," Mario pushed on, trying to find Sophie's eyes again. "You made me a better man," he smiled weakly.

"What part of shut up don't you understand!" Clarice shouted as she pushed the gun even harder against his skull, except it was already too late.

Sophie's pupils were shrinking, and the blue shined like a diamond beacon being held up to the light. The redness retreated, reverting her skin back to the paleness of the moonlight.

"I'm sorry," Sophie said, as tears ran silently down her cheeks.

"Don't be," Mario assured. "See you on the other side," he smiled.

"ENOUGH!" Clarice screamed.

The gun shot echoed down the empty streets outside. What was left of Mario's body fell forward before Sophie. She closed her eyes quickly and sucked in a breath of shock as blood splattered all over the front of her. Sophie stood still with her eyes held tightly closed. She panted as she tasted his blood in her mouth.

There was a deafening silence in the abandoned warehouse until Clarice's hyena cackling broke it. Sophie opened her eyes to find the woman before her with her head tossed back, laughing as she celebrated the life she had just taken.

Mario's life. The last living guardian Sophie had. The man who had raised her when her parents had been taken from her.

"Sophie," her mother begged in her ear. "You can't!"

Sophie wiped the blood of her loved one away from her lips. "Watch me," she growled as she took off like a bullet to take out the murderous woman before her.

Twelve

The atmosphere changed immediately, as excitement coursed through Clarice's body like an electrical current. She quickly kicked off her heels and took aim at the girl rushing towards her. Clarice fired the gun and watched as Sophie simply side stepped out of its path as she continued to charge Clarice.

"Interesting," Clarice said, as a smile curled up the end of her lips and she took stance in preparation.

Sophie jumped and jammed her left heel into Clarice's face, swinging her body around to sit on her shoulders. She yanked the string out of her hoodie and held it over Clarice's neck to strangle her, but Clarice bent over and flung Sophie's body against a pillar in front of her. Sophie groaned as she hit and slid down to the floor.

"I think you underestimate me," Clarice chuckled.

"Not as much as you do me," Sophie whispered as she got to her feet.

She yanked a button from her jacket and launched it into Clarice's throat, fracturing her windpipe and forcing her to stumble back. Sophie stood up, studying her as she grabbed her throat and gasped for air. She was in no hurry to take this woman's life. She deserved to be tortured, as she had tortured Mario before Sophie arrived.

Clarice broke into a gasping laugh. She knew the look in Sophie's eyes. It was the same look Clarice had when she took her own first life.

"We're not so different, you and I," Clarice gasped with a smile as she stood up straight and she stared into Sophie's eyes. Adrenaline took over her body, and she no longer felt pain coming from the cracked pipe inside her throat. "You think you're better than me, but really you're just like me," she wheezed as she took stance.

Sophie looked at what remained of Mario's body as it laid in the middle of a lake of blood. "I beg to differ," Sophie said flatly. Her emotions completely numb and lost from her body.

"If you say so," Clarice shrugged, waiting patiently for Sophie to come for her.

Sophie took off running towards Clarice, doing a summer sault, and picking up more speed as she ran. She jumped to kick Clarice in the face again. Clarice countered, grabbing her foot and twisting it before flinging her across the floor.

"Is that really the only move you've got?" Clarice asked sarcastically.

Sophie rolled and was quickly back on the balls of her feet with one hand balancing her and the other arm up in the air. She smiled her

Cheshire smile. "I guess we're going to find out," she said, looking at Clarice with determination. She stood up and took stance.

"You're just as cocky and wrong as your mother," said Clarice with a wicked smile. She quickly grabbed an ice pick from the table next to her and charged Sophie.

In what felt like slow motion, Sophie blocked every attack and jab Clarice had given her. However, it was the speed that caught Clarice's attention.

She quickly dropped to her knees and sliced Sophie's side as she slid across the floor. Sophie was too numb to feel the blood that now oozed down her side. She simply tilted her head and studied Clarice.

"Sophie, please!" her mother begged inside Sophie's mind. Her daughter was no longer with her. "Jack!" Sophie heard Jess call out, but she didn't care what her mother had to say. She only cared about making the woman before her feel the pain she felt just moments ago.

Sophie walked straight up to Clarice as she swung wildly to push Sophie back. Sophie just raised her leg and kicked Clarice in the chest hard enough to push her into the pillar behind her and crack it.

"Sophie, STOP!" her father demanded.

"She killed Mario," Sophie responded, with no emotion in her voice. She grabbed Clarice by her hair as she prepared to jam her skull onto the concrete floor.

"ENOUGH!" she heard her mother scream.

A female hand grabbed Sophie's hand and pushed it high into the air, forcing Sophie to let go of Clarice.

"Go!" Jess snapped to Clarice over her shoulder.

Clarice staggered to her feet and took off running. Sophie was right. Clarice had completely underestimated her. She smiled wearily as she staggered out into the dark, empty streets, got into her car, and drove out of the city. Sophie was special indeed, Clarice thought to herself as she eagerly headed home to tell her father.

"She's getting away!" screamed Sophie at her mother.

When she attempted to chase Clarice, a bright light filled the warehouse and pushed Sophie all the way to the other side of the building. It took a moment for Sophie to get her bearings.

"You're choosing HER?" Sophie cried out to her mother with rage like she'd never felt before.

"No," her mother snarled. "I choose YOU!" Jess snapped back at her daughter. "And now I have to see if I can reverse the damage you have already caused."

Sophie went to yell a response, but Jess was already gone, leaving Sophie to scream into the emptiness. A cry that was heard all the way into the streets of downtown, as she sobbed hysterically for the lifeless body before her.

He heard the elevator door open and got into position. James' heart raced uncontrollably out of his chest. The room was covered with candles and rose petals, thanks to Tina. She had bought him a nice button-down white shirt and some khaki dockers, so he was a little more dressed for the occasion. James took slow, deep breaths as he focused on the pattern on the hotel carpet below him. The door before him opened and closed.

It didn't register to Sophie that James was on the floor on one knee with a ring box open in his hand, or the words that would come out of his mouth.

"I know that this is not an ideal situation," James started, keeping his eyes focused on the floor so that his nerves didn't get the best of him. "But I have loved you from the first day we met," he pressed on. "I don't care who or what is after us as long as we are together. I want to grow old with you. I want to sit on rocking chairs on a porch watching the sun go down," James rambled on. "I want to have the love that our parents have, and I know I can only find that with you. Sophie," James said, taking a deep breath, "will you marry me?"

When he brought his eyes up to meet hers, he stopped breathing. Sophie was covered in blood, and she looked like a traumatized animal trying to escape its hunter.

"Sophie," James said, slowly. "What happened?"

Her eyes darted around the room wildly as she kept her back pressed up against the door.

"Soph," James whispered softly. "Whose blood is on you?" he asked, trying to keep his own panic under control.

Sophie gasped for air and continued to look around wildly. Then she ran towards the wastebasket and threw up what felt like everything she had ever eaten in her entire life. James dropped the ring box on the floor and rushed over to hold her hair back. He stroked her back until her body stopped heaving.

Hearing the commotion, Tina and Ben came through their adjoining door. "What's…." was all Tina got out. They both froze at the sight of Sophie gasping for air over the waste basket covered in blood.

"Grab the bag," Ben ordered Tina. When his wife didn't move from shock, Ben used a softer tone. "Go get the bag, Tin. Sophie needs us." Tina backed away in horror and rushed to get the medical bag.

Sophie's eyes finally came back to focus as she leaned her head against the side of the bed. The light flickered softly from the massive collection of candles that engulfed the room. She felt the soft rose petals beneath her sweaty palms. However, it would be the blue opened ring box and the shine that came from the diamond ring inside that would catch her full attention.

Tina came in with the medical bag, and Ben ordered James to get a wet rag as he sat down next to Sophie. "Where are you hurt, Soph?" Ben asked gently.

"My heart," Sophie said, letting out an uncontrollable sob. Ben went to raise her shirt to look, but Sophie grabbed his hand and stopped him. "It's not mine," she said, blankly staring at the ring on the floor.

Ben's stomach dropped immediately, taking a good guess on who the blood belonged to. He heard Tina drop to her knees behind him. James rushed in and handed Ben the wet rag.

"Let's get you cleaned up," Ben said softly as he went to wipe the blood from Sophie's face. Sophie used her free hand to stop him. "We need to wipe your face," Ben said, a little more firmly, fighting the urge to violently throw up himself.

Sophie continued to stare at the ring box. She let Ben's hand go free. She still held onto the hand above her heart. Sophie was as cold as death itself. James pulled her hair back as Ben gently wiped away death from her face. She was obviously in shock, but so was everyone else.

"Sophie," James whispered.

Sophie just started to shake her head no aggressively. James reached out to pull her into his arms, but she crawled forward quickly, out of his grasp. Sophie was mentally numb as tears fell silently down her freshly cleaned cheeks.

His stomach dropped immediately. James knew what was coming, and he couldn't let it happen. He waited a minute before trying again.

"Honey," James whispered softly as his voice cracked.

Sophie looked each of her loved ones in the eyes. Clarice's voice rang in her ears. "Love gets people killed." Panic consumed Sophie's body and soul as her bottom lip quivered.

"Sophie," James begged. "Don't…" he pleaded, reaching out for her.

Sophie scrambled to her feet, and she began slowly backing up towards the door. "I can't…" she choked out before she grabbed her bag, flung the door open, and was out of the building before any of them could stop her.

James fell silently to his knees, still reaching out for Sophie as he rocked back and forth in silence. His heart completely shattered, and his body an empty shell. He curled up into the fetal position, unable to respond to Ben shaking him and calling out his name.

Tina took one look at her friend and took off running after Sophie. "SOPHIE!" she called desperately to a girl that was long gone. Tina stood in the dark and empty street, looking frantically around her. "SOPHIE, PLEASE!" she screamed as long as she could before falling to her knees and bawling as life spiraled out of control around her.

Sophie was already three blocks away when she heard Tina's cry of pain wake the dead, but she couldn't go back. She couldn't keep anyone safe. They were all going to die, regardless. They had a lesser chance of doing so without her.

Sophie used the crowbar out of her bag to unlock the car and yanked the door open. She threw her bag in the backseat and quickly hot-wired the car like Mario had taught her, before heading down the empty street towards the highway.

"Do you remember the coordinates?" she heard Mario's voice ask her in her ear.

Anger built up inside Sophie. "Of course," she retorted.

"Sophie Lee," she heard her mother warn.

"One ghost at a time, please!" Sophie snapped back sarcastically.

"How about no ghosts at all!" her mother scoffed in return.

"Let her be," she heard Mario interject. It remained silent for the rest of the trip to Colorado.

The vision of James on one knee, nervously confessing how he wanted to spend forever with Sophie, flashed before her eyes. Sophie gasped at the image as devastation consumed her soul. She numbly reached over and turned the radio all the way up. Britney Spears' "Oops, I Did It Again" blared from the speakers as Sophie sped down the empty highway, desperately blinking away the tears that streamed down her face.

Clarice didn't bother to obey the law as she drove frantically towards the private airport. She was only a few minutes away. Her father would be so pleased with what she had discovered about his precious Sophie.

The old man had made claims over the years that Sophie would be unlike any other team member, but there had never been any actual proof. Jess interrupted Clarice's order to drown Sophie on her birthday. Although Clarice had always known Sophie to be faster and more graceful than any human she had ever fought with, it wasn't until now that she could confirm her father's suspicions.

Sophie could fling Clarice against the pillar as if she was nothing. Clarice took a shallow breath through her cracked throat and ribs as a reminder. The only question was, did they have to tap into her anger issues to make her "gifts" active, or did she possess them without a trigger?

Clarice raced up the tarmac, grabbed her bag from the back, and rushed onto the plane. "Go!" she ordered the pilot, who waited for her to return. When Clarice sat down, she found herself suddenly extremely exhausted and needing a nap. She pushed back the seat, closed her eyes, and fell into a deep sleep.

When Clarice opened her eyes, the same wooden door as before was in front of her. "You're too late," Clarice yelled. "Your secret is out!"

"Open the door," Jess ordered.

"Screw you!" Clarice yelled to no one.

"Open the damn door!" Jess demanded.

Clarice wasn't sure what possessed her to actually open the stupid thing, but when she did, it flooded her with light straightaway. Once her eyes adjusted, Clarice found Jess standing before her with her arms crossed and mad as hell.

"I'm telling him!" Clarice blurted out, knowing exactly what Jess wanted.

"You know you shouldn't and why," Jess said, glaring at Clarice. "It will be so much worse for her."

"I don't care about your stupid spawn!" screamed Clarice, spitting while she yelled. The venom obvious in her tone.

"That's fine. Considering I just spared your life, I'm pretty sure you owe me," Jess said, staring at Clarice with heat.

"I don't owe you a damn thing!" Clarice hissed.

"Please tell me what it was that I ever did to you!" Jess said, exasperated. "I have done nothing but love you like a sister, Clarice, and you know it," she said, laying on the guilt.

"Yeah, OH so loving," Clarice grimaced at her.

"Seriously?" Jess asked, as her anger grew. "I know you didn't have the best upbringing, but all things considered, I did my best to fill your mother's shoes."

"My mother?" Clarice accused. "You know NOTHING about my mother or what she did!" she yelled.

This screaming match was getting Jess nowhere. She was going to have to figure out how to reason with Clarice. The surroundings changed to the training room. A younger version of both of them were practicing their fighting skills.

"Your ghost tricks have no effect on me," Clarice immediately retorted as she refused to take in what was being showed to her.

"That's fine," Jess shrugged as she turned to watch the two practice. Young Clarice knocked down Jess before instantly holding out her hand to help young Jess get back to her feet.

"You were always there for me," Jess said, softly. "What happened to us?"

"You know exactly what happened," Clarice snapped. A button that still had a sensitive trigger.

"I couldn't stay forever," Jess whispered. "You should have gotten out, too. I'm sorry I didn't take you with me," she added.

Clarice heard the pain in her voice, so she turned away. It was too hard to look at her like this, anyway.

"But you did," Clarice said, quietly.

"Did you know what he did to me?" Jess suddenly asked her.

"No," Clarice responded honestly, unable to look Jess in the eyes.

"I didn't think so," Jess said.

The response surprised Clarice.

"He never played fair," Jess added softly.

Clarice didn't move. She knew exactly what Jess meant.

"You were always the favorite," Clarice mumbled.

"You were my favorite," Jess said with a smile.

Clarice froze. She'd never been someone's favorite. She wasn't sure how she felt about it. Part of her felt warm, like never before. The other part was guessing it was a lie to try to manipulate her.

"I'm not trying to manipulate you," Jess added.

"Get out of my head," Clarice warned.

"I'm not," Jess shrugged innocently. "I'm just being honest."

"I can't save her," Clarice said flatly.

"Yes, you can," Jess replied, just as flatly. "It won't bring you what you want," she added bluntly. "He's not capable. He never was."

"You don't know anything," Clarice retorted, although she knew Jess was right.

Jess sighed heavily. "I can't make you do the right thing," she finally said. "It won't bring you what you want, and Sophie will pay the ultimate price, greater than either of us ever did," Jess warned.

"She's a pain in the ass anyway," Clarice shrugged, but her heart oddly tugged for the girl, knowing Jess was right.

"Do what you have to," Jess said, full of sorrow. "He will not stop once he has her, though...If I have to choose, I won't be able to choose you if you continue to try to destroy her," she said firmly.

"I know," Clarice said in a low voice.

"I will always love you," Jess added before she walked away.

Clarice was once again caught off guard. Her heart had never felt this much confliction since the day Jess left for good.

"I didn't know!" Clarice called out to her. She didn't understand the sudden need in her chest to make sure Jess knew Clarice had been clueless to what her father had done to Jess so long ago.

Jess stopped, but didn't turn around. "I didn't think so," she said, softly. "And now he gets to do it all over again, and more, with my daughter. Only you can choose if he doesn't."

Jess walked away into the light and disappeared.

Clarice was pushed back through the door. However, she

remained just on the other side of it once it closed. “I didn’t know!” Clarice yelled again, not sure who she was trying to convince. Jess or herself.

Sophie only stopped to put gas in the car. After a little over nine hours of driving, the roads were becoming narrower as they wound through the mountain landscape. Snow had already been falling for days, and if she wasn’t so dead inside, she would appreciate the surrounding view.

Sophie carefully pulled into an abandoned parking lot and switched into her snow boots. She was thankful they had done some shopping the day before. She paused for a second to reflect just how south her life had gone in less than twelve hours, before she threw her bag on her back and abandoned the car she had stolen.

The snow was deep, but Sophie was in no hurry. She waded her way to their cabin before digging away enough snow to get the door open and sliding in. From the outside, it didn’t look like much. Just a simple log cabin with a minimal deck, surrounded by trees and snow in the middle of nowhere.

Sophie locked the door out of habit more than anything and started a fire in the fireplace. The inside looked like a mansion compared to the outside. With wooden ceilings, floors, and walls minus the granite stone fireplace. It was a beautiful, unsuspecting two-story hideout in the middle of the Rocky Mountains of Colorado.

There was a large brown leather couch on a decorated rug positioned in front of the fireplace, with two mauve cloth covered love seats on either side. A chandelier hung in the center of the vaulted ceiling providing plenty of light, with medium-sized windows sporadically placed in order to see who or what was coming from either side.

Sophie slipped out of her wet and bloodied clothing and added it to the flames, before turning around to inspect the liquor options on the far back wall. She paused by her bag to pull out the iPod James had bought her as a gift and slip her AirPods into her ears. Sophie ran her finger slowly over the dusty bottles lining the opposite wall before smiling and grabbing the Malibu rum from the shelf.

"Oh good," Sophie said, smiling. "It's full."

She unscrewed the bottle, threw the cap into the fire, and began chugging the coconut warm liquid as she blared pop music into her eardrums.

"Real mature," she heard Mario's voice from behind her. She didn't bother to turn and look.

"Coming from the dead man who got himself killed," Sophie yelled over the blaring music as she continued to dance in front of the fire in her black laced underwear and chugging rum straight from the bottle.

"You're going to hate yourself in the morning," Mario lectured suddenly in front of her with his arms crossed in front of his chest.

"I hate myself plenty right now, thanks," Sophie retorted, puffing in his face and turning to dance in the other direction.

"I know you're mad," Mario started as he leaned up against the bar in front of the glass shelves containing alcohol. He was facing Sophie despite her desire to keep him at her back.

"Nope!" Sophie yelled in a very high pitch. "I'm pissed!" she slurred in a voice loud enough to wake the dead.

"Well, this is certainly going to teach me," Mario said sarcastically as he rolled his eyes.

"Screw you!" Sophie yelled, staggering towards him and shoving her finger towards his chest. Mario quickly side stepped her. They were very clear. No touching.

Sophie glared at him, before slamming the empty rum bottle onto the bar. She started humming the song her dad used to sing to her.

"Like sparkling wine," she sang off key. "Don't mind if I do!"

Sophie squinted at the bottles before her. "Hey!" she yelled. "Stop moving!"

Mario sighed heavily and crossed his arms impatiently. "Hardly drinking means you get drunk faster," he called out. "And you are already very drunk," he reminded her.

"Wells you're....you're....you're not heres to serves me, so who cares!" Sophie said, slurring her words.

She found a red wine with a gold infinity symbol that had a slash through it on the black label with no words. Sophie giggled immediately.

"How appropriate," she chuckled as she staggered to the couch in front of the fire.

Mario eyed her suspiciously. "What's so funny?" he asked with curiosity.

"This!" Sophie declared, holding the bottle up to show him. She squinted at the bottle, sighed heavily with a frown, and turned the bottle so that the label was facing Mario. "Infinity is never forever, just like love," Sophie professed loudly.

"What's that supposed to mean?" Mario asked her with a raised eyebrow.

"The cycle of life is forever divided between good and evil," Sophie shrugged as she yanked the cork out of the bottle and forced the warm liquid down her throat.

"How is love not forever?" Mario asked, trying to distract her.

Sophie exaggeratedly drew the bottle away from her lips and sighed while rolling her eyes dramatically.

"Love can never conquer all," she said sarcastically. "And good never wins in the end," Sophie pouted before putting the bottle back to her lips to consume more of the liquid that numbed her pain.

Then something unexpected caught her eye.

"Hey!" she slurred loudly. "There's numbers in here," Sophie declared as she frustratedly tried to hold the bottle up in different directions and spilled red wine everywhere.

"Oh, for God's sake, SLEEP!" Mario ordered, putting his finger to her forehead.

"No fa..." was all Sophie got out before he forced her into a deep sleep.

Thirteen

Sophie opened her eyes and waited for the multiple doors before her to stop moving around. "Very funny," Sophie slurred.

"Oh, goodie," she heard Mario state sarcastically. "You're still drunk here, too. Open the door, Kid."

"No!" Sophie said, pouting and crossing her arms in front of her chest.

"Save the two-year-old tantrum for someone else," Mario warned. "Open the damn door."

"I don't want to see her," Sophie declared to the sky. She heard a heavy sigh for a reply.

"It's just you and me right now," Mario assured. "Now open the door."

"They have to stop moving first," Sophie slurred and squinted to make them into one.

"Lord, help me," she heard Mario pray to himself softly, followed by silence.

Once the doors became one, Sophie opened the door and stumbled through. They were still oddly in the cabin, but Mario was cooking in the kitchen. The smell of food made her want to vomit. Sophie staggered into the kitchen and fell into the nearest chair before her.

"You could have changed the scenery at least," she mumbled.

"Yeah, well, you could still be sober and stop being a pain in my ass, but here we are," Mario said, frustratedly over his shoulder. "It's my first time," he muttered. "Cut me some slack."

"It shouldn't be your anytime," Sophie mumbled back. Mario let it slide.

He turned with a plate full of cheesy eggs and hash browns. "Eat," he ordered as he purposely threw the plate onto the table. Sophie cringed at the sound and grabbed her head. "Take those while you're at it," Mario said, nodding to the two aspirin suddenly next to her with a glass of water.

"I'm going to throw up," Sophie said, quickly covering her mouth.

"Drinking two full bottles of alcohol will do that to you," Mario said, crossing his arms and leaning against the sink. "Eat," he said, again.

Sophie glared at him. Mario didn't waver. "I don't like you very much right now," she mumbled and stared at the plate before her.

"Yeah, well, the feeling's mutual right now," Mario snapped back.

"Eat."

Sophie scowled back at him. She saw the throbbing vein in his neck pulse as he tried to hold back his own temper.

"You'll feel better, contrary to what your stomach is saying. Just eat," Mario said, bitterly. "Please," he added more softly.

Sophie looked at the plate before her and slowly picked up the fork. Despite her beliefs, Mario was right. The grease seemed to soothe her stomach as she swallowed a small fork full of the hot cheesy eggs. Sophie didn't dare admit it out loud, though.

"Listen, Kid," Mario started. "I know you're mad, but..."

"I'm not mad," Sophie laughed hysterically. "I'm P..I..S..S..E..D," she screamed to the sky as anger engulfed her entire being.

Mario paused. He knew her pain. Mario could feel it even more in this realm, and he didn't like it at all. How was he supposed to help her when he could feel how much heartbreak she was going through? Mario knew Sophie couldn't breathe from all the pain, because neither could he.

"You were all I had," Sophie sobbed at the realization. "And now you're gone," she choked.

"Oh, Kid," Mario whispered. He still couldn't touch her to console her. "I'm not the only one," he said, choking up.

Sophie's eyes changed dangerously black. "Where is she anyway?" she snapped.

"Cooling off," Mario snapped back. "Where do you think your stubbornness and temper come from?" he added with a chuckle.

"It's not funny," Sophie mumbled.

"What's not funny is this whole rebellious teenager crap," Mario retorted. "It was bad enough to live through it when you were actually a teenager," he said, glaring down at her. "Grief doesn't give you permission to be an asshole," he added in his fatherly tone.

"I can grieve however I want!" Sophie shouted. "I'm pretty sure I earned the right to do so at this point in my life."

"Not when time is running out, and you've left people in danger," Mario warned.

"Screw time!" Sophie screamed back. "I can't keep anyone safe! And who the hell decided that I had to be the one to do so!"

"When gifts are given, much is expected," Mario stated firmly.

"Gifts?! Are you freaking kidding me right now?!" Sophie laughed hysterically as a mad woman in need of a strait-jacket.

"Are you done, Princess?" Mario asked, still keeping his arms crossed to prevent him from touching her.

Sophie looked murderously at Mario. It's a good thing he was already dead, he thought to himself. He knew she hated it when he used it, but it was the best word he could come up with to call Sophie out on her over dramatic tantrums. Mario did the same with Jess. God, she hated it too. Mario smiled at himself, which didn't help him with Sophie's mood.

"He's going to find them, and he's going to kill them," Mario stated bluntly, to get their focus back on track.

"They were dead the moment they met me," Sophie uttered angrily as she shoved another fork full of food into her mouth. Despite her anger, the food was helping her feel better.

"And what about James?" Mario asked casually.

The image of James on one knee before her, so nervous to ask her to spend the rest of their lives together, flashed before her eyes. Sophie put the fork down and stared at the floor. "I can't save him," she finally whispered.

"Of course not," Mario said bluntly. "How can you when you don't even try? I mean, why not just hand deliver him to the man with the cane right now?" he added for good measure. "It would make the end much quicker for James, and doesn't he at least deserve that much? What better way to show him how much you care for him? The price for having the courage to love you, accept you, and the shitshow that comes with you. Seems like an equal trade, don't you think?"

Sophie glared at Mario, and he glared right back. Jess and Jack would probably handle this much better than he was, however, they weren't available. Much like they hadn't been available for half her life.

Mario had to make up his parenting skills as he went, and if he gave her anything less than the harsh truth, Sophie wouldn't know she was dealing with the real him.

Sophie broke the staring contest first. Not her usual MO, but she was tired. These interactive dreams didn't tend to give her much rest, and she was exhausted. Tired of fighting with ghosts. Mostly, she was tired of fighting with herself.

James deserved a hell of a lot better than what Sophie gave him. Granted, she was in shock and not handling the last few hours well at all, but he did still deserve better. And now he was left alone. Running from the same psychopath she was, only without her so-called 'gifts'.

"You're right," Sophie mumbled, and quickly shoved food into her mouth.

"I'm sorry, what was that?" Mario pushed.

"You are right," Sophie said, with a mouth full of food.

"Can't give it to me even in death, huh?" Mario smirked.

Sophie swallowed her food. "You are right," she said, sighing dramatically.

"Duh," Mario replied, shrugging, as a smile easily escaped watching her being tortured. "I forgot how much fun this is," he said, smiling.

Sophie grimaced at him, but it only lasted for a second.

"You're the pain in the ass," she added, and shoved more food into her mouth.

"So, where would they go next?" Mario asked, getting down to business.

Sophie thought for a second. "We were supposed to head to New Mexico for warmer weather," she said, with her mouth still full. "I don't know if they will still go," she said, looking at her plate and swallowing.

"Mario?" Sophie asked after a second.

"What?" Mario replied, producing a map of the United States and putting it on the table before her.

"Why did you tell Tina to go to Kansas City?" Sophie asked, not looking him in the eye.

"I didn't," Mario stated as he stared at the map. "Tina said, you wanted me to meet at the house," he added as he tilted his head to look at the map. "Was there a specific place to meet?" Mario asked her, distracted about getting Sophie back with her friends.

"I didn't ask you to go to Kansas City," Sophie said, slowly.

Finally comprehending what was taking place, Mario stopped to look at her and blinked.

"Tina sent a message saying that you were going to check in on your parent's place and we needed to meet. You had new information you needed help with," he said, slowly, quickly realizing how eager he had been to see her. Mario didn't even see the trap that had been laid.

"Tina got a message from you saying to meet in KC," Sophie said, watching him. "Then she got another one saying to meet at the warehouse," she whispered.

"Clarice was already at the house," Mario said. "She was waiting for me."

"So, who sent the messages?" Sophie asked quietly.

"Clarice isn't that tech savvy," Mario declared. He thought about all the information he had on the people in Sophie's life currently.

Sophie watched his face change as he came to the same conclusion she did. "I don't think she would," Mario tried to clarify.

"She's the smartest person I know, and knows everything about computers," Sophie added slowly, shaking her head.

"She would never do that to you, though," Mario tried to anchor her.

"Unless they got to her first," Sophie added. "He can be very persuasive. We've seen it," she added with warning.

"Tina wouldn't do that to you," Mario said, in more of a question than a statement.

"And she's got James and Ben," Sophie whispered in panic.

"Her own husband and friend?" Mario asked her, still unsure but unable to come up with another name at the moment.

"I have to find them," Sophie said, standing up. "Send me back," she said, looking at him.

"I don't know how!" Mario said, honestly in panic.

"Sleep, Peanut," she heard her mother say. Before she could protest against her mother being the one to help, Sophie felt Jess' finger on her forehead and she was snoring under a blanket on the sofa in front of the fire.

ಌ

The buzz of a flickering florescent light rang in Eddie's ears. His eyes felt swollen shut. His mind was foggy, but he felt a soft bed beneath him. What happened? The memory of his encounter with Clarice flashed before his closed eyes.

"Sophie!" Eddie croaked as he sat up immediately. His head throbbed in protest of his actions.

"She's fine," he heard an unexpected voice come from the other side of the room. Eddie closed his eyes again to help his swimming head calm down.

"So, is this where I die?" Eddie asked bluntly.

"Not yet," the old man replied. "Despite my daughter's misdirected beliefs, she does not determine which of my employees live or dies."

"Why save me then?" Eddie asked, slowly opening his eyes.

The room was mostly dark, minus the dying florescent light above him. Across the room sat the old man, holding his cane in front of him for balance. He tilted his head in amusement as he studied Eddie.

"Because we're more alike than you know," the old man said with a slight chuckle. "This will be the last time," he warned before getting up to exit. “Choose your side wisely, dear boy,” he said softly over this shoulder before he left Eddie alone.

Eddie wasn’t sure what to think. That was the nicest he had ever seen the old man be in his entire time spent in this hellhole. Eddie would be dead if it wasn’t for the old man.

Helping Sophie only ever got him closer to death, and for what?

Fighting for a girl who had long forgotten he existed? The old man was right. It was time to choose a side. It was time Sophie fought her own battles. She needed to learn what it meant to toss the wrong people off to the side.

No one had spoken in the last twenty-four hours since Sophie left them. No one knew what to say. It was James who broke the silence. “We should head to Albuquerque,” he smiled as he began packing his things.

“What for, exactly?” asked Ben, confused.

“We have to meet Sophie,” James said bluntly. His fingers lightly danced over the ring box before he picked it up and put it securely in his bag.

Ben looked at Tina for help.

“I’m not sure Sophie will meet us,” Tina said slowly.

James just shook his head no.

“No,” he said, simply. “She will come. When she’s ready,” James declared, putting the last of his clothing into the bag and heading for the bathroom.

“I think she broke him,” Ben whispered, his concerns to his

wife.

"Well, it doesn't hurt to play along," Tina said, studying James with concern. "Whatever happened at the warehouse was clearly not good," she whispered. "And we don't know how Mario died." Her voice cracked at the thought.

Tina knew Sophie didn't do it, although she didn't know who did either. There was nothing to go off of, other than a headless body lying in a pool of blood. She didn't think she would ever stop throwing up when Tina saw Mario.

Ben had stayed with James, and Tina snuck out to see what clues she could find. Mario had sent her the message late that afternoon for Sophie to meet him in a warehouse in the West Bottoms. It was an odd part of town, just west of downtown Kansas City in an area that housed empty haunted houses and antique stores, mostly.

The Uber driver informed Tina that she had just missed the best haunted houses around. Tina preferred them over the horror that she was about to find.

A table of instruments suited for torturing, and Mario's dead body. The only clue that anyone else had been there was a set of size 8 high heeled red shoes strewn behind a metal chair, but no hint who they belonged to.

"I wiped brain matter from her face," her husband hissed at her.

"Well aware," Tina hissed back. "But until we know who else was there, it's not safe to split up just yet," she said, more softly.

"What do you mean it's not safe to split up?" James asked curiously as he came out of the bathroom, only catching the end of the conversation.

"James, Honey," Tina said, slowly. "We're not sure who all the players are right now," she tried to explain.

"Sophie said, never to travel together," James said, shaking his head and putting stuff into his bag.

"Yes, but Sophie's not here," Ben tried.

James stopped packing his bag for a moment. "She will be," he shrugged and continued to finish packing.

"Did someone come visit you?" Tina asked, trying to determine if it was shock or a ghostly influence pushing him at the moment.

"Listen," James said, turning to face his friends. "Sophie has just lost her last parental connection," he said, with sorrow in his voice. "She needs to process, and then she will be back. We can't let her down in the meantime," he shrugged.

Shock it was. Tina looked at Ben and shrugged. "Albuquerque it is. However, it will be together," she added firmly. "You can still keep your distance. We're riding the same bus," Tina added with authority.

James agreed and looked out the window as his friends gathered their things.

"She'll be back," he whispered to himself. She had to come back. Right?...

Sophie woke up with a full belly, and only a slight hangover. "Thank you," she whispered to the ceiling of the cabin. She already knew the best way to figure out if Tina was actually on their side or if she had changed teams without them knowing.

Sophie picked up the empty rum bottle and red wine bottle.

She rubbed her finger over the gold symbol. She had seen it somewhere before. Her pounding head just wouldn't tell her where.

Sophie tossed the rum bottle in the trash. She got ready to throw the wine bottle after it, then something caught her eye. She carefully turned the bottle as she held it up to the light.

There were numbers carefully etched into the glass just under the black label. If she hadn't drunk the entire bottle, she would have missed them completely. What were they?

Her throbbing head pounded louder. She went to the kitchen to find some aspirin. Two pills laid on the table next to a glass of water and a note in Mario's handwriting.

Please take these and don't argue. Love, M

"Yes, Sir," Sophie mumbled as she tossed the aspirin into her mouth and took a sip of water to help wash them down. She stuck out her tongue to the ceiling so he would know she swallowed them properly. There was no response to her childish display. Sophie turned her attention and squinted at the wine bottle. A piece was missing.

Realizing she was standing in the living room in only her black lace bra and underwear, she grabbed her bag and emptied its contents onto the couch. The piece of paper with the sentences fluttered out and caught Sophie's eye. She grabbed it before it touched the couch and opened it up.

The tune of her father's song suddenly rang in her ears. She hummed it as she read each sentence. Suddenly, she froze. "Like Sparkling Wine," she whispered and looked at the empty wine bottle on the table. They weren't random sentences. They were song lyrics.

Lyrics to THEIR song. And pointing at the now empty wine bottle with numbers etched inside.

"Are you kidding me?" Sophie said to herself.

She grabbed the wine bottle and stared at the numbers etched inside of it. Latitude and longitude coordinates and a code. Hiding here in the rendezvous location should something ever go wrong. That's why the SD card didn't have it. It was never meant to.

The man with the cane was never to have the end product, but her father never could just not finish what he started, either. Jack didn't know how. So, what now?

Sophie turned to look around the cabin. Something had already gone wrong. Seriously wrong. Despite her finding it by drunken accident, didn't mean that she could leave it out in the open either.

Although the mission had altered, it didn't mean that this shouldn't still be dealt with. That's why her father gave her the necklace. He needed her to do what he never could.

Throwing it in the fire didn't guarantee success. She needed something else. Sophie flung open the front door and was greeted with snow and a body slicing icy wind. She shoved it closed immediately.

"I really need to put some clothes on first," she muttered to herself as she raced to the couch.

"Please do," she heard Mario beg in her ear. She smiled warmly; thankful he was still with her.

Once she was properly layered, she set outside to find the tools she needed. Luckily, she was able to find them quickly and headed back inside to start a fire. As the flames grew, she took the empty bottle in her hand. "Opa!" she yelled for good cheer as the bottle shattered into pieces.

Sophie carefully pulled out the shards that contained etched numbers on them and tossed the rest into the fire. She grabbed a wooden bowl from the kitchen and placed the shards in it. Then she quickly wrapped her hand with gauze and tape from the emergency kit in the bathroom.

She sat at the table and took a deep breath before grabbing the rock and slowly turning the shards of glass into dust. When not a single trace of numbers remained, Sophie carried the dust to the fire and watched it burn, keeping the numbers in her memory for another day.

"Good job, Kid," she heard Mario whisper.

"Well, we can deal with that another day," Sophie answered, putting her hand on her hip as she watched the flames dance in the fire. "I've got bigger problems to deal with," she said.

The man with the cane could wait. She had to figure out how to meet up with James and Ben and test her suspicions of Tina out. With final resolve, Sophie moved to the couch and picked out the burner phone.

She didn't trust Tina, and she didn't know if James would even speak to her after leaving him like she did. She closed her eyes and took a deep breath in and out before dialing a number.

"Hello?" the male voice answered in confusion.

"It's me," Sophie whispered. "Are you alone?"

Ben was in the bathroom collecting their things when the burner phone he had left in his pocket vibrated. The number was

Sophie. "Hello?" he answered slowly and confused.

"It's me," Sophie whispered. "Are you alone?"

"Yes," Ben said, slowly standing up and closing the door.

"Everything alright?" Tina hollered at him.

"Tell her yes," Sophie instructed.

"Yeah," Ben hollered, confused. "Just need a minute," he added. "Are you okay?" he whispered to Sophie.

"As much as can be expected," Sophie answered honestly.

"James has lost it," Ben hissed at her.

"I know, I'm sorry," Sophie whispered back. He heard her guilt over the phone. "Ben," she said, slowly. "I need to know where you're going next."

"James wants to go to New Mexico," Ben whispered, watching shadows of feet move outside the door. "He thinks you'll meet us there," he said, frowning.

Sophie smiled. James still wanted her to meet them. That had to be a good sign, right?

"Ben," Sophie ordered, "don't tell anyone I called."

"Why not?" Ben asked, confused.

"We don't know who all the players are yet," she said, with sorrow in her voice.

"Tina said the same thing just a few minutes ago!" he exclaimed.

"Ben!" Sophie hissed. "Promise me. Not a word."

"Fine," Ben sulked.

"And Ben..." Sophie whispered.

"Yeah?" Ben replied.

"See you in New Mexico," she said, with hope before the line went completely dead.

Ben stared at the phone in his hand. Why couldn't he tell anyone Sophie was coming? What was going on? Well, at least she didn't sound as crazy as James currently was. Unless she already called him. Maybe that's why James knew she was coming? Ben shook his head and flushed the toilet for good measure before heading out to meet his wife.

"You alright?" Tina asked, considering him suspiciously.

"Yeah," Ben said, in a daze. "I wouldn't go in there for a while," he grinned at her.

"You're so gross!" Tina laughed at him and went to finish packing.

Fourteen

Clarice was pacing her room, furious at the information she had received the second she stepped off the plane. Eddie was alive. Her fool of a father had saved his pet, yet again. Despite her disclosure that Eddie had been conspiring the entire time to help Sophie escape their attempts to bring her in. No matter what Clarice did, the troll remained. How was absolutely EVERYONE else more important than his own blood to him?!

Her fury had distracted her from giving him the news she knew he desperately wanted. Clarice just wasn't sure if that was her only excuse at the moment. Jess' words haunted her conscious.

She honestly didn't know what all her father had done to Jess until after she was dead. Not like she could have done anything about it, anyway. At least, that's what Clarice tried to convince herself was the truth.

Clarice never went against her father, minus the one time she tried to walk out. He purposely used Sophie to bait her back in, and she could never walk away again. They both knew it.

Clarice's mind wandered shortly at a life outside of the tunnels, smiling, and hanging out with Jess and Jack. Would their lives have been different if she had stood against him, too?

"No," Clarice answered herself, knowing the only result would have been two dead girls instead of one. She survived by keeping her mouth shut about her mother's murder. She did nothing to stop him from murdering Jess and Jack. She helped in the quest to capture their daughter. Clarice did whatever he asked, like the loyal dog she was, because it was easier than dealing with the fact that he only knew how to use her and nothing more.

The old man never gave her enough credit. Clarice was smarter, savvier, quicker, and stronger than anyone else he had on staff. She may not know as much about computers as Eddie did, but that didn't make her any less valuable. Clarice could manipulate any person who crossed her path. Well, anyone excluding her father. And Jess.

Jess was the one person Clarice never had to manipulate. They had grown up training together and were well aware of each other's strengths and weaknesses. They worked together often.

Even when Clarice got so frustrated with her father about the constant comparison, Jess never hesitated to remind her she was just as valuable. She really did like Jess. Sophie, however, was a different matter.

She wasn't sure why Jess felt the need to come to Clarice to save her enhanced spawn from her father. Jess couldn't possibly love her like she had claimed if she was asking Clarice to sacrifice herself for her damn daughter!

Her anger grew as she tried to convince herself that Jess was just manipulating her to her death, but a part of her knew exactly what Jess was really asking of her.

Not just to save her daughter from being hunted even more. Rather, not to be a lab rat like Jess herself had been. Clarice wasn't willing to accept it, yet deep down she knew Jess wasn't asking her to sacrifice herself for someone she loved more. Jess was asking for history not to repeat itself, with Clarice doing nothing.

The stakes were higher, because the test results were not dormant in Sophie like they had been in Jess. Neither subject asking to be different at all, but forced to be something they weren't. Something Clarice was all too familiar with. Jess knew it too and was guilting Clarice with her past.

She picked up a book laying on her desk and screamed as she threw it against her door. "I can't help you!" Clarice shouted to no one. She had survived this long by doing what he asked of her. Not by Jess. Rather by her father. A ghost would not take her life for going against it. Her father, on the other hand, was a different story.

The image of him reprimanding her in front of everyone about trying to kill Eddie flashed before her eyes. Everyone in the lab had smirked at her being scolded like a child before them. It was degrading, and he knew how much that would hurt her more than physically abusing her, which is exactly why he had done it. To remind Clarice that she was nothing without him. Nothing.

"I can't help you," she whispered, trying to convince herself, but her feet didn't move towards the door either. For the first time in her life, Clarice questioned which side she was going to choose...

Albuquerque, New Mexico, was proving to be quite warmer than Kansas City. The trio watched the sun welcome them as the bus crossed state lines. They each kept to themselves and made it look like they were not traveling together. It was ingrained at this point; they were experts at the dance.

Ben checked in first while Tina and James scouted the town a bit to collect more supplies. He tossed his bag on the bed and went to look out the window. They had one room this time, double beds.

"Hello, old friend," Sophie said, coming out of the bathroom. Ben jumped in surprise.

"Give a guy a heart attack, why don't you!" Ben hissed at her while clutching his heart.

"Sorry," Sophie giggled.

He eyed her cautiously. "You seem to be doing well," Ben said slowly.

"Grief was a faster process than expected," Sophie smiled, knowing his concern. "It helps when the ghosts follow you through life," she added, winking.

"Still. Tina went to the scene. She said it was definitely horrific," Ben said, staring at the floor. "I'm so sorry for your loss," he said, looking into her blue eyes.

"Thank you," Sophie whispered back.

"The others are getting supplies. I'm not sure how long they will be," Ben stated. "So why don't you tell me what's really going on?"

Sophie hesitated. She wasn't sure she could tell him she thought his wife was on the other side. Not until she had some proof, of course.

"Mario didn't send us those messages," Sophie settled on.

"Yeah, we've figured that out," Ben said. "Any idea who did?"

"Not yet," Sophie answered honestly. "But I'm working on it," she added. "Did Tina get the second message alone or was she with you?" Sophie tried to ask casually.

"I think she got the second one alone, because it came while she was in the store and she came out to show it to me," Ben said, thinking back. "Why?"

"Just trying to track down the timing to limit the options," Sophie shrugged. She sat down on the bed and put her feet up. "How is he?" she asked hesitantly.

"Scaringly well," Ben said, knowing she was asking about James. "I don't know if it was shock or what, but he always knew you would meet us here. Told us to pack up and get here and wait," Ben shrugged. "Didn't faze him a bit," he said, observing her.

"Did you know?" Sophie whispered softly.

"He didn't tell us," Ben stated clearly. "But, yeah, we knew he had it."

"What made him think to do that?" Sophie asked softly, looking at Ben for answers.

Ben walked over and sat on the bed next to her.

"He's been in love with you since the first day you met," Ben said softly. "When you're a guy and you find the love of your life," he said, "you really want to get a ring on her so you can declare to the world that the girl that knocks your socks off is yours," he added with a soft shoulder bump. "We don't know anything else."

"But me?" Sophie asked. "I mean, I love the guy. I just don't exactly have a life that allows me to walk down the aisle right now," she added softly.

"No one said, 'right now', Soph," Ben said, looking at her. "For James, it's more of letting you know you are the only person he wants to spend the rest of his life with. The only reason he didn't do it sooner was he thought you would run."

Sophie looked at him and the guilt he saw was overwhelming.

"He is well aware of the life we're living right now," Ben pushed on quickly. "You've met his parents," he chuckled. "He just wants that kind of relationship, but he'll take it however he can get it. Mostly, it's his way of showing you you're the only one on this planet for him. Even if the ceremony isn't until later, or never happens at all. He just wants you to know. Well, that and everyone else when they see the ring," Ben laughed.

Sophie looked at him, confused.

"It keeps other men from thinking they have a chance at something we love." Ben winked.

Sophie breathed out a breath she didn't realize she had been holding.

"I guess I didn't handle it very well, did I?" Sophie asked him.

"Well, the timing was God awful for both sides," Ben assured.

"What am I supposed to do now?" Sophie asked.

"Let him have a do-over," Ben shrugged.

"A what?" Sophie laughed.

Ben sighed dramatically before responding.

"You're going to have to wait for the awkwardness to pass about you being back," Ben said firmly. "Lucky for you, James is ridiculously understanding and never blamed you for a second. So, just wait," he shrugged.

Sophie frowned in confusion.

"Let him propose again when he thinks it's the right time," Ben clarified. "And try not to run," he added, bumping her in the shoulder again.

They both turned when they heard the door unlock and open. To both their surprise, it was James on the other side. When James' eyes met Sophie's, he dropped everything in his hands.

"Hi," James whispered softly with a smile.

"Hi," Sophie whispered with a smile back.

"Please tell me that wasn't dinner you just dropped," Ben said, scrambling to pick up the bags James had dropped onto the floor.

James didn't respond. He stood as still as a gravestone.

"Oh, for Pete's sake!" Ben grumbled. "Sophie, do you promise not to run if James, here, comes into the room?"

Sophie giggled. "Of course not."

"Good!" Ben said, shoving James further into the room and putting the bags on the table by the door. He grabbed his jacket. "I'm going to give you a moment to get your act together before my wife comes back," Ben said, winking at Sophie and closing the door behind him.

"I'm sorry," they said in unison, then laughed uncomfortably and stared at the floor.

"I'm sorry I couldn't stay with you," Sophie whispered, focusing on the floor to help distract her from the amount of guilt engulfing her.

"I know," James whispered back. "I get it. I'm sorry for your loss," he said, taking a step towards her. He was dying to hold her again.

Sophie sensed his hesitation and figured she'd earned it. It would be her responsibility to help him get his courage back. "I wouldn't mind a hug," Sophie offered with a shrug.

James closed his eyes and took a deep breath before walking over to the bed and pulling her into his arms. He gently combed her hair with his fingers and traced her arm lightly with his fingertips.

Sophie didn't cry like she thought she would. Maybe she was still in shock, or simply incapable of crying anymore tears for her godfather. Instead, she absorbed James' warmth and the love he offered to her unconditionally as she closed her eyes and drifted off to a deep sleep.

Sophie opened her eyes to the wooden door. So much for getting some rest. She sighed deeply as she reached out for the doorknob.

"Are you going to tell him?" she heard Mario ask her eagerly.

"Let me get through the freaking door first," Sophie laughed.

"Oh, yeah, right," she heard Mario tell himself.

Light flooded around her, and it took a second for her eyes to adjust. She found Mario at the cabin table with a map stretched out over it, and a notebook with some scribbles on it.

"Whatch ya working on?" Sophie asked, taking in the scene.

Mario tapped the end of the pencil on his chin.

"Well, I'm really curious who all took part in my death," he said, studying his notes. "Clarice is pulling someone's strings, and we need to figure out who," he added firmly.

"Who exactly is Clarice?" Sophie asked for clarification. "And how do you know her?"

Mario froze. Jess begged him not to tell her. She had to find out for herself, or it might shut her down completely.

"Clarice and Jess grew up working for the man with the cane," Mario shared.

"How did he find mom in the first place?" Sophie asked.

Mario panicked. Of course, Sophie would ask all the questions he wasn't allowed to answer.

"I met your mom in her teenage years," Mario added, trying not to lie. "They were huge into using teenage ops back then because they were less suspected than adults," he shrugged. "Definitely more impossible to control with raging hormones and all," he chuckled. "Your mom worked with the same government agency I did. We did a mission overseas together. Your mom saved my butt," Mario said, reminiscing with a smile.

"I'm sure this is going to get somewhere eventually," Sophie chuckled.

"The man with the cane hired her and Clarice to do freelance gigs on the side," Mario continued with a frown. "Clarice was a couple of years older than us. She had a really screwed up childhood, with an even worse father," he added. "Your mom took pity and always tried to get Clarice to be the best version of herself, but the old man was always favoring your mom and throwing it in Clarice's face. So, the rivalry goes way before your time, Kid," Mario shrugged.

"So, what am I dealing with exactly?" Sophie asked, crossing her arms in front of her chest. She knew she would take Clarice's life with her own hands for what she took from Sophie. There was no need sharing that information with anyone though.

"Clarice is smart. She's not extremely tech savvy, though," Mario said, deep in thought. "That's why I know she was the puppeteer and not the puppet. Unfortunately, she was trained to be one of the best manipulators on this planet. It's just a shame she uses it for evil instead of good," he frowned.

"What else?" Sophie asked as casually as possible.

"Psychopath runs in her blood," he warned. "She's never to be underestimated."

"So, she stated," Sophie said, frowning, remembering her threat.

"She will never fight fair, no matter who's on the other side," Mario said bluntly. "You are to avoid her at all costs," he warned.

"Little late for that," Sophie retorted.

"Yeah, I know," chimed in Jess in frustration as she entered the room. "Hello, Mario," she said, with a hint of warning in her voice.

"Jess," Mario answered nervously.

"So, what are we meeting about?" Jess asked casually, looking around the room.

"It's not against the rules," Mario mumbled. The look Jess gave him silenced him immediately.

"Talking about your bff, Clarice," Sophie said, with sarcasm.

"Watch your tone, Daughter," Jess warned.

"Well, this meeting isn't for you, so you can go," Sophie said, turning her back on her mother. Mario stepped between the two of them.

"There are more important things to deal with right now, Ladies," he said, nervously.

"She's protecting a murderer," Sophie scoffed. "YOUR murderer, to be exact!"

"I'm protecting YOU, ungrateful daughter!" Jess hissed at her. "You had no business fighting her," she stewed.

"And why not?" Sophie demanded.

"Because they only suspected you were different!" Jess yelled back. "You went and gave them the proof they needed to come and take you!"

"They only wanted the key!" Sophie retorted.

"YOU ARE THE KEY!" Jess screamed back in frustration.

Sophie froze. "What?" was the only word that could come out of her mouth.

"Okay, I think we just need to take a second and breathe," Mario tried to referee.

"What did you say?" Sophie asked, looking at her mother in complete shock.

"She said you're the key, and she's right, Peanut," Jack said, coming in to help Mario.

"What the hell?" Sophie said, sitting in the nearest chair.

"You were never supposed to fight Clarice," Jack said, kneeling before her. "They suspected and tried to drown you at the pool to see what happened, but your mother intervened," Jack added softly, looking over at his wife. "The satellite was the last project I did," he continued, looking back at Sophie. "You were right," he whispered quietly. "I gave it to you so that when it was time you could destroy it, because I couldn't."

Jess went to leave again. "Stay," Jack ordered to her over his shoulder.

It wasn't often Sophie heard her father order anything of her mother. She knew she had to listen to what was being said.

"He wanted to turn it into a weapon," Jack continued. "Once your mother and I realized that you had gained your gifts, we knew you would be the greatest weapon for him. The goal was for him to never find out. Unfortunately, fighting with Clarice has made that impossible," he said, looking into Sophie's eyes. Not with blame. Simply with his 'let's come up with a plan' face he wore when he was working on his projects.

"I'm sorry," Sophie whispered to him. "I didn't know."

"I know," Jack said, patting her on the knee. "We should have done better at telling you the whole story," he said, more so to Jess than to Sophie.

Jess remained quiet as she sat on the couch with her arms crossed and looking at the flames dancing in the freshly lighted fireplace.

"I think that's enough for today," Jack said with a smile. "Get some rest, Peanut," he whispered as he touched her forehead and sent her body back through the wooden door into a deep sleep.

Once Sophie was gone, Jack stood up and turned to face Mario and Jess.

"Jess," Jack said, "it's time to put your stubbornness aside and decide who you're going to fight for."

Jess glared at Jack with fire glowing in her eyes. "You know damn well who I would choose," she hissed.

Jack smiled. "And you," he said, looking at Mario. "You need some more lessons. Ready?"

"Yes, Sir," Mario sulked. "Can you show me how to send her back?" he asked with sudden eagerness. "That's a really cool trick to get her to stop fussing."

Jack chuckled as he put his arm around his friend. "Sadly, there are rules for that too."

"Figures," Mario mumbled.

They walked away into the darkness.

"Coming?" Jack asked his wife.

"In a minute," Jess called over her shoulder.

The boys left her to her thoughts and fire that danced before her, but it flickered in and out of sight. She tilted her head to study it with curiosity.

"So close…." a disturbing voice came from the other side.

Jess jumped up from the couch and stared even harder at the fire. "You will not take her," she growled back.

"Watch me," the old man's voice warned before the fire went out and Jess was left in the darkness alone. Or so she thought….

Sophie woke to the sunlight sneaking in through the small crack of the hotel curtains. She rolled over to an empty bed. Tina and Ben were still sleeping in the bed next to her. James was nowhere to be found. Her heart sank for a minute. She knew she had to earn his trust back, but she didn't like the space that had grown between them.

Sophie rubbed the sleep out of her eyes and crept out of the bed to get cleaned up in the bathroom. A hot shower would do her good. Jess' voice kept ringing through her ears....

"YOU ARE THE KEY!"

And because of her inability to remain in control, Sophie had put everyone in even greater danger than when they started. The man with the cane knew, and there was nothing Sophie could do about it now.

She was a little irritated that her parents just hadn't bothered to be honest with her from the very beginning. Sophie would have known better. There was plenty of blame to be shared by all parties at this point.

Sophie needed to get to the bottom of what exactly it was she could actually do. Some sort of baseline to work off of. Maybe her friends would have ideas of just exactly how to accomplish that. First and foremost, though, she needed to find out which side Tina was playing on.

She let the hot water run over her body, as she braced herself against the shower wall and let her mind wonder. The memory of Mario being killed before her eyes seemed to haunt her less and less. She assumed because he hadn't actually left her, and that comforted her knowing that she still got to have him in her life, even if it wasn't physical.

Mario had given hints that Clarice and her mother went back as far as teenagers. She would definitely have to get more information so she could learn as much about Clarice as possible.

She didn't share with anyone that she would take Clarice's life in return for Mario's. No one had lectured her just yet about it, but that probably had to do with more pressing matters that had to be dealt with.

Suddenly, the memory of little Edward flashed before her closed eyes. She briefly wondered if he was even still alive. If he was, did he even remember her? If he wasn't, was it because of her?

Sophie's heart quickly grew heavy and, to push the negative away, the vision of James kneeling before her came into view. James. She knew, considering the circumstances, running seemed like the best option at the time. Sophie wondered what she would have said, if she hadn't just lost Mario before her by Clarice's hand.

A vision of Sophie in a white dress, walking down the aisle with Tina as her Maid of Honor and Ben as the Best Man, as she approached James in a suit wearing his boyish grin.

Yes. Sophie would have said, 'yes', and would still say 'yes' with her life as dangerous and unexpected as it currently remained. Sophie thought about the conversation she had with Ben earlier.

"No one said, 'right now', Soph," Ben had said, looking at her. "For James, it's more of letting you know you are the only person he wants to spend the rest of his life with. The only reason he didn't do it sooner was he thought you would run."

She would have never run from James. Sophie cringed as the water ran down her face, because that was a lie. She already had. Technically, she wasn't running from him specifically, though.

Sophie was running from costing any more lives. She was running from her problems, not the man that she loved with every breath she took. Now, she would have to spend however long it took proving that point of clarification to him.

The door cracked open.

"Hey," she heard James speak softly. "I got everyone breakfast. Just join us when you're ready."

"You could join me instead," Sophie offered.

There was a deafening silence, only broken by the sound of running water.

"Don't you want to have some alone time?" she heard James question both himself and her motives in one single sentence.

"I've had a lifetime of that," Sophie mumbled, kicking herself for offering.

The silence was painfully awkward. Just when she couldn't stand to take any more of it and was getting ready to tell him to go, Sophie heard him slip off his shoes and unbutton his jeans. Okay, she thought. Don't panic. Take it slow. This is a good first step, she convinced herself.

The hot water had filled the entire bathroom up with steam, so Sophie could barely see him when he pushed back the curtain and slipped in behind her. Her breath immediately picked up with anticipation of what to do next.

"I'm so sorry," Sophie started with a sob she didn't expect to be escaping from her mouth. She couldn't seem to face him being this vulnerable and naked.

"Ssshhh," James said, as he lathered up a washcloth with body wash. "I'd like to wash you," he added as more of a question than an actual statement.

"I could use it," Sophie said with a soft smile.

She kept her back to him and felt the warm washcloth circle on her back, shoulders and arms. James carefully washed her whole back side while keeping his distance. Sophie's heart ached to be closer to him, but this was the price she was going to have to pay until he chose otherwise.

James eased her hair off to the side as he ran the washcloth down her neck. Sophie moaned in appreciation. Unexpectedly, he pushed his body up against her, and she felt his erection throb against her backside. He wrapped one arm gently around her waist and circled the washcloth around her eager breasts.

They rose and fell in time with his rhythm, and Sophie melted against James, willing for him to take whatever he wanted from her. He kissed her gently on the neck as he continued to move south. Sophie's body vibrated against him, and he couldn't help but love every minute.

Suddenly, James dropped the washcloth and took a step back. Sophie almost fell all the way on her back in the tub with the sudden gap between them. She wanted to protest, but knew she had no right. Instead, she braved facing him as they both seemed to catch their breath.

"I'm sorry," James whispered, unable to look her in the eyes.

"I'm not," Sophie said, observing him.

James raised his eyes to look at her only for a brief second before staring back at the floor of the tub.

"I'll let you finish," James mumbled as he prepared to exit the shower.

Sophie knew she shouldn't have. She knew she should have respected his need to give her space, but she didn't care at the moment. She grabbed James' hand, reaching for the curtain and pushed him against the shower wall, with her mouth feverishly claiming his for her own. Sophie pressed herself up against him as she ran her hands eagerly through his hair.

James froze instantly, unsure of what to do. Then he gave into the heat of the shower and their need for each other. He wrapped his arms around her and pulled her as close to him as physically possible. His erection throbbed to the beat of both their hearts as they impatiently explored each other as if they were meeting for the first time.

"I need you," Sophie whispered in his ear.

James moaned with acceptance and spun her around to help balance her back against the shower wall. He grabbed her legs and pulled them around him as he kissed her so deeply she lost all oxygen to her brain.

"Are you sure?" he asked her urgently when he pulled back. He looked deep into Sophie's eyes for the truth from her.

"Yes," Sophie said, with an assuring smile.

James nodded and crushed his mouth against hers once more, sliding into her since she was already wet and eagerly waiting. He began moving slowly and carefully, giving her time to adjust. Sophie gasped and threw her head back, moaning her appreciation for his willingness to give her what she so desperately needed. James nibbled on her neck gently as he went deeper and deeper.

"Oh, James!" Sophie went to call out, but she felt his mouth impatiently drowning out her scream. They shook and moaned in unison as she exploded around him and he came along with her.

Sophie laid her head on his shoulder as he held onto her and allowed them both to catch their breath. She wiggled a bit as she was still tingling from him being inside her.

"Wow," Sophie breathed out.

"You didn't have to," James said, unexpectedly in shame as he pulled out and placed her down safely. The shower was becoming quite cold suddenly.

"I wanted to," Sophie pleaded. "I've wanted to since I got back," she said, in embarrassment.

"Really?" James asked, shocked.

Sophie pulled him close to her, placing her head on his forehead.

"I ran from myself," she pleaded. "Not you," she added in a whisper. "I understand if you need time, though."

Sophie kept her eyes closed, knowing she probably didn't want the answer he was about to give her.

"I figured," James whispered back after a minute. "I don't blame you. I just had terrible timing," he added, frustrated.

Sophie giggled, and it lightened his heart with the sound.

"We should probably go have breakfast before we turn into prunes, though," she giggled.

James pulled back and looked deep into her eyes.

"I just need a little time," he confessed.

"I figured," Sophie said with a weak smile. "We've got some crap to deal with anyway," she shrugged. James turned off the water, and Sophie stepped out first. "You'll never believe what I found," she added over her shoulder as she toweled off.

"Do tell," he said with a smile.

"Let's have breakfast first," Sophie laughed as she got dressed.

She ran a brush through her wet hair and threw it into a ponytail.

"I don't know if this helps you at all," she said slowly as she reached for the bathroom door.

James looked at her, puzzled.

"I would say 'yes'," Sophie said, smiling weakly with a shrug and hurried out the door, leaving James gaping after her.

"Nice shower?" Tina asked with an eyebrow raised at her friend as she came out.

"One of the best," Sophie said, sheepishly, forgetting Tina was on her list of things to take care of.

James finally exited while running a hand nervously through his hair. Tina and Ben watched him with curiosity.

"Well, this should be interesting," Ben whispered to his wife. Tina quickly elbowed him in the side to be quiet.

"Sorry that I left," Sophie started as she stared at the floor. She still felt incredibly guilty for leaving them behind. "It was just a bit much to handle," she said honestly and shrugged.

Sophie looked down at the necklace, closed her eyes to concentrate on opening it, and tossed the SD card to Tina once she was done. Tina looked at her with confusion.

"I don't think I should have this on me," Sophie said, watching Tina's face for any clues. "If something happens, the man with the cane will get it for sure. I think you should take it and do with it what you think is best."

Tina looked at the tiny card she now held in her hand.

"You've always had it," she said, in confusion.

"That's why I shouldn't," Sophie shrugged. "If things continue to go south, they will assume that I have it and it wouldn't be good for them to be correct."

"Good point," Tina said, still looking at the card in her hand.

"Maybe we could send it to someone to hide it for us?" Ben offered.

"That just means putting more people in danger," James pointed out.

Tina closed her hand and simply said, "I'll take care of it," and put the SD card in her pocket.

"I'm sure you will," Sophie said, softly watching her friend closely, but no clues were given.

"So, what now?" Ben asked, looking around the room.

"I need help with something else," Sophie said reluctantly.

"What's up?" James asked, giving her his boyish grin.

"Well, none of us know what it is I can actually do," Sophie started again slowly. "And I think the only way to actually know would be to run some sort of tests."

"I don't think it's wise to take you to a lab of any sort," Tina cut in immediately.

"Yeah, my thoughts too," Sophie agreed. "Surely you have some old school stuff we can try?"

"I don't like this," James said, straightaway.

"She's right," Ben interjected. "We have to test her to know what she can and can't do if it comes down to that." Ben turned to James and put his hand on his shoulder. "We can go easy, and if anything happens, you have a doctor on hand." he winked. "It's not like she takes long to heal," Ben added for assurance.

"I don't think we need to be putting her life in danger either," James frowned.

"I will be honest and let you know when we need to stop," Sophie assured. "Quite frankly, it's hard to prepare for a fight if we don't know what tools we actually have on our side," she said with authority.

"I don't like it," James mumbled again.

Sophie crossed the room and put her hand into his and squeezed.

"I need to know what I can and can't do, so I know what I CAN do to keep you all safe," she said, softly stroking his arm.

"It's not your job to keep us safe," James quickly protested.

Sophie grabbed the back of his head and pulled him into a gentle kiss.

"Yes, it is," she said, when they parted.

"I still don't like it," James frowned.

"Noted," Sophie said, smiling back.

"So how do we do this?" Ben asked Sophie.

"We should make a list based on the facts that we already know," Tina interrupted. "Do our research, and see what we can come up with," she said, shrugging. "Tell us 'no' when we cross a line," Tina warned Sophie. "But the broader the testing we can do, the better."

"That's my nerd, girl," Ben said, kissing Tina gently on the lips.

Well, this would be another good way for Sophie to find out whose side Tina was on, but whatever they found would be leaked to the wrong side if Sophie's suspicions were correct. Either way, Tina was going to be the most useful with this task. If she was on the wrong side, Sophie would have a heads up on what he was looking for in her as well. It was going to have to do.

"Let the games begin," Sophie said, shrugging.

Fifteen

Clarice had been home for a few days, and still managed to say nothing. She told herself she needed to cool off about the stupid troll living to tell the tale, but Clarice wasn't sure that was entirely true. She glared at Eddie as he took his place in front of the computer monitors on the wall.

"What's up your butt?" Eddie asked her flatly.

"You're breathing," Clarice scowled.

"I can't help it if I'm the new favorite," Eddie shrugged.

"Don't get too comfortable," she said with a wicked smile. A chill went down Eddie's spine. Clarice had something in order to be so blatantly confident. He tried to tell himself he didn't care what it was. However, he did care. Eddie shook his head and got back to work.

"What's the latest?" Eddie asked Clark, who was very sour at Eddie's return to taking the lead.

"Nothing yet," Clark mumbled with annoyance.

"What have you been doing while I was fighting for my life?" Eddie poked at him.

"Your job, better than you!" Clark snapped back.

"Clearly, since she's still MIA and it's been days," Eddie laughed at him, shook his head, and went back to staring at the screen.

"Jerk," Clark mumbled under his breath.

"Making all sorts of friends," Clarice mocked.

"Can't be everyone's favorite," Eddie said with a smile and a shrug. Clarice's blood boiled. She hated that he always could get under her skin.

"What's the update?" barked the old man from the shadows behind them. He had entered without them noticing.

"Apparently, nothing," Clarice replied excitedly, waiting for her father's wrath to shine.

"Please explain to me why I hired you to find me someone if you cannot do so?" the old man warned. No one said a word and kept their faces forward. "Clark," he said, dangerously calm. "Please stop by my office in an hour. I believe we have something to discuss."

"Of course, Sir," Clark responded with a smile at Eddie.

"Glad to see you back, Edward," the old man said, before everyone heard his cane grow distant in the tunnels.

"We'll see who stays his favorite," Clark boasted.

Something told Eddie he wouldn't be seeing Clark after his visit to the old man's office. Eddie and Clarice had been the only ones to return when they were called. Clarice called a thousand times more often than Eddie. Clark had earned his sentence, Eddie told himself. He felt no need to save him from himself.

As for being the so-called "favorite", Eddie wasn't sure how he felt about his role. He had yet to discover why the old man felt like keeping him alive, but Eddie didn't really feel the need to question it right now, either. He should have been dead a long time ago. He was pretty sure they both knew it. Eddie was guessing his lives had all been used up, though, and it was best to just keep his head down and do what was asked of him.

Sophie had left him. That much he knew. She hadn't looked for him, either. Amnesia or not. All helping Sophie got Eddie was nearly dead. It was time to stop caring for those that stopped caring about him a long time ago and accept his fate.

"Goodbye," Eddie mumbled under his breath in sorrow.

Only Clarice heard him. She looked at Eddie, studying him carefully. They both knew Clark would not be returning, but she was pretty sure Eddie wasn't saying goodbye to the eager tech.

"I have to get to work," Eddie told Clarice, making her even more skeptical.

She stepped back to study him in silence. Clarice knew the tone. She knew the behavior. The troll was officially broken. Whatever her father had done in her absence, she realized Eddie would not be a problem for her anymore. He had officially accepted his new role. Sophie would get no more help from him from now on.

Clarice didn't poke at him. She didn't have to. He was finally one of them. The only question was, was Clarice still one of them too?

They headed downtown for the library. There wasn't as much concern about being on the public library's internet stream, since what they were looking for could be general research for almost any student. Everyone divided to conquer the most coverage.

Although Sophie spent little time learning computer hacking, she did know how to track an IP address. She monitored Tina's searches while she looked for stuff for herself at the same time. They had divided the list of animal genetics that Dr. Cox had listed to them, but Sophie encouraged them to stretch as far outside of the box as possible. Everyone was so engrossed with their tasks at hand that they missed lunch and dinner all together.

The lights flickered above them. Sophie tensed up instantaneously until she saw the librarian give her a friendly wave. It was their warning that the library was closing.

"I'm starving," Ben said, rubbing his growling stomach.

"Yeah, me too," James replied, rubbing his stomach as well.

Both had their bags on their back, and their arms full of papers and books.

"I completely lost track of time!" Tina exclaimed, who was shushed by the librarian.

"Let's find something to eat," Sophie suggested. "We need to stay covered. We don't know who's watching," she warned. It was still good practice, even if they were being watched by one of their own.

"Slate Street Café is supposed to be good, and has an upstairs wine loft," Ben said with a smile.

"Did you research for Sophie, or just for food?" Tina chuckled.

Ben stuck his tongue out at his wife. Sophie smiled, but desperately hoped she was wrong about her friend. Everyone bundled up and headed for Slate Street Café.

They could only have a quick bite before the place closed down. From the outside, it was just a typical beige barn styled building that had clearly been converted to a community hotspot. Once they entered, bright lights, a wooden floor, with various sized white tables, and dark wood chairs welcomed them. There was a small red staircase that led to the wine loft.

A polite young woman with long chestnut-haired pulled back in a ponytail, wearing all black attire, gave a shy smile and showed them up the stairs. A tall, slender woman with a deep chocolate bob and caramel highlights greeted them with eyes to match. She was wiping down the wine glasses that had clearly just been cleaned.

It was carpeted upstairs in a dark mauve, and various leathered stand-alone chairs were scattered on one end for socializing, along with a few small tables and chairs scattered around. A small bar provided wine tastings with the bartender. Lamps hung from the rafters over the bar with scattered recessed lighting in the ceiling turned low to provide mood lighting. Wooden shelves stacked against the wall next to the bar, with various knickknacks on them.

They picked a table in the back out of habit, keeping their backs, as much as possible, to the wall to see who was coming their direction. No one discussed their findings. Instead, they shared more childhood stories and all the different trouble they had found themselves in growing up.

According to Tina, James was always a lady's man. Though he never seemed to get caught for any of the mischief he caused. Tina took the credit, even though the boys protested it was usually Tina that was the chief troublemaker.

Sophie shared some of the places she remembered going to with Mario. Her missing memories seemed to come back more and more, despite Mario no longer being with her physically. Sophie assured them she was the typical dramatic and rebellious teenage girl. She laughed as she told them how Mario tried his best with the no-nonsense parenting style and even called her "Princess" when he felt she was being too dramatic. However, he could never keep it up for very long, and went back to being a softy once her tantrum was over.

Everyone was relieved to hear her talk so fondly after losing someone so cherished just recently. Ben still worried if she would break at any moment, but Sophie remained calm whenever speaking of her time with Mario.

Ben reached into his bag for a notepad and added to his list of "gifts" he had already discovered as she talked. Sophie was too lost in her memories to even notice.

They hung out for about an hour, then headed back to the hotel. Ben held onto Tina as they walked along the sidewalk. James kept his hands in his pockets. Sophie's face fell a little at the realization that they couldn't just go back to the way things were prior to Mario's death. She sulked and kicked what rocks she found along the way.

Unexpectedly, Sophie felt James slip his arm through hers so they could walk together. She smiled weakly at him. She wasn't sure if it was his actual idea, or if he just sensed her pain, but she would take it either way.

"I just need some time," James whispered as a reminder.

"I know," she replied softly.

Sophie watched the streets with her eagle eyes, noting the black unmarked van that seemed to follow them as they headed back to the hotel. She quickly memorized the license plate; already pretty sure it would come back a ghost.

"What's up?" James asked, seeming to always read her mind.

"Black van," Sophie whispered back.

"Yeah, I saw it earlier, too," he informed her. "When I went out for breakfast," James added.

"Did you tell Ben and Tina?" Sophie asked.

"No," he confirmed. "I thought it might just be me."

"Looks like another player has joined the game," Sophie said.

"Yeah, but for which side?" James asked wearily.

"Looks like we're going to find out," Sophie said, as the van pulled up alongside James and Sophie. They had allowed a safe distance between them and Ben and Tina to not look like they were traveling as a group.

Tina looked over her shoulder. Sophie shook her head 'no' so they would keep walking. The tinted window rolled down while the SUV slowed to an almost complete stop.

"Do you happen to know the way to San Francisco?" asked an elderly gentleman who was very similar to Mario.

He had a grey beard and mustache, gold earrings in both ears, and a bandana on his head covering thinning long grey wavy hair. He wore a black leather jacket and a t-shirt with a large skull on the front of it. Sophie froze at the phrase. There was something familiar about it.

James looked at Sophie for a clue, but her eyes glazed over. "We're not from the area," he offered politely, "so we're not much help."

"I didn't ask you," the man said, as he continued to stare at Sophie. "Do you happen to know the way to San Francisco?" he repeated to her.

"His favorite song," Sophie whispered softly to herself before responding, "No, but if I do, I'd love to wear some flowers in my hair."

James stared at Sophie as if she had lost her mind.

"Long time no see, Sophie," the man smiled.

"Long time no see, Cecil," Sophie smiled warmly at the man.

"Wanna go for a ride, Kid?" Cecil asked her.

"We'd love to," Sophie said, softly.

Cecil stared at James. "I'm only here for you, Kid," he said, looking James up and down to size him up.

"We're a packaged deal," Sophie said, smiling her Cheshire smile at him.

"He said you'd say that," Cecil mumbled. "Get in."

The side door opened with a couple of other men dressed in biker gear sitting inside.

"Come on," Sophie said, tugging on James' arm.

He looked at Ben and Tina, at Sophie, at the men in the van, and back at Sophie.

"Mario sent them," Sophie whispered. "Their bark is worse than their bite," she giggled.

James looked at Ben and Tina, giving them a weary smile to try and assure them as he climbed in the van. Sophie turned and winked at them both before following suit and closing the door. Ben and Tina both stood gawking as their friends climbed into the mystery van without protest. Cecil saluted them as he drove by.

"What the hell?" Tina asked while Ben just stood with his mouth open as the van turned the corner and disappeared out of sight.

James kept a hand on Sophie's leg during their ride to wherever they were going. He eyed each character carefully, but Sophie just sat back and waited for them to stop. The windows were tinted black, and there was no way of knowing where they were exactly, when suddenly, the side door jerked open.

"Where is she?" a woman called behind a crowd of mostly male motorcycle enthusiasts.

Sophie hopped out first and was instantly pulled into the arms of a tall, slender woman who had grey hair past her waist pulled back in a ponytail. She wore jeans and a black t-shirt that matched Cecil's.

The woman pulled Sophie back to survey her from head to toe with her aging eyes. "It's been too long, Child," the woman stated bluntly as she inspected Sophie for any injuries.

"I missed you too, Donna," Sophie smiled as she was pulled into another hug.

"Who's the boy?" one of them shouted, jabbing their thumb in James' direction.

"This is James. He's Team Sophie, so don't make me hurt you," Sophie replied, glaring back at the man who asked before tossing her head back in a laugh. "Be nice, Daryl," she warned with a smile.

James awkwardly held out his hand to Daryl, who stared at it for what seemed like an eternity before he took it.

"Mario sent word you were here," Donna cut in. "How can we help?"

"Who are these people?" James whispered in Sophie's ear.

"They're friends of Mario's," she whispered back. "We're in excellent hands," she said, winking, but James wasn't exactly convinced. Looking around the garage, he noticed a lot of small arms mixed in with the typical tools needed for fixing bikes and cars.

"Actually, I do need help with something," Sophie smiled sweetly. She grabbed Donna's elbow and walked her across to the other side of the garage.

James noticed the three large men walking around him to inspect him. "Hey fellas," he laughed nervously.

"What are your intentions with our Sophie?" Cecil cut to the chase.

James was a little thrown off by the question.

"Are you deaf?" Cecil demanded, and James suddenly realized the meaning of the passive aggression that he had been receiving.

"Quite honestly, I plan on marrying her, or at least keeping her safe until my last dying breath," James shrugged and relaxed at the intent of the group. They clearly loved Sophie as much as he did. They had some sort of past with her, and they brought him to see if he was worthy.

Daryl huffed a chuckle. "You? Keep her safe?"

"I'm more than I appear," James smirked.

"How long have you been around, Boy?" one of them grunted.

"I found her in the woods several months back," James answered honestly. It did no good to lie to these people. "She got injured, and I brought her to my parents' house to heal. We've been together ever since," James said with a wicked smile, letting them know it was more than just some fling. "And her father gave me his permission already," he added for good measure.

It wasn't a lie. Jack pulled him aside and asked him the same question. What were his intentions? He was pleased with the answer and gave James their blessing.

Daryl looked at Cecil, who appeared to be deep in thought. "Jack gave you his blessing?" Cecil repeated.

"Yes," James confirmed. "It's hard to explain, but he did."

Everyone waited for Cecil. You could hear a pin drop; the silence was so deafening.

"Well," Cecil said, slowly. "If Jack and Mario approve, then I do too," he said, sticking his hand out to James. He pulled James into a hug immediately after he took it. "But if you ever make her even the slightest bit unhappy," Cecil threatened into James' ear, "my boys and me are going to give you a visit, if you catch my drift."

"Yes, Sir," James said, with a smile.

Cecil patted him on the back and pushed him out of reach.

"Hungry?" he asked James.

"We just finished eating. Thank you," James declined politely.

"Beer?" Daryl asked.

"Certainly," James gladly accepted.

"Absolutely NOT!" everyone heard Donna exclaim on the other side of the garage.

"It needs to be done," Sophie stated bluntly. "I will be safer knowing," she added for good measure.

"I don't like this one bit!" Donna declared.

"I don't either," James announced.

Donna jerked her head to eye James with skepticism.

"But we do have a doctor with us, and you know she won't take no for an answer," James shrugged before taking a sip of his beer.

The men looked between James and Donna for answers. They didn't get any.

Donna turned to Sophie. "I'm not happy about the idea, but he's right. You're going to do it, anyway. It might as well be under my watch," she said grimly. "I do like him though," she winked and tilted her head in James' direction.

"Thought you might," Sophie giggled.

It was settled. Cecil's gang was going to provide some added "testing equipment" and a warehouse for their lab. At least this way, general weapons, most likely held by Clarice's teams, could be fully tested. Now, to just see what she was actually capable of....

"I don't like this at all!" Tina said, in hysteria. She had been pacing the hotel room for the last couple of hours after James and Sophie climbed into an unmarked van.

Ben kept his eyes closed as he focused on the man's face, who was in the driver's seat. He knew he had seen him before. He just couldn't figure out from where for the life of him, no matter how hard he tried to focus.

"How can you just sit there and nap?" Tina yelled.

"I'm not napping," Ben said, giving up and opening his eyes. "I was trying to focus." Tina looked at him like a wild animal. "I have seen him somewhere before. I just can't remember where," he added in defeat.

"That's it!" Tina shouted, pulling the laptop out of her bag, popping it open, and frantically typing. "If we can get a picture from one of the traffic cameras, we can trace him!"

"You know Sophie will keep him safe," Ben said softly.

"I know," Tina whispered. "But if we lose her, we lose everything."

Ben didn't know what Tina meant by that. He only knew his wife wanted the best for her friends. That's one of the many reasons he loved her so much. He went back to closing his eyes to focus as his wife feverishly typed on the laptop to track down the mystery man. The sound of the lock on the door being unlocked by the electronic key had them both jumping. They looked urgently at each other before staring back at the door.

"Are you kidding me?" Ben yelled when he saw Sophie walk in with James in tow as if nothing had happened.

"What?" Sophie asked, confused.

"What?!" Tina yelled, jumping off the bed. "We've been worried sick for the last couple of hours since we witnessed the two of you climbing into an unmarked van with strangers!"

Ben rushed over to hold his wife down. He knew that tone, and so did James.

"Sorry, Tin!" James interjected. "Mario sent reinforcements, and we got caught up in that. I'm sorry I didn't call," he said, gently rubbing his hands up and down Tina's arms to soothe her.

Tina mumbled under her breath, but no one could understand her as she walked to the other side of the room to give herself some space. Sophie observed her.

"So, who are these reinforcements?" Ben interrupted.

"It's Mario's old biker gang," Sophie answered, not taking her eyes off of Tina. "They're able to help provide a warehouse and some testing equipment," she said matter-of-factly. Tina stopped pacing, and Sophie watched for clues.

"That's it!" yelled Ben. Everyone stared at him. "The driver is a friend of Mario's and was at his bar often during the summer!" he replied in triumph.

"Well, I guess that's something," Tina offered with a frown, ignoring her husband's sudden revelation. "Are you sure you still want to do this?" she asked, turning to Sophie and looking her straight in the eye.

"It's better that we know what we're dealing with," Sophie shrugged. "We need to determine my strengths and weaknesses."

"That's true," Tina said, suddenly in thought.

It made Sophie a little uneasy with how quickly Tina was willing to "test" her. However, she couldn't determine if it was the naturally inquisitive side of her friend, or because the man with the cane needed answers. Either way, Sophie couldn't chance letting her guard down.

"They're off the grid," Sophie continued. "So, we won't draw any attention. I hope you have your ideas ready," she said wearily.

"Let's just get something to eat and relax," James replied, desperately wanting to change the subject. It was bad enough that the woman he loved wanted them to treat her like a lab rat in order to find out what she was capable of. They didn't have to talk about it constantly until then.

"So, what do you want for your last meal?" Ben joked, but swiftly was slapped in the stomach by his wife.

Sophie giggled to ease their minds. She loved their banter, even if she couldn't trust it at the moment.

"Italian?" she offered.

"Something tells me you'll need the carbs," Tina smiled wearily.

"Pasta it is!" James exclaimed as he headed to the laptop to find some delivery options.

"Do you still have the SD card?" Sophie asked, hoping to sound casual.

"No," Tina said flatly, not giving anything away.

"What do you mean, 'no'?" Ben asked.

"I sent it to a friend for safe keeping," Tina shrugged and gave no more details.

Ben looked at Sophie, confused, but Sophie was too busy dealing with the pit in her stomach. Had Tina sent it directly to him? Or would she send it through an unknowing suspect? Sophie suddenly lost her appetite, however, forced herself to eat all the same. It would do her no good to let Tina know she was on to her.

Sophie had promised she would not attack him if James slept in the same bed with her, but she couldn't stand the thought of him sleeping on the floor or in a chair. James reluctantly agreed, although kept his front to her and a pillow in between them.

Sophie wasn't sure if James didn't trust her or if he didn't trust himself. She secretly wished for the latter. However, when Sophie closed her eyes to get a good night's rest, she found the wooden door instead.

"Oh, come on!" Sophie whined. "I need sleep before tomorrow!"

"Open the door, Kid," Mario warned.

"You're lucky I like you," Sophie mumbled as she reached for the doorknob. The light that greeted her was warm like he used to be. "Now, what?" she sighed.

"Sorry to bother you, Princess," Mario said, sitting at a table with his feet up, hands behind his head, and rolling his eyes.

"Don't start with me," Sophie said with a chuckle.

"You're really gonna do this?" Mario asked seriously.

"We need to know," Sophie said. "We both know that."

"Yeah," Mario said, taking his feet down and sitting up straighter. "I'm just worried," he added honestly.

"I have a doctor on site," she offered as a consolation.

"A doctor can't help if you're dead," Mario retorted, glaring at her.

"Well, I don't intend to go that extreme!" Sophie laughed. There was an awkward silence between them. "I need to know," she finally whispered.

"I know, Kid," Mario whispered with a weary smile. "Why do you think I sent you my best people?" he said, leaning back and putting his feet back up.

"Yeah, Donna's not happy with me either," Sophie mumbled.

"We're just looking out for you, Kid," he reminded her.

"I know," Sophie replied with a smile. She pulled out the chair across from him and sat down. "So, what's so important you're interrupting my beauty sleep?" she asked, looking at Mario skeptically.

"I have found nothing to support your suspicions of your friend," Mario said, shrugging.

"So, you're Team Tina then?" Sophie said, a little hurt.

Mario put his feet down again and leaned over the table.

"First and foremost, I will ALWAYS be Team Sophie," Mario replied firmly. "But you have a lot of team members, and right now she only has two," Mario said, shrugging.

"She sent away the card," Sophie reminded him.

"I'm aware," Mario said, unfazed. "I'm looking into it. Just because Tina sent it away like you thought she would doesn't mean she sent it to him," he said, staring at her intently.

"It doesn't mean she didn't," Sophie retorted.

Mario shook his head and laughed.

"You have enough enemies to worry about," Mario warned. "Let me worry about this one," he added sternly.

Sophie looked at him with great determination. Mario sighed overdramatically. "I didn't say let your guard down, Princess. I said, let me look into it," he groaned.

"And how can you play detective as a ghost exactly?" Sophie asked, doubtingly.

"A hell of a lot better," Mario said, winking at her. "Now, get some rest." He stood up to walk towards her. Sophie pulled back her head in hesitation.

"Do you know how?" she asked, half teasing and half concerned.

"Brat," Mario retorted before he touched her forehead, forcing her back through the door and into the deepest sleep she'd had in a long time.

Sixteen

Can I just say one more time that I am one-hundred percent against this?" James asked nervously.

"Duly noted," Sophie said, smiling and kissing him on the cheek. "So, what's first?"

"Maybe start with things we can test easily?" Tina offered.

"Okay," Sophie replied. "What do you have in mind?"

"Some things we know," Ben said in his doctor's voice. "Fractures only take days to heal, while broken bones take almost a week," he stated as he made notes on his list. "So, we don't need to break anything today," he added in a warning tone.

"Okay, Dad," Sophie giggled.

"Well, we know she's fast," Tina said with a smile. "Feel like a run?"

"I mean, I guess," Sophie said. "But how are you going to measure?"

"That's what I'm here for!" Daryl said with a smile. "Hop in!" he said, climbing into the car he had brought.

"You want me to race a car?" Sophie asked with a chuckle.

"A car made for drag racing." Daryl smiled a defiant smile. "I haven't lost a race yet!" he declared proudly. The trio climbed into the car.

"Maybe you should get a head start," Sophie teased. She had no clue how fast she actually was. The challenge thrilled her all the same.

"Suit yourself!" hollered Daryl out the window as he took off.

Sophie counted to ten slowly before she took off after the car. She squinted her eyes as she pinpointed the image ahead of her. She breathed carefully as she enjoyed the breeze whipping through her hair as she ran. It impressed Sophie when she caught up to the car rather quickly.

"Um, guys," Ben said, pointing to the speedometer.

No one said a word. The dial continued to creep up steadily and was currently at 70 mph.

"How fast do you think she can actually go?" Tina whispered.

"We're about to find out!" Daryl said in excitement as he pushed on the gas pedal.

Sophie maintained speed with the car. She had to stop looking over, because all she saw was the back of their heads as they watched the dashboard like hawks. It made her more curious than excited and caused her to slow a bit, so instead she kept her eyes in front.

She hadn't been running long, but Sophie was feeling the speed leaving her body physically. She didn't know exactly how fast she was running; but that speed would not last for long distances. It was still information needed. When the energy completely was gone, Sophie slowed down to a jog, and eventually leaned over to rest her hands on her knees while she caught her breath. Daryl slowed down and circled back.

"You were almost at 85 mph!" yelled Ben with excitement.

"You okay?" James asked, rushing to her side with concern.

"I'm fine," Sophie assured. "Just not a distant runner at that speed," she said, honestly.

"That coincides with the characteristics of a cheetah," Tina announced for everyone. She pulled out her own list and made a note. "I wonder if you hunt the same," she said, tapping the pen against her chin deep in thought.

"I'm sorry?" Sophie asked her.

"Hunt," Tina repeated, as if that answered the question.

"Hun…" Ben started.

"Oh, sorry!" Tina said, realizing she needed to clarify. "Cheetah stalk their prey by staying low on the ground, and grabbing them by the throat to suffocate them," she said matter-of-factly.

"Let's save that test for later," Sophie said, in sudden disgust.

"Suit yourself," Tina replied with a shrug.

"Isn't doing all this testing in one day going to wear you out?" James pointed out.

"I'm okay," Sophie assured.

"He makes a valid point," Tina said. "It will be hard to test everything if you're exhausted through part of it."

Sophie's gut called to her. Tina was a little too invested in this testing, and she didn't feel like it was as much for Sophie's benefit as it was for Tina's.

"You're safe as long as you're here," Daryl said. "Take all the time you need."

James didn't intend to have the torture stretched out. He had mentioned it so that they would rethink and maybe not finish, but his plan was quickly backfiring in his face.

"Or we don't have to do it all," he offered, knowing no one would support him.

"Nice try," Sophie said with a smile of determination.

They agreed she would rest in between so that they had a better understanding of what she was capable of. Some things, Sophie purposely kept to herself since she couldn't shake the feeling that Tina was all too eager to test her limits to the fullest.

Over the course of a couple of days, it was determined that, based on the animal genetics Dr. Cox had listed in New Orleans, Sophie had an interesting mixture of talents.

Sophie had Ben add sensitivity to smell to the list, which concurred with a grizzly bear. It turned out Sophie was stronger than even she knew as well. She could yank a car door off the hinges and pry open a windshield with her bare hands. However, the thickness of metal definitely determined if Sophie could bend it or not. A car door, yes. A rafter beam, not so much.

Grizzlies are also more aggressive when defending themselves and loved ones such as cubs. Sophie didn't admit just how much she could relate to that characteristic, but made a note to herself. She would need to monitor herself when fighting.

Cheetahs also had what they called a visual streak. This

allowed them to locate prey against the horizon. Sophie confirmed she could do just that. They spent one day just testing how far she could actually see. It seemed if she really focused, she could see almost five miles away. If she couldn't, it was closer to three miles.

Near the hotel, they had climbed to the rooftop to run some other tests on her eyesight while her body physically rested. Even Sophie was fascinated that she could see ants crawling on the ground despite her being 10-stories high. Compared to her friends, objects directly in her line of sight were apparently magnified, and she saw the brightest of colors in everything.

"Well, you'll never have to wear glasses," Tina had pouted, knowing she needed to get some for herself.

Ben guessed she had an extremely efficient circulatory and respiratory system that assisted in her healing process. Her bone marrow replaced itself rapidly and effectively, as if it had a mind of its own all together.

They couldn't deny her excessive cat genetic influences with the way she leapt, landed, and walked. Sophie gave any woman trying to portray Cat Woman a run for their money.

Despite Ben's attempts, Sophie was not a subject for telekinesis. She could move nothing with her mind, make people do things, or read people's minds.

"We'll come back to this," Ben kept saying.

"Dead horse," Sophie said, with a chuckle every time they tried.

They kept a log of how much she slept afterwards, too, so they would have a better idea of how long it took to recuperate. Physical tests took less time to bounce back from than the mental tests. Ben assured her it was only because she had used her physical "gifts" more often, and her body had already adapted.

Donna fussed over her every time they returned to the garage, while Cecil spent a lot of time with James. Sophie wasn't sure if it was Mario's doing, or if Cecil loved him almost as much as she did.

No one visited her while she slept. No wooden doors. No Mario. No parents. The only thing that she noticed was the occasional touch on her forehead, forcing her into a deeper sleep. Sophie realized this was their way of forcing her overactive brain to be silenced and allow her to get the rest she needed. Although Sophie hadn't always appreciated it in the past, she was thankful for the added help.

Tina often started an argument with her during the tests. She kept insisting that they needed to know if anger increased the intensity of Sophie's "gifts" versus just being calm. Sophie hated to admit it, but Tina had a point.

Although anger definitely increased Sophie's abilities, it also caused her to lose control faster. She would have to find the delicate balance between being enhanced and crossing the point of no return. She would have to be careful, because losing control meant she lost purpose and the wrong lives would be taken.

They had spent five days testing everything they could think of. Sophie had tried to test some things on her own but got busted by James. He was so furious with her when he caught her holding her hand over the flame of the stove.

James made her swear to never do another test without him present. Sophie loved how much he cared. She also knew he wasn't willing to push the limits either, if it meant she might get hurt. James had fought her the whole way through the process, but she understood. If the shoe was on the other foot, Sophie would do the same.

"Hey," Sophie whispered to James once she knew Tina and Ben were out like a light.

"Hhhmmm," James mumbled, half asleep himself.

"I promised to never do a test without you, but I need to do one more," she whispered softly in his ear.

"Now?" James asked, trying to rub his eyes awake.

"Yes," Sophie assured. "I'll make it worth your while," she smiled.

"I doubt that," James countered with a frown.

"I can go without you," Sophie offered.

"Just give me a second," James mumbled.

Sophie grabbed her tennis shoes and quietly slipped them on while she waited patiently for James to regain his awareness of reality.

"Aren't you going to get dressed?" James asked, confused.

"Don't need to," she said with her Cheshire grin.

James sighed and reluctantly followed her. He wasn't sure if he should be excited or concerned once he realized they were heading to the hotel pool.

"What exactly do you have in mind?" he asked nervously.

"I think being in the desert has kept us inside the box," Sophie said, slowly. "We need to test the water too."

She tried not to shiver. The last time Sophie voluntarily went near a pool was on her fifth birthday. They all knew how that turned out. She had avoided large bodies of water minus swimming with James at his parent's house.

"You okay?" James asked, noting her hesitation.

"Just not a fan of pools," she admitted honestly.

"Oh. Yeah," James responded, realizing what Sophie was referring to. "So, what are we doing?" he asked her, trying to change the subject.

"I need you to time me," Sophie said, slipping off the boxers and t-shirt of his she still wore when sleeping, leaving her black laced bra and panties on.

"Time you doing what?" James asked in sudden alarm.

"I think they tried to hold me under the water to see what would happen," Sophie said, looking at him, unsure of his reaction.

James remained quiet for what seemed like an eternity.

"Okay," he finally said. "But I'm pulling you out the second I feel something is going wrong."

"I expect nothing less," Sophie said, smiling at him as she turned to face her fear.

"Hey," James whispered in her ear before spinning Sophie around to face him. "I love you," he said, staring deep into her eyes before he grabbed her and pulled her into a deep and passionate kiss.

"How do you expect me to test my ability to hold my breath if you take it all away before I get in the water?" Sophie breathed when they parted.

"Sorry," James smiled weakly. "You needed to know."

He stepped back to give her space. James knew this was something she had to do. He also knew there was no way he could change her mind. At least now she would have something to think about as she sat at the bottom of the pool.

Sophie turned around to face the pool again. She closed her eyes and took a deep breath before she dived into the deep end and crossed her legs to wait. Sophie took a moment to watch James pace above her. She took comfort in knowing he wouldn't allow her to drown herself and looked around the bottom of the pool while she waited and enjoyed the peace and quiet. Memories flashed before her eyes.

Memories of herself as a child, spending time with her parents. Training with her mother. Her father teaching her how to focus her senses. Playing with Edward at their house. Saving Edward at school. Training at various facilities around the world while traveling with Mario. Meeting James. Their first night together, followed by a glorious day after. And every intimate time after that. Him on one knee before her proposing.

Then something happened. Sophie saw her parents lying dead on their kitchen floor. Giselle's limp body in her arms. Bill's eyes staring back at her as his body grew cold on the Jumpin' Jack Power Plant floor. Simon, so proud of every kill. Mario, with Clarice holding a gun to his head, chased by his body lying in a pool of blood.

Then she saw an old man, with half his face burned off across from her and looking her directly in the eyes. His eyes glittered with excitement. His laugh started low and grew creepily louder as he seemed to hold her paralyzed with his glance.

Sophie suddenly couldn't breathe. She began gasping for air, but instead allowed water to enter her lungs. She was frozen. Unable to move her legs and swim to the top. He was drowning her. Just like he tried to do when she was little.

Panic consumed her body. She was going to die here. The way he had intended all those years ago, and she had let him. Her head filled with darkness, and she felt the life leave her body.

Suddenly, arms were wrapped around her and she was being

pulled to the surface. She felt James pull her out of the pool and begin CPR on her. Why couldn't she respond?

"Sophie Lee," she heard her mother order. "You open your eyes right now!"

"I can't," Sophie thought. Something was not letting her. She felt James beat on her chest and desperately breathe into her mouth, but her body refused to help him.

"Sophie!" she heard Mario and her father call to her.

"Don't you dare die on me!" she heard James yell at her.

Her mini me was suddenly crouching before her and staring at her oddly, tilting her head. Disappointment consumed her face.

"I thought you were better than this," the little girl said with a frown.

"A little help here!" Sophie thought desperately.

"Help yourself," the little girl retorted. "We've BEEN helping you!" she pointed out angrily. "And now you're just letting him win."

The little girl crossed her arms in front of her chest and shook her head dismissively. Anger brewed from Sophie's core.

"What a disappointment," the little girl said rudely as she rolled her eyes. "So many lives taken. All for absolutely nothing," she said, mockingly, as she sat down, crossed her legs, and stared at Sophie as if she was nothing more than pond scum. Sophie felt her anger grow. "I guess you really are nothing," the little girl continued to taunt her. "You're not worth anyone's time, especially James's," she added. "At least you'll be easy to get over once he realizes you weren't worth fighting for in the first place."

"Stop it," Sophie mumbled as she tried to get feeling back into her body.

"Who's going to make me?" the little girl laughed back. "It's bad enough you're going to let Clarice get away with murdering Mario. Mario. I mean, it's not like he ever did anything for us anyway," the little girl continued.

Frustration and anger stirred deep within Sophie. "Please stop," she begged.

"And don't even get me started on mom and dad," the little girl continued talking to the sky, ignoring Sophie completely. "Mom just gave birth to us. Both died to keep us safe, and you could care less," she shrugged.

"Stop it," Sophie said, more forcefully, not realizing that the anger was helping her to get her life back.

"And we can't forget good old Bill," the little girl pushed on, waving her hand in the air as if she were swatting a fly away.

"Enough!" Sophie demanded, getting closer to a yell.

"Gee, at least no one else has to lose their life now," she said, suddenly looking at Sophie with a wicked grin. "Oh, wait…" the little girl said, pausing.

"Enough!" Sophie yelled.

"Don't tell me," the little girl yelled back at her. "Tell HIM!"

"ENOUGH!" Sophie screamed out as she rolled over and coughed up the water that she had swallowed from the pool.

"I'm sorry, I was just trying to save you," James said, pulling her into his arms and rocking her.

"I wasn't talking to you," Sophie whispered with exhaustion.

James froze for a second before slowly rocking her in his arms while he waited for her to catch her breath.

"What happened?" he whispered once she could breathe

normally again.

"I don't know," Sophie answered honestly. But she had an idea. "How long was I under?" she asked, to change the subject.

"Over an hour," he reported.

"Not too shabby," she smiled warily.

"Let's not try it again," James sighed as he held her tightly against him.

"Deal," Sophie whispered.

James went to pick her up to carry her back to the room.

"No," she said, grabbing his shirt in her hands. "A promise is a promise," she said with a smile.

"What?" James asked, puzzled.

"I know you said you needed space, but right now I need you," Sophie said, with desire oozing in her voice.

"You almost drowned!" James yelled wildly. "Have you lost your mind?!"

"Please," Sophie begged.

She almost lost her life. She needed to feel alive again. She needed to feel safe again. She needed to feel him.

"I think that's going to be a little difficult with our current sleeping arrangements," he sighed.

He could hear it in her voice. This wasn't about having sex. This was her needing to prove that she loved him and couldn't stand the thought of losing him. Although he loved that she still thought of him that way, this was hardly the time or place.

"Please," Sophie begged again.

James looked her in her eyes and saw the fear and the pain coursing behind them. She needed him to take it away. She needed him to make her feel safe and loved again. She needed him, period.

James never took his eyes away from hers as he carefully picked her up into his arms. He collected her discarded clothing in one hand and began carrying her back down the hall. Sophie looked back at the disappearing pool in confusion.

"Trust me," he whispered with desire and heat thick in his voice.

She laid her head on his shoulder and rested for what she thought was going to be a passionate session of lovemaking. Instead, she woke up to him placing her down just outside of their hotel door.

"I thought," she started to say.

James held up his hand to silence her. Once inside, he took her hand and led her to the bathroom, closing the door behind him. Alright, bathroom it was. She smiled wickedly at the last time they had shared the bathroom. Electricity coursed through her veins as her heart sped up with anticipation.

James sat on the edge of the tub and drew a hot bath. Sophie's eyebrows came together as the gesture quickly replaced excitement with frustration.

"Seriously?" she whined.

"Ssshhh," he reminded her while he kept his focus on the bath. "And strip," he added.

Sophie put her hands on her hips as disappointment replaced her frustration.

"Strip," James ordered again, not looking at her. Sophie sighed heavily and began taking off her already soaked underwear. "Get in," he commanded when she was done. She glared at him but got into the tub. "Sit up," he said, and waited for her to obey.

"You're very bossy," Sophie mumbled, although she honored his request. He pulled off his own soaked t-shirt and boxers before grabbing the luffa and slipping in behind her. Sophie was not prepared for what came next.

"Do you remember the first time we met?" James asked out of nowhere.

"Of course," Sophie answered, confused.

"You wanna know what I remember?" James offered.

Her curiosity peeked. They had never really talked about it before. "Sure," she said, trying to sound casual and not alarmed.

James took his time loading the luffa with body wash and lathering it up really good. He began washing her back while he talked.

"It's difficult for a man to admit when he makes a mistake," he started slowly.

Sophie straightened immediately and was ready to flee the tub. She no longer wanted to hear what James had to say. She couldn't take the rejection that she felt was coming.

James noticed her reaction, of course, but kept calm and relaxed as he continued to wash her body. He picked up her hair to give him better access to her neck.

"I always assumed that I could find a relationship just like my parents had," he continued.

Sophie's grip on the edge of the tub tightened, and she was about to jump out when she felt his legs clamp around her tightly to hold her in place.

"They picked me to join the CIA," he continued somberly.

Sophie could easily have escaped him; however, this was clearly something he needed to tell her. After everything, Sophie owed him to listen to whatever he needed to confess. James felt her resign and loosen her grip on the tub. He made no reaction to give her a hint where this was exactly going.

"That just left a sour taste in my mouth," he continued softly. She could hear the frustration in his voice. "Then I met Helen," James pushed on. Sophie's body tensed for a split second as she remembered the woman she had met at the ball. "She was fake, but I was too blind to see it," he said, as he used his left arm to wrap around her waist and pull her close to him to wash her front. "I was emptied by my CIA stint, that I assumed finding someone to keep safe and care for was more my style."

Sophie suddenly realized that they had never had the chance to talk about his past, or anything private, for that matter. She listened with curiosity, trying to ignore the heat that pulsed from her core at his touch.

"Everyone told me she wasn't the one," he sighed. "But I'm a little stubborn when I think I'm right, and I ignored all the signs," James continued. Sophie heard the frustration with himself more than anyone else come through his statements.

"When I found out that she was sleeping with Curtis, I was too numb to even care. My heart had already stopped at that point," he said sadly. "However, she did me the biggest favor not showing up for our wedding."

Sophie's chest tighten, but she blinked away the tears that suddenly filled her eyes. This was his story, and he wanted her to hear it. She would give him what he needed and remained quiet as he talked.

"I had a lot of odd jobs," he chuckled, seeing memories Sophie was blind to. "Although something was still missing," James shrugged. He continued to wash Sophie as he talked. "Tina had dragged us to another stupid party, and I was about to lose it all together," he stated. "So, I went for a walk."

Sophie's lips curled into a smile as the night played out before her. "I heard a noise," James said, grinning. "Then something took off running before me. I honestly thought it was a drunk idiot at first, but there was something about the shadow figure I couldn't resist. So, I ran after it," he stated with excitement coming through his voice.

"You kept up pretty good," Sophie said, impressed.

"You had a head start," James retorted, trying to sound defensive and failing miserably. "And you scared the crap out of me when you grabbed me and shoved me against the tree," James chuckled lightly. "But God, you were the most beautiful woman I had ever seen," he whispered.

Sophie's heart raced again as she listened to his version of the story.

"It was more than just your looks," James added quickly. "There was something about you that made all the emptiness leave my body," he tried to explain. "My heart beat like never before. I didn't realize just how dead I had become inside before you woke me," he whispered as he lightly traced her arms with his fingers. Sophie felt him grow hard against her, but she didn't dare move.

"Being chased by bad guys will do that to you," she whispered, completely distracted.

"I realize they were there, but it was you that had my focus," James whispered in her ear. "For the first time in my life, I wanted nothing more than to know everything about you, and to keep you safe," he added lovingly. "Even though I never will be able to," he said solemnly as reality set in.

Sophie stopped as her heart suddenly shattered. He wasn't just protesting the tests to keep her safe. For the first time, she realized

James was also protesting because it hurt him to know how much more normal he was compared to her, and that was most likely making him feel like he was less of a man for her.

Sophie hyperventilated as anxiety took over. He would not leave her because he lost love for her. He was going to leave her because he felt like he had nothing to offer her.

"Hey!" James said, pulling her from her thoughts. He pulled Sophie as close to him as humanly possible and squeezed her to calmness. "What's wrong?" he asked.

"I just realized why this is so hard on you," Sophie whispered in a half sob. "I understand why you need distance."

"I don't think you do," James replied in shock. "Yes, it's hard watching you put yourself in danger on purpose right now. And, YES, it's even harder realizing that you will always be able to save yourself before I could ever be of any use," he mumbled through his frustration.

A sob escaped her mouth before she could stop it, and she threw her hand over her mouth to prevent more from seeping out. James immediately wrapped his arms and legs around her, cocooning her in his love.

"I'm not looking to leave you," James assured her, quickly realizing where Sophie's panic might be coming from. James waited patiently for his words to sink in. "It's just hard trying to figure out what value I can provide you so that you can understand how much you give to me," he finished, kissing her on top of the head.

Sophie digested his words. She always had a tendency to forget how hard being in her life was for other people. Finding out she had so many "gifts" didn't help matters. She finally knew why her friends and the man she loved gave up everything to stay with her. It wasn't fear of being killed or trying to keep her safe.

It was because she had unknowingly provided something to each of them that made them want to return the favor. It wasn't just protection. It was her love, empathy, protecting the weak, and standing up for what was right as James would inform her as he continued to soothe her in the tub.

When the water grew cold and their bodies started to prune, James wrapped her in a towel before going to grab some clothes. They spent most of the night whispering. Sharing their hopes and dreams, and the future they envisioned having together. It surprised Sophie that James had the same desires to grow old and rock in rocking chairs on a porch surrounded by mountains too.

They spent the entire night sharing things they had never shared before. Sophie shared her fears of not being able to keep them safe, and what it felt like to lose Mario before her eyes. She confessed things she hadn't even confessed to herself yet.

Sophie remained silent about her suspicions about Tina. She knew better than to share what she couldn't prove about his best friend, no matter how far he had helped her understand where he was at and where he wanted to get to.

Ben snored loudly on the next bed, but Sophie would be too engrossed in talking to James to notice Tina was still awake. Listening to every word that was being whispered.

Seventeen

Algos sat at his desk, numbingly rubbing the picture etched into his gold ring. He spent little time looking back, but today his mind wondered while he waited for Clark to enter his office.

Angie's face flashed before his eyes. Not growing up as a child, but rather the moment he showed up at her door as a young adult, having been released from the system. The look of shock mixed with horror had brought much pleasure to him when she answered the door and realized it was him.

He remained innocent and told her he simply wanted to talk for a second. Angie reluctantly let him in, watching him with great uncertainty as he wondered around her living room looking at old photos. Photos of her with his biological father, smiling a weak smile, but their eyes showing a grief and horror that he had put there long ago.

However, before he could enjoy reliving Angie's death, it was the memory of the day Jim took Algos and Peter to ride the subway and visit Jim's mother that suddenly took over. His grandmother was on her death bed, and Jim needed to say his goodbyes. Angie was sick with the flu, or so everyone thought, which meant Jim had to take the boys with him on the visit. Algos was five, and Peter was three, and Jim had his hands full more than even he had realized.

Peter was just like any other annoying little brother, who looked up and idolized Algos the second he was brought home from the hospital. At first, Algos' motivation was simply to take the pest out himself, but his mother was smarter than he gave her credit for. She had interrupted him as he tried to suffocate Peter as an infant with a pillow and made sure Peter was never left alone with Algos again. So, he changed tactics.

Clarice always thought she was the master at manipulation, but Algos was the true master. He had been practicing long ago, with Peter being his first attempt. Peter was a good first candidate, mostly because Peter had something that was referred to as a conscious and soul. Something Algos didn't gain from his parents. Despite his loyalty to his older brother and his childhood innocence, Peter protested often at the beginning of every mission Algos gave him.

Peter wasn't nearly as fascinated by death as Algos was as they grew up. Murdering animals, skinning them (dead and alive), and performing his own autopsies were frowned upon. So, Algos had to learn early on how to not get caught and leave evidence behind unless he wanted someone to actually find it.

Algos proved early on to be too smart for his own good, always reading and asking his teachers and parents questions no child should have been asking. Occasionally, he heard the phrase, "That boy's just not right," yet most people never could wrap their heads around his true potential. However, Algos knew exactly what he was capable of.

Science held his fascination the most. Family members would say they had a "future doctor in the family" when they would attend family functions, but Algos had no desire to save anyone. He was more fascinated by how much the body changed when life was taken from it.

"Hold on to your brother," Jim had warned, forcing Algos to keep Peter close to him. He placed his hands on Peter's shoulders and stood behind Peter amongst the crowd as they waited for the subway to arrive.

"Train is fast!" Peter had shouted in excitement.

"Yes, train is fast," Algos replied with annoyance.

"Keep me safe?" Peter had asked Algos over his shoulder.

Algos rolled his eyes impatiently. "Yeah," he grunted in response.

Peter turned to watch for the subway as he wiggled under Algos' grip with excitement. How could someone be so excited to ride the subway? Algos thought to himself. Being stepped on and elbowed by strangers while the smell of urine and dirt stung your nose. Algos had glared at the random strangers pilling in close as they heard the subway train getting closer.

He despised being this close to people. He despised people in general. There were plenty of more exciting things to be doing than this. Peter's bouncing with excitement only made him angrier. Algos didn't want to be here. He wanted to be home watching the effects of his man-made poison had on his mother's body.

The sound of the subway train grew louder as it approached, giving Algos a headache.

"Train is fast!" Peter tried to scream over the noise. Algos' resentment for his little brother grew quicker than ever before.

"Train is fast," Algos mumbled as he waited just before the train reached them to give his little brother the slightest push that no camera or witness would catch.

A woman screamed as the train sped past before slowing down to a complete stop to allow passengers the ability to exit and enter. But it was too late. Peter was gone. They said the driver had an immediate heart attack when blood splattered the windshield, blocking his view.

Jim shook as he stared at his oldest son, who had become his only son within seconds. Although nothing would ever be proven otherwise, the look in Jim's eyes told Algos that he had witnessed enough to know it was no accident. Algos didn't care.

"He slipped," Algos had said, shrugging innocently before bouncing up and down, just like Peter had done just seconds ago. "Train is fast," he giggled under his breath.

It would be the first time he had taken a life in front of witnesses, and he would quickly learn that it was much more exciting to take a life when there was someone else to watch.

"Train is fast," Algos said, chuckling as he stood staring out the window that watched the lab below. A timid knock came from the other side of the door. "Enter," Algos belted.

"You called for me?" Clark asked with a mixture of excitement and fear.

"Yes, yes," the old man said, never taking his eyes off of Eddie while he worked. "How are you adjusting, my good boy?" he asked enthusiastically.

"Quite well, Sir," Clark answered, making the mistake of relaxing.

"I hear you were in charge while young Edward was out," the old man stated, already knowing the answer.

"Yes, Sir," Clark answered too confidently.

"And yet you haven't been able to find a trace of Sophie the entire week he was out," the old man stated with a hint of warning to his voice.

"I got further than Eddie would have!" Clark replied defensively. The old man's lips curled at the silent competition Clark held himself in with Eddie.

"That's rather hard to determine," the old man stated flatly.

"I'm better than he'll ever be," Clark mumbled to himself.

"Unfortunately," the old man declared when he turned around.

Clark stopped breathing immediately at the sight of his face up close and personal. He had heard rumors, but the old man purposely stayed in the shadows, and rarely showed his face to his employees.

"A loss is still a loss, isn't it Clark?" the old man finished with the left side of his mouth curling up in a half smile.

"I supposed so," Clark stuttered in shock.

"I don't like to lose," the old man said, bluntly.

Clark began backing away towards the door. "It's only a loss if I don't get back to work," he rattled off in panic as he began searching for the doorknob frantically with his hand behind his back. He knew better than to turn his back on the old man.

"Oh, you'll get back to work," the old man assured with a look in his eyes that Clark had only heard about. The look of excitement, desire, need, and murder all wrapped in one. "Just with less body parts than you started with," he laughed a deep throaty creepy laugh as he limped towards Clark.

Clark screamed and pleaded for mercy before turning quickly to desperately find the door to escape, but it was too late. He felt a small prick in his right leg that caused him to fall over on his left side. He looked down in panic, since he could no longer feel his leg.

Suddenly, an unbearable burning sensation spread from his hip quickly down to his toes. Clark screamed at the sudden agony that consumed him as he fought to undo his belt buckle and pull down his pants. His skin seemed to dissolve before his very eyes, and all he saw was his thigh muscle staring back at him. In a panic, he began yanking his pants off over his shoes. The old man just curiously watched him.

"Charles!" he called out.

"Yes, Sir," replied an elderly man who looked nearly on his death bed himself, standing next to Algos in an extremely worn butler's tux.

"Make note," the old man declared. "This dose seems to be a little too potent."

"It appears so, Sir," Charles stated dryly, not even looking at Clark.

"HELP ME!" Clark begged, but Charles' face never moved from its resting expressionless state.

"It simply accelerates and takes all the fun out," the old man whined like a child whose toy had been taken away.

"You will do better next time, Sir," Charles responded flatly as he held out his hand to retrieve the cane from the old man.

"We need to figure out how to get more than one dose in there too," the old man stated, showing his frustration.

"I will let the good doctor know," Charles said, before exiting the room.

When the old man turned around, Clark was already dead.

"Damn," Algos muttered. "Send someone for the body!" Algos yelled over his shoulder.

He really needed to get the dose perfected before he could use it the way he intended to. He sighed and clenched his jaw in annoyance before heading back to his chair.

Algos observed Eddie as he worked. Not because he was worried. He saw the same thing Clarice did. A broken man accepting his new role. Pride swelled inside Algos' chest.

Finally, he could have the son he was always meant to have. Not like the one he had made with Clarice's mother, but the one he knew he could groom. Algos smiled as he idly rubbed the symbol etched in his golden ring once more.

Sophie opened her eyes to the wooden door before her. She didn't even realize that she had fallen asleep talking to James.

"Open it," her mother ordered.

"Hello to you, too," Sophie grumbled, but opened the door and waited for her eyes to adjust to the flooding light. She was in an abandoned warehouse somewhere. No one else was with her.

"You're in more danger than you know," Jess said, walking

beside her with her arms crossed defensively and staring straight ahead.

"I didn't know!" Sophie protested. Her mother just held up her hand to silence her.

They both heard the echo of the cane enter the room before they actually saw him. Jess left Sophie to stand before him. Sophie watched closely, with both confusion and curiosity at what played out before her.

"Hello, Jessica," the old man sneered.

"You cannot have her," Jess hissed.

"But can't I?" he asked with a creepy declaration that made Sophie's blood run cold.

"She's not what you desire her to be," Jess said flatly.

"I don't know what you are referring to," he shrugged innocently.

"You know exactly what I'm referring to," Jess roared, letting her anger escape into her voice. "She's just as normal as I am."

"I highly doubt that," the old man said, studying her carefully.

"You will have to kill me before you can have her," Jess said, sticking her chin out definitely.

"That can be arranged," the old man said, with nothing behind his eyes and a complete lack of emotion. Sophie shivered at his behavior.

"Bring it on," Jess said, with her wicked smile and taking stance.

"Mom, no!" Sophie yelled, but no one acted like they could hear her.

"It's a memory," Jack whispered sorrowfully, coming to stand next to Sophie.

"You're going to attack a helpless, disabled man?" he laughed a creepy laughter as he tilted his head at her. His eyes remained blank. This man had no conscious or soul.

"Not at all," Jess said, tapping into her ability to hunt prey.

Jess' eyes changed, too. The breathing that was showed by the rise and fall of her chest became almost nonexistent. Sophie held her breath as she watched her mother turn into a stone-cold predator before her very eyes. Sophie felt her blood turn cold within her and wondered if this was what she looked like when she lost control.

The man suddenly rolled his eyes in boredom. "You fool no one," he sighed dramatically.

"Never underestimate a mother's love," Jess replied hauntingly as she waved for the man to attack.

"I'm not fighting you," the old man laughed at her.

"Then you will die," Jess said, matter-of-factly.

"I hardly doubt that," the old man laughed. They all heard several footsteps heading their way. He had clearly brought backup, or a team, to take her out altogether.

Murderous laughter escaped Jess' throat. Sophie looked at her dad, who stared at the floor, unable to see whatever was about to take place. Several figures dressed in black attire quickly surrounded Jess.

Sophie was not prepared to see what came next. Every single person, minus the man with the cane, came at her mother all at once. Sophie wanted desperately to not watch, but she couldn't seem to move her head. Now she understood why her father couldn't watch.

Jess, ever so gracefully, took off each team member one by one. She grabbed the arm of the person who went in for a punch and pulled them past her while she gut-kicked another that charged her. She quickly broke the arm she held in her hand and tossed them aside as if they were a simple rag doll. While the first two fell back, three more went in for an attack.

Sophie stood still, holding her breath, as she listened to bones crack and necks snap. She did not know how lethal her mother truly was and quickly made note to always keep herself on Jess' good side. Sophie absorbed every action like a sponge, as excitement coursed through her veins like acid. Jess was amazingly graceful, despite leaving a pile of bodies in her wake.

Sophie noted that the old man simply backed away, but never took his eyes off her mother. She saw the look of pride and excitement for every life that Jess took. Thriving on it, as if it were the only reason he lived and breathed.

Sophie quickly grew sick to her stomach. She looked back at her mother and was disturbed to see the excitement that reflected in her own eyes. Jess had always instilled the importance of every life mattering, yet as Sophie watched her mother not hesitate to take the lives around her, she realized that her mother also had a darker side to her. A side that even Jess feared to nourish, and Sophie knew nothing about.

Sophie tried to convince herself that depending on how long the man with the cane had her in his possession, it was something he had instilled in her. But she wasn't entirely sure, because she knew a dark monster grew within her as well. Sophie had felt it take over when she watched Clarice torture Mario before her. Did evil live in all of them? Or had he made sure each of them carried it so he could exploit it? Sophie twisted her head to throw up at the scene playing before her.

"You're missing the point," Jack whispered, suddenly staring down at her.

"And what point is that?" Sophie said, a little irritated as she wiped the leftover vomit from her mouth. "Mom was a badass?" she retorted sarcastically.

Jack's face quickly went from sorrow to anger, and even Sophie took a step back from him to put space between them.

"I didn't raise you to be so ungrateful," he said, with his voice mixed with frustration and disappointment. It cut Sophie to her core.

When she looked back at her mother, there was a pile of dead bodies behind her and she panted as she stood once again before the man with the cane.

"You. Will. Not. Have. Her," Jess stated once again.

"That's not your decision to make," the old man shrugged.

He held up his cane, and a dart shot out from the bottom. Jess spun and ducked just in time to miss it before she grabbed some sort of liquid and a lighter from her belt. She quickly squirted the liquid on the old man and tossed the lit lighter onto him. Half his face was suddenly in flames, and he screamed in agony as his skin quickly melted off.

"I WILL stoop to your level if I have to," Jess said, hauntingly lacking any emotion before she turned her back on him and walked away. The man with the cane ripped off his suit jacket and hurriedly put himself out.

Sophie stopped breathing. She couldn't believe all the things she had witnessed in just a quick few minutes. The scene disappeared before her eyes, and only Sophie and her father remained in the emptiness.

"She went against everything she stood for to keep you safe," Jack said, looking straight ahead at nothing at all. "Maybe it's time to put that anger back where it belongs," he added before walking away from his daughter.

"What if I can't control it?" Sophie called out with a much more disturbing thought weighing on her mind.

Jack hesitated, but kept his back to his daughter.

"Then you might as well be his," he shrugged before flipping his hand and pushing Sophie out the door.

Sophie gasped as she sat up.

"Hey," James whispered. "You okay?"

Sophie reached over the side of the bed and began violently throwing up into the trashcan next to her. James sat up immediately to help hold her hair back.

"What's wrong?" he asked in alarm.

Ben and Tina sat up at the sound of Sophie hurling her guts out, and Ben rushed to inspect her at once. Tina eyed her carefully.

"We did too much today, didn't we?" Ben mumbled as he waited for her to stop throwing up. "Get a glass of water and cool washcloth," he ordered Tina. Although she hesitated, she did what her husband asked.

James stroked Sophie's back. "What happened?" he asked her softly.

"Bad dream," Sophie mumbled as the memories continued to flash before her eyes.

Ben felt her forehead and quickly grabbed a thermometer. "You have a fever," he declared, concerned and confused.

"I just need to lie down," Sophie said, weakly, passing out before her head ever hit the pillow.

Eighteen

"Are you ready to tell me?" the old man asked, forcing Clarice to jump. He had entered her bedroom without her noticing, because she was still thinking about Jess.

"Tell you what?" Clarice asked, with a hint of nervousness in her voice.

"What happened in Kansas City?" he asked hauntingly while sitting on her bed.

Clarice was immediately alarmed. Not once in her entire life had he come to her room to sit on her bed and talk to her. Forty-plus years of her life told her this was a blatant set-up, but she couldn't fight the urge to see how this was going to play out.

"I killed Mario," Clarice shrugged, not giving any emotions or anything else away.

The old man looked up at her and studied her. "You know," he said, slowly. "I don't think I've ever told you, but I was always glad between the two of you you're the one that remains."

Clarice couldn't save the shock from crossing her face. She was pretty sure her heart stopped beating all together. Alarms were going off inside her head, but warmth flooded her body.

A smug smile crossed the left side of his face. He had her.

"You handled this matter nicely," he added for good measure. "Minus Edward," he added with a warning.

Clarice was too busy basking in the first compliment he had given her since the day she was born to be irritated with his favoritism for Eddie.

"I gained intel while I was there," Clarice blurted out eagerly.

"Oh?" the old man asked casually.

"Yes," she said with a wicked, knowing smile. "Everything you thought about her was true," she whispered with excitement.

"Oh," the old man said, in a bit of shock.

He wasn't sure what Clarice had been hiding exactly, but this was definitely not what he suspected. He reminded himself that getting mad and torturing her simply for keeping it from him would not get him the result he desired.

"How so?" he asked, trying to keep the excitement out of his voice.

"The strength is definitely not dormant," Clarice stated, grabbing her side in remembrance of being thrown against the pillar. Her voice was just now getting away from being so raspy.

"Anything else?" the old man asked, raising his good eyebrow at her.

Clarice thought for a second.

"Speed," she stated as she replayed the scene before her eyes and thought about how effortlessly Sophie had blocked Clarice's most powerful punches.

"Interesting," he replied, deep in thought.

"Her anger is strong," Clarice warned.

"Aren't all of ours?" the old man chuckled, as if he found this very amusing. He went to leave her room.

"We can use what she already has," Clarice begged, as she chased after him. He simply turned and patted her on top of her head as he would any other loyal dog before he turned to walk out.

"What have you done?" she heard Jess whisper in despair within her head.

"He loves me," Clarice whispered to herself, despite her head knowing very well that it was a complete lie. There was no response from the ghosts of her past. "He loves me," she whispered again. Only this time, it was more out of desperation to convince herself that what she had just done would be worth it.

"Something's not right," Sophie heard Ben whisper in concern.

"What is it?" Tina asked curiously.

"She has a fever," he stressed.

"So?" she asked.

"A fever is a sign of your body fighting off an infection," she heard Ben state bluntly. "Roger made sure she would never get sick."

"So, what if she's fighting something else?" James asked in a panicked realization.

Sophie couldn't open her eyes. She couldn't move. She waited for the wooden door to appear, but it never did. She remained on fire and in complete darkness.

Clarice was headed to her father's office when she heard voices coming from the other side of the cracked open door.

"Do you think she'll actually be an asset?" an unfamiliar voice asked.

"She's as close to Sophie as possible. She's perfect," the old man said, with satisfaction coming through his voice.

"What are you going to do once she's brought in?" the stranger asked.

"There will be tests, of course," the old man stated excitedly.

"Don't you worry she will not survive?" the stranger inquired.

"If I made one, I can make more," the old man said with a shrug.

"Isn't she worth more alive than dead?" asked the stranger with obvious concern in their voice.

"I guess we'll find out," the old man replied coldly.

Clarice's stomach dropped. What had she done?

Tina was living at the library, trying to find possible answers to why Sophie suddenly could not respond for the last couple of hours.

Ben continued to monitor her vital signs, and James nodded off occasionally in the chair he had placed next to her as he held her hand.

When he went to force his eyes open, he found the wooden door standing before him. He shoved it open without hesitation.

"She won't wake up!" James called out as he shielded his eyes, waiting for them to adjust.

"I know," he heard Mario declare gloomily.

"She's not answering us either," Jack announced.

James looked around to find Mario and Sophie's parents all in the room together. Mario and Jack sat at a table looking over papers, while Jess remained distant in front of the fireplace on the other side of the room.

"She needs to move soon," was Jess' only response.

"It's hard to move when she's unconscious!" James exclaimed wildly.

"Do you think it was the tests?" Mario asked Jack.

"No," Jack assured. "She was fine right before.

"You don't know for sure, though!" James shouted in panic. "No one knows!"

"Sit down," Mario said, in a half order to James.

He knew the look of pure panic all too well, and James needed to get his focus back. Mario got up and poured James a drink.

"Drink," he ordered before he sat back down.

James looked from the drink to Mario and glared. He knew Mario was just trying to help, but James couldn't think of how drinking would help anything. He looked back at the glass and slumped into the empty chair before slugging the brown warm liquid before him. He felt his nerves slowly calm.

"Ideas?" Mario asked, looking between Jack and Jess.

Jack looked towards his wife, but she kept her back to them all.

"We can't just sit here," James said frantically.

"We don't have a choice," Jess said, softly staring into the fire.

"I don't accept that!" James yelled in frustration.

"Let's just talk this out," Jack offered, but the look his wife shot him silenced him immediately.

Mario watched in silence as if caught in the middle of a nightmare. He shoved his chair back as he stood up in his own frustration and walked over to the shelves behind him. He snatched a bottle of wine and slammed it on the table.

"Tell him," Mario ordered Jess.

She remained silent with her back to them all.

"Tell him!" Mario ordered again with more force.

James looked wildly around the room. Mario continued to stare at the back of Jess' back, willing her to turn around, while Jack kept his eyes on the table in front of him.

"Tell me what?" James demanded as he turned to face Jess' back with Mario.

After what felt like an eternity, Jess dropped her head and sighed heavily.

"Do you see the symbol on the wine bottle?" Jess asked softly.

James jerked his head back to the wine bottle and saw the gold infinity sign with a slash through it.

"So?" he asked in confusion.

"How much do you remember of your final training with the CIA?" Jess asked casually, still not turning around.

"All of it," James mumbled, annoyed that they were still playing games with him when their daughter's life was on the line.

"Do you remember the Daniel Cord case?" Jess asked, giving no emotion.

James froze for a second at the name. Daniel Cord was the worst case that he had ever studied.

Daniel was a sixteen-year-old boy that had a career as a narcissistic psychopath. He had started his journey as a child by being a fire starter and animal torturer. He was bullied often for his sexual inadequacies as a teenager and showed chronic low self-esteem. This eventually led Daniel to becoming a stone-cold killer before ever reaching adulthood.

No fear, and no remorse for the lives he took. Daniel believed the victims knew the reason he attacked them, and he stopped at nothing to take a life in order to achieve his goal. No guilt. No conscious. No soul.

"I do," James said, slowly, not sure where this was going.

"Algos is on an even higher level," Jess said, with a frown. "He's obsessed with total control and gaining the power over life and death." She continued to stare into the fire as she shared the history of the man that had raised her most of her life.

"He gave himself the name Algos Hersteller at nine," Jess continued, emotionless. "Having already murdered his brother and father, and eventually moving on to his own mother. That symbol is his version of the family crest," Jess said, finally turning around to face everyone.

"He strives to break the line between life and death, and control it all," she said, blankly. "He believes he can achieve it through Sophie," Jess stated, finally blinking again. "And now that his suspicions about her have been proven, there's nothing we can do."

"What do you mean, there's nothing we can do?" James asked madly. "Even psychopaths get caught," he declared angrily.

"Not him," Jess whispered before turning her back on them again.

"So, we're just giving up?" James asked in outrage.

"Absolutely not," Jack assured as he placed a hand on James' to help calm him down. "It just makes things a lot trickier," Jack said, letting his own frustrations seep through.

"There are rules in death," Mario inserted. "Algos is trying to break them. We're just not sure how or when," he said with a frown.

"Is he messing with Sophie now?" James asked in full panic.

It was bad enough he couldn't physically keep her safe. How the heck was he supposed to fight a psychopath on a field he didn't have access to?

"No," Jess assured. "This is her own doing."

"I'm sorry," James cut in. "Did you say her own doing?"

"With Sophie's enhancements come faults," Jack whispered. "One being that when she gets overwhelmed, she shuts down for her own protection. But we don't know why she's currently shutting down," he added, sneaking a glance at his wife.

"She saw something in her sleep," James said, suddenly realizing what took place in Sophie's last hours.

He saw Jack stare at Jess momentarily before looking at the table again.

"What did you show her?" James asked in a whisper.

No one made eye contact with him.

"What did you show her?" James yelled in more of an

accusation than a question.

"Nothing to cause this," Jess whispered, not entirely sure that was true.

"What did you show her?!" James demanded for the last time.

Jess dropped her head and sighed once more.

"She needed to see that I do everything I can to protect my daughter," she said, slowly. "It was only the last fight I had with him alone," Jess added flatly. "I left a mark," she said, smiling to herself.

"Seriously?!" James shouted in anger.

"We believe Sophie is concerned she isn't as pure as she actually is," Jack cut in with a rush. "She's worried she will cross a line that she can't come back from."

"Sophie would never kill someone that didn't deserve to be taken," James defended.

Jack gave a weary smile. "We all know that, but I'm afraid that Sophie isn't as sure."

"So how do we help?" James asked urgently.

"We were wondering if you could take a stab at it, Kid," Mario said, with an encouraging smile.

"Me?" James asked, confused. "How am I supposed to do that?"

"Love is more powerful than you realize," Jack said, looking at the back of his wife. "Anger can push you temporarily, but love will always be the greatest fuel of all. It provides us balance," he said, not taking his eyes off the back of Jess.

"Balance keeps us from going mad," Mario added.

"So, how do I balance her?" James asked eagerly.

"That, my boy, is something you're going to have to figure out," Jack replied, still staring at Jess as if he was trying to get her to turn back around with his eyes. "Everyone is different, with different needs, and different things that pull us back to being centered. Only you will be able to find out how you can provide that for her."

"I don't know that I'm the one to offer that for her," James stated quietly.

For the first time, he allowed himself to relive the feeling of pain from Sophie leaving right after James had proposed to her. He had understood, but it still left a mark. He just never took the time to deal with it because it hurt more than he wanted to admit.

"Did she ever tell you that Simon was ready to kill her when a vision of you came to save her?" Jess asked suddenly.

James looked at Jess' back in shock.

"Your love is the only reason she is even with us now," Jess said, not turning around as she stared into the fire. "You get to her when we fail," she whispered, a little hurt by the fact. "So, you need to decide if you're going to fight for her, or do the curtesy of leaving her," Jess added bluntly.

"What she means to say is…" Mario quickly cut in.

"I said exactly what I meant to say," Jess said, coldly. "I have a daughter to save. With or without you."

James was taken aback by her sudden coldness. He wasn't sure what Sophie saw last, but it was clear Jess felt she was to blame. Even if she wouldn't admit it to herself. They thought James would be the one to keep Sophie safe. Maybe not from the man with the cane, but definitely from herself. James looked down at the table while he contemplated his options.

"We don't have all day," Jess barked coldly.

James gave her a glare before turning to Jack.

"Send me back," he said defiantly.

"Does that mean you're fighting with us?" Mario asked hesitantly.

"Send me back," James commanded Jack without answering. Jack searched James' eyes for an answer, but only saw defiance.

"Good luck," Jack whispered as he touched his forehead and James was pulled back through the door.

"Was that a yes?" Mario asked in confusion.

"We're about to find out," Jess said in a whisper as she refused to turn her back on the fire before her.

Nineteen

James gasped for air when he came to. Ben watched him with concern.

"Let me guess," Ben said, dryly. "A ghostly visit?"

"Of course," James mumbled.

"Helpful?" Ben asked with anticipation.

"When are they ever?" James retorted with frustration.

"So, no?" Ben asked lightly, already knowing the answer.

James glared at his friend before hopping up to pace the room and think.

"So, what did they say?" Ben pried.

"She's doing it to herself," James muttered, deep in thought.

"I'm sorry, what?" Ben asked, not sure he heard his friend

correctly.

"Yeah," James said to him with a frown. "They showed her something that really upset her, and she shut herself down."

"What the hell?!" Ben yelled before composing himself to check her vitals again. "I thought they were supposed to be helpful," he muttered as he took her blood pressure.

"That's what I said," James said.

He paced a few more times before his eyes lit up. He raced to her and leaned really close while whispering something Ben couldn't hear into Sophie's ear.

Ben watched with curiosity, but didn't pry. James always got to Sophie better than anyone. Of course, it would be James to help her pull herself out of whatever this was. They both held their breath as they stared at her, willing her silently to come back.

Sophie breathed in deeply, but remained in her sleeping trance. It was up to her to choose to wake up. All they could do was wait for her to decide life over death.

Sophie wandered around in darkness, looking desperately for a door, but none appeared before her.

"Hello?" she called out, but no one responded.

Sophie heard James' whispered words, and her heart jumped at the sound of them.

"I can't get back!" Sophie screamed out into the darkness.

"Can't you?" asked a little boy sitting on a patch of grass, gazing at her.

"Edward," Sophie whispered, recognizing the figure before her instantly.

"So, you do remember," the little boy retorted with a sarcastic tone and a frown to match.

"Of course, I remember," Sophie whispered in a bit of shock at seeing him. The phrase "there always has to be a door" rang through her ears, but she couldn't control what was happening any more than her need for oxygen.

The little boy looked at her with doubt.

Sophie was a firm believer in the fact that everything happened for a reason, so she did what she thought was needed by him.

"Do you remember the time we put a smoke bomb in Ms. Grubb's desk for giving you an F and calling you dumb?" Sophie asked with her Cheshire grin, and crossing her arms in front of her chest.

The boy looked up at her with an instant smile before quickly composing himself into a doubtful frown.

"Yeah," he muttered softly.

"Blowing up Mr. Peterson's car definitely got me in trouble with mom," Sophie said, with a frown. "But it was totally worth it!" she whispered with excitement, assuring the little boy she remembered plenty.

"You got in a lot of trouble for that one," the little boy lit up as he giggled. After a second, his face dropped. "But then you left," he whispered.

"Not by choice, I assure you," Sophie said, carefully walking towards him to sit on the patch of grass with him. "You were my friend," she added with a smile. "And I miss you every day."

"You do?" the little boy asked in shock.

Sophie smiled and nodded in confirmation.

"I even wonder if you're still alive and okay," she added softly.

"Oh, I'm alive," the little boy replied with a triumphant smile. "Just not okay," he added with a frown.

"Do you know where you are?" Sophie asked him gently, trying to find out more information to help her.

"No," the boy frowned. "But it's really dark and cold here," he said sadly.

"Edward, can you tell me what's around you?" Sophie asked, suddenly feeling panic consume her.

"I go by Eddie," he said, sticking out his chest and putting his chin into the air with determination.

"My apologies," Sophie responded, trying not to giggle at his reaction. "Can you tell me what's around you, Eddie?" she corrected.

"It's boring down here. There's no windows or games to play," Eddie replied with disappointment. "And he's creepy," he added in a whisper.

"Who's creepy?" Sophie asked in alarm.

"You know who," the little boy whispered, looking to the ground.

"No," Sophie gasped.

"Come find me," the little boy begged, suddenly looking at her, lost, and pleading for her to come save him. "You have to come now!" he yelled.

He jumped to his feet and backed away slowly and in obvious fear.

"Eddie, you need to tell me what's around you," Sophie begged.

"He's coming," the little boy whispered in terror, before turning away to run off into the surrounding darkness.

"Eddie!" Sophie called out, reaching for him, but he was already gone.

Her chest tightened, and she was struggling to breathe. She placed her outstretched hand on her chest as she gasped desperately for air. She heard the echo of the cane hitting some cement floor as it grew louder. He was coming.

"I will find you," Sophie whispered in determination before she squinted her eyes closed and screamed, "ENOUGH!" to force herself awake.

Sophie sat up suddenly, gasping for air. James and Ben rushed to her instantly.

"Are you okay?" James asked in panic as he stroked her back to soothe her as Sophie fought to catch her breath.

Just then, Tina came through the door with a huge smile on her face. Sophie turned to her and glared.

"Where is he?" Sophie snapped at her.

Tina took a step back in shock and fell against the closed door behind her.

"What are you t-talking about?" Tina stammered in fear.

"You know exactly what I'm talking about," Sophie snarled.

Confused by Sophie's reaction, Ben raced to Tina and threw his body in front of her for protection.

"Sophie, what are you talking about?" Ben asked nervously at her sudden need for blood shining in her eyes.

"I will find him, with or without you, so you might as well tell me," Sophie barked at Tina.

"Calm down," James ordered, confused at her sudden reaction

towards their friend.

"What the hell is wrong with you?" Tina asked in panic.

"I know you work for him!" Sophie blurted out in anger.

"For who?" James asked, trying to put himself into Sophie's line of sight and take her off of Tina while they tried to get to the bottom of whatever Sophie thought was going on.

"Oh, HELL NO!" Tina yelled as she threw her bag down and prepared herself to fight. Ben spun around and tried to hold her arms down at her side.

"Breathe," Ben said, nervously.

"You set us all up," Sophie continued in a tremulous voice. "Mario is dead because of YOU!"

"What?" James asked in disbelief, turning his own head in Tina's direction and unsure of what to believe.

"I did no such thing!" Tina screamed back.

"I think we just need to take a second," Ben interjected, raising his voice to be heard over the current yelling match.

"She's accusing me of working with HIM!" Tina yelled wildly at Ben.

"Why do you think this?" James asked Sophie, looking deep into her eyes.

"The messages only went to her and Mario," Sophie rambled. "She sent off the SD card as soon as I gave it to her. She's the reason he's...." Sophie couldn't finish the sentence.

"You've gone MAD!" howled Tina. "I didn't ask for those messages to only come to my phone! I didn't ASK for them AT ALL!" she yelled. "And I sent the SD card to a coworker in Oklahoma!" Tina finished, crossing her arms defensively.

“I need to find Edward,” Sophie pleaded with James, not caring about the words coming from Tina’s mouth. Her gut was never wrong, despite people insisting otherwise.

“Who?” James asked, very confused.

So much screaming was taking place, they didn’t hear their burner phones go off inside their bags.

“Explain this to me,” James begged, trying to get to the bottom of the mess.

Sophie’s ears caught the high-pitched chirping sound as each phone rang a second time.

“Hold on,” she said, holding up her hand, trying desperately to listen. She was sure she heard something. She just didn’t know what or from where. Then Sophie heard it again. She jumped up and raced to her bag.

Tina glared at her, but heard her own phone go off at her feet. She bent down to grab it. The boys looked confused at each other, then heard the chirping sound as well. Everyone got their phones and opened them to read the message.

We’re coming for you. You won’t win. -E

“What the hell?” Ben asked, staring at the message.

“What is this?” James demanded.

“We need to move,” Sophie said, staring at the phone in her hand.

“I’m not going ANYWHERE with YOU!” Tina yelled.

“Then die,” Sophie said flatly as she grabbed her stuff and headed for the door.

"WHAT THE HELL IS GOING ON?" screamed Ben, losing control.

"They're coming," Sophie said, flatly. "And they have Eddie for a hostage."

"Eddie, as in YOUR Eddie?" Tina asked, suddenly changing her tone.

Sophie looked at Tina, full of grief and regret. "I'm sorry," she whispered before she walked out the door.

"Wait!" James yelled after Sophie.

"We're not safe," Sophie said over her shoulder as she continued to walk down the hallway.

"Where are we going?" Tina called after her, forgetting her anger instantly.

"Las Vegas," Ben called after everyone. Sophie stopped walking to turn around and face him.

"Why Vegas?" she asked, surprised.

"It's the last place Eddie was seen alive," Ben said bluntly.

Sophie looked at him with wildly confused eyes.

"Your dad asked me to find him. I didn't have much to go on, and I'm not even sure this is the right Eddie since I don't have a clue what he looks like," Ben added quickly. He knew Sophie's wrath and didn't want to be on the other side of it.

They watched as relief crossed Sophie's face. It was a start.

"We're going together," Sophie said, quickly turning and looking at Tina.

"I don't think that's the best id...." was all Ben got out before Tina held her hand up to silence him.

"The boys can go together," Tina said, not taking her eyes off

Sophie.

Sophie nodded in confirmation before turning around to make her way to Vegas. It was time to find Eddie. She had put it off, unknowingly, long enough. Tina walked beside her in complete silence.

"I don't feel very good," Ben whispered to James.

"Well, at least it's easier to hide a body in the desert," James laughed nervously.

"I prefer my wife not to be the one to get buried," Ben retorted sourly.

"Sophie wouldn't do that," James smiled wearily. At least he prayed she wouldn't.

The girls flew to arrive faster, slipping in the mix of a bachelorette party that was boarding. The boys would travel by land. Ben was not excited to give Sophie and Tina so much of a head start with both girls being upset with each other. However, time was quickly running out, and neither girl would listen to his pleas or excuses.

"Don't go too wild on me," James smiled uneasily, before he kissed Sophie gently in the shadows of the parking garage.

"I'm not sure this is the best idea," Ben whispered desperately to Tina for the last time on the other side of the garage.

"I'll be fine," Tina smiled before giving him a gentle kiss.

"Call me immediately if you're not," Ben warned. "I don't care if you use the plane phone either," he added.

"Not much you're going to be able to do while we're thousands of feet in the air, Honey," Tina chuckled. "Stop fussing.

"But she thought," Ben started.

"I know what she thought," Tina said sternly. "Frankly, I would have suspected the same," she said with a shrug. "I haven't exactly been truthful with her," Tina admitted. "We'll work it out," she winked before walking away before Ben could protest anymore. "Ready," she said flatly to Sophie.

"Yep," was the only reply Sophie offered. They grabbed their bags and headed inside.

"Come on," James said, putting his hand on Ben's shoulder. "Let's see if we can beat them," he said with a competitive attitude. Ben laughed hysterically, not sure how his friend planned on beating an aircraft.

"Sure," Ben chuckled, picking his bag off the floor and following James to the entrance of the parking garage.

The girls entered the plane and quickly found their seats. They listened patiently to their departure instructions, then Sophie took to staring out the window.

"You realize this is the shortest flight ever, right?" Tina said with sarcasm as she kept her eyes on the girls in front of her.

"Not short enough," Sophie chuckled as she wiggled nervously in her seat.

"I'm sorry," they said, in unison, turning to face each other, and laughed at the awkwardness between them.

"I'm sorry," Sophie tried again.

"Me too," Tina smiled.

"I'm still trying to get used to trusting people," Sophie confessed, playing with her fingers in front of her.

"Well, I haven't exactly earned it lately, either," Tina admitted, mimicking Sophie's gestures. "I'm sorry he's gone," she whispered.

"Well, he's not really gone, and kind of more of a pain in the butt now," Sophie gave a nervous chuckle.

"Oooo, I did not think about that!" Tina said, suddenly in surprise.

"Mario did say he was Team Tina," Sophie smiled at her nervously.

"I knew I liked him for a reason," Tina laughed as she sat back to relax a bit.

"I think I have a bigger problem," Sophie professed quietly.

"Oh?" Tina replied, turning to her friend and giving Sophie her full attention.

"I'm not sure I'm always the one in control," Sophie started slowly.

"I don't understand," Tina stated, confused.

"I think 'he' is inside me somehow," Sophie whispered in a strangled voice.

"Oh, Sophie!" Tina said, quickly pulling Sophie into her arms.

"I can't explain it, but I'm not okay," Sophie sobbed softly as she pushed the words out.

Tina pulled her back immediately. "You ARE okay," Tina demanded.

"But I'm NOT!" Sophie stated more firmly. "And doubting myself is causing me to doubt people closest to me, including you," she added, full of guilt.

"You're going to have to give me more than that," Tina stated. "And we only have 58 minutes before we have to get off, so just start from the beginning."

Sophie looked around nervously. They sat right in the middle of the bachelorette party who had already begun to "get their drink on" as they sang songs and exclaimed how exciting it will be to see

Thunder from Down Under at the Excalibur. Tina sensed her hesitation.

"They will not notice," Tina giggled. "And if we can get to the bottom of it before we get off the plane, I'll take you to the show," she said, winking.

Sophie looked at Tina with shock.

"What the boys don't know won't hurt them," Tina shrugged casually, forcing Sophie to giggle herself.

And for the first time, not even with James, Sophie confessed her darkest fears to the girl who had long forgiven her for accusing her of working on the other side. Mostly because Tina had a secret of her own. She just wasn't ready to share it yet....

Twenty

The girls didn't make it to the show, but Tina insisted they would return to do so at a later date. Sophie just laughed and rolled her eyes. It felt good to have her friend back.

The boys arrived sooner than expected, but they wouldn't spill the beans on how they achieved their success. Sophie would have been annoyed at the secrets if she didn't have more pressing matters to deal with. She needed to find Eddie.

Vegas was an awful place to hide in. Especially in the casinos. There was no way of getting around the endless cameras that security monitored constantly looking for thieves, drunks out of control, and sins being committed 24/7. It was the city where people gave into their deepest and darkest desires, no matter the cost. The perfect place for the man with the cane, but not the Eddie Sophie remembered.

"So, where was he last seen?" Sophie asked, keeping her head down and walking as quickly as possible to get to the safety of their room.

"Walking out of this hotel," Ben smiled with satisfaction, even if he had to keep his head down.

"Nice," Sophie smiled with pride.

"I thought you'd like that," Ben added. "Meet you in a bit!" he announced before suddenly veering off to the left and into the crowd of men playing craps.

Tina sighed heavily. "I'm going to smell like so much smoke," she whined before turning on her heels and heading for the slots.

"I think I will try my luck at Blackjack," Sophie smiled wickedly.

"Aren't we going to the room?" James chuckled.

"You are," Sophie said, with a wink, before she headed for the tables, leaving James to go to the room alone. At least on camera.

After an hour, Sophie caught up with everyone in the room. They had adjoining rooms again this time. The boys were sitting on a king-size bed watching tv, while Tina was working on the laptop at the desk per usual.

"Took you long enough," James muttered, but couldn't hide his happiness.

"I got distracted." Sophie shrugged casually as she pulled her hands out of her pockets and tossed her winnings on the bed at them.

Ben gasped. "You card counter!" he yelled, pointing at her accusingly.

"I am no such thing," Sophie said, defensively, but no one

seemed to buy it.

Tina was engrossed in the computer screen before her.

"Whatch ya looking at?" Sophie asked her noticing her withdraw.

"How old did you guess Eddie to be when he was here last?" Tina asked her husband without moving her eyes from the screen.

"Probably seventeen or thereabouts," Ben offered. "Why?"

"How would you describe Clarice?" Tina asked Sophie as she continued to stare at the screen.

"What did you find?" Sophie asked in a panic as she walked towards Tina.

She just pointed to a young man with short brown hair, wearing a pair of jeans, and an old black Metallica t-shirt and worn tennis shoes. He was standing in front of a limousine with a woman who had on black high-heeled shoes, black stockings that emphasized her athletic legs, a black short skirt, and a red silk short-sleeved blouse. It was unbuttoned far enough to show her perky breasts in a black lace bra underneath. She had long blonde hair that was curled just past her shoulders.

"Wait for it," Tina whispered, and as if on cue, the boy looked directly into the camera before him and mouthed, 'Help Me,' before getting into the limousine never to be seen from again.

Sophie threw her hand over her mouth before dry heaving violently. She had nothing on her stomach to give up, which was her only saving grace at the moment. She fell to her knees, gasping for air in between, trying to throw up. Her eyes quickly filled with tears that ran down her cheeks.

Eddie begged for her, and Sophie never came. Her gut was now attacking itself, because she never kept looking for him. Sophie had the occasional memory, but never followed through on checking up on him. Her parents told her to keep him safe, and she did nothing. Nothing.

The room spinned violently around her. James grabbed Sophie, and she hung on for dear life as guilt completely consumed her. He had him. The man with the cane had Eddie, and it was Sophie's fault.

"Stop it!" she heard Tina yelling in her ear.

"I can't," Sophie cried out.

"You can and you WILL!" demanded Tina.

The room slowed down a bit, but Sophie continued to gasp and try desperately not to throw up.

"You are no good to Eddie, acting like a dramatic princess!" Tina commanded.

The room stopped spinning almost immediately, and Sophie started slowing down her breathing.

"Okay, Mario," Sophie retorted once her senses calmed the heck down.

"I thought you'd like that," Tina beamed suddenly.

"I think we're going to have to find a better way to not go on overdrive," Sophie said with a slight chuckle as she shook her head. The more she learned about herself and her "gifts" as her parents would say, the more they seemed to spiral out of control and knock her to her knees. There had to be a better way.

"Okay," said James, taking charge. "Clarice clearly targeted him, and convinced Eddie to go with her somehow," he stated the facts.

"And he knew he still needed to leave you one last message," Ben interjected.

"But it wasn't one last message," Tina declared loudly. Everyone looked at her in question. "Look," she said. "I didn't feel comfortable about the messages either, and I knew someone had been watching Sophie all these years for the team to track her like they did."

"Eddie," Sophie whispered.

"I think he believed Mario was in trouble and directed everyone to Kansas City," Tina continued. "I think that's why he told us to leave last time, too."

"But why wait so long?" Ben asked.

"It's not exactly like they would let him communicate without consequences," James offered. "He probably has to make sure he's always covering his tracks."

"We need to find him," Sophie said in desperation.

"Or not," Tina cut in.

Sophie jerked her head to stare at Tina with her mouth open in shock.

Tina threw her hands up in the air so that Sophie knew she wasn't trying to cause problems.

"I just mean, we let Eddie find YOU. If he's always the one watching you, he would see you were here, and he would know you're trying to find him," Tina shrugged.

"Not a bad idea," Sophie contemplated.

"Except the man with the cane will also know you're here," James pointed out with a frown, hoping she would see the whole picture.

"Eddie's priority right now," Sophie declared without hesitation. "But we need to prove we're looking for him, so where all was he seen in the last week of being here?"

"I'll make a list," Tina said, sitting down again and let her fingers type feverishly. She used facial recognition software to locate Eddie in the sea of people who were here to try and get lucky without getting caught doing their sins.

"This doesn't help find him now," Ben pointed out nervously.

"Showing him I'm looking for him will encourage him to reach out again," Sophie said.

"And possibly get killed," James warned.

"We'll have to take the chance," Sophie said. She'd already left Eddie once. She couldn't afford to do it again.

"Stop making a list," Ben ordered Tina, making them all freeze at his sudden outburst.

"Why?" Sophie demanded.

"It won't take a list," Ben mumbled.

James knew exactly where he was going.

"If you sent him a message the same way, we would get to him faster," James said slowly.

"We'd have to move immediately," Tina warned. "And we don't know where to head to."

"I hear Utah has some amazing skiing this time of the year." Ben shrugged.

"We just got here!" Tina sighed dramatically.

"I thought you said we were coming back," Sophie laughed.

"Yeah, but it's not like we can go plan a bachelorette party right now," Tina pouted.

Ben looked at James, but he just looked at the floor and blushed. Sophie tried to hide her smile, but failed miserably.

"We'll make the time for it, if the time is needed," Sophie

replied, winking at Tina.

"Deal!" Tina yelled, clapping her hands as she jumped up and down. Sophie didn't know what Tina had planned, but she convinced herself she'd be in excellent hands.

"Book the tickets, Hun," Ben told his wife. He shook his head and laughed at Tina's need to interfere.

"On it!" Tina called out and went back to the laptop.

"Are you sure you're ready to do this?" James asked Sophie softly.

"It's overdue," Sophie whispered back.

"Then let's go find him," James said, smiling at her.

"Done!" Tina called out.

"Ready?" James asked everyone.

Everyone nodded eagerly except Sophie, who looked lost in her thoughts. She tossed her bag to James.

"I'll meet you on the bus," she said with a Cheshire smile.

James suddenly felt a little panicked and unsure of what was to come, but he knew he could trust her with his life and for him...that was good enough.

Sophie waited for everyone to have a safe enough distance ahead of her since she was unsure how close the latest team had been hunting for her. She walked into the bathroom and sighed heavily. So much for keeping her vibrant hair a secret.

She peeled off her jacket and tied it around her waist. She pulled the scrunchy off her wrist and pulled her hair into a ponytail.

"Are you sure?" she heard Mario ask her nervously inside her head. Sophie's smile grew wide and determined.

"More than ever," Sophie said as excitement coursed through

her veins.

"Be careful, Kid," Mario whispered defeated as Sophie turned to walk out the door.

For the first time in years, she took her time strolling through the hallway. She ran her fingers lightly on the faded wallpapered walls. She smiled and waved at every camera she passed.

When she reached the craps table, Sophie took the dice from a man's hand, blew on it, and rolled as she smiled at the people in shock around her before grabbing a drink off the cocktail server's tray and waltzing past them all. She did absolutely nothing to hide.

Sophie wiggled her fingers and winked as she said hello to every security camera in her path. When she finally stepped out the front door and onto Freemont Street, she held her hands up high and breathed in the stale air of alcohol, greed, and despair before dropping her arms and turning to face the same camera Eddie had.

"I'm coming, my friend," Sophie said, smiling and showing all the love she could show through her eyes. She turned around and whistled while she walked down the crowded sidewalk without a care in the world about being caught.

Eddie nearly fell to the floor at her blatant declaration, and he hurried to blink the tears that had filled his eyes. Sophie was coming to save him. After all these years, she was finally coming for him. Panic quickly set in as Eddie realized he was not the only one in the room. He wasn't the only one watching Sophie pretend to suddenly be free.

Clarice stood in the corner and held her breath. She clinched her fist tightly as anger quickly warmed her blood.

"You stupid fool," she breathed out.

She didn't know what Sophie was up to, but it was already too late. The switch flipped inside Clarice, and the deep hysterical laughter that grew louder by the second made everyone shiver that stood before her. Revenge never tasted sweeter inside her mouth.

"I'm coming for you, too," Clarice cackled before spinning on her heels and heading to her room to grab her travel bag.

"Well, well," the old man sneered from above them all. "Look who's decided to finally come and play," he said, tilting his head and watching Sophie's display meant to taunt him. He would do such great things with her finally at his side.

The old man absentmindedly tapped his ring against his cane, losing sight that the boy before him was no longer broken and had switched to the side he had always been destined to be on. Sophie's.

James watched Sophie from afar. He couldn't help but enjoy her humming all the way to Bakersfield, a couple of seats ahead of him on the bus. Sophie was back to being hidden under her hood by the time she arrived on the bus, but whatever she had done, she was definitely proud of herself for it. James smiled and shook his head. God, he loved that girl.

Sophie occupied herself with the latest book she had found, *The Pearl in the Darkness,* by Santana Saunders. She found the story of the world coming to an end due to giving up religion to be quite relatable. Although James encouraged her to stick to rom coms considering they had enough thrilling suspense going on to last them a lifetime.

Sacramento was a thirteen hour ride, and Sophie was far too excited to sleep. So, she hummed and read, sitting next to an elderly woman who was thankfully keeping to herself.

When the bus finally arrived in Sacramento, Sophie stood in the aisle to stretch.

"Need a break?" she heard James whisper from behind her.

"I wouldn't mind stretching my legs," Sophie smiled as she grabbed her bag and headed off the bus.

They wandered separately around the convenience store close by. "Do you have some change?" she heard Tina ask her from behind.

"Actually, I do," Sophie smiled and went to reach into her bag for some money. Just as she did, her body weakened, and she suddenly felt nauseous.

"You okay?" Tina asked her in alarm.

"I'm not sure," Sophie replied honestly.

"Let's get a room and you can lie down," Tina said, grabbing Sophie by the waist and leading her out immediately.

James had to fight the urge to rush towards her. There were too many cameras on them, but the sight before him had him sweating. Something wasn't right.

Tina carried Sophie to a taxi. "I think we need a room nearby," she declared loudly for the boys to hear her. "My friend over did it. Do you know what's by?" The large Hispanic man rattled off a couple of options and Tina repeated which one they were headed to before helping Sophie into the car.

"What's wrong?" Ben asked behind James while he hid his face from view with a magazine. James leaned on a pillar near where the taxi was speeding off.

"I don't know, but it doesn't look good," James said uneasily as he forced himself to keep staring at the ground as they rode past them. "We need to get there asap," he said, tensely before flagging down his own cab. Ben went into a separate car while keeping a safe distance.

When they got to the room, James burst through the door first. "What's wrong?" he asked without stopping as he rushed to the bed Sophie was currently laying on.

"I honestly don't know," Tina said, concerned as she kept a cold washcloth on her now feverish head. "Something's going on inside for sure"

Ben slammed the door closed and opened the medical bag immediately to take her vitals, but there would be nothing they could do for her. Sophie was no longer the one in control...

Twenty-One

Clarice wasn't sure what was happening. All she knew was she needed to lie down. She staggered down the hallway in desperate need of her bed. Clarice felt like someone had suddenly drugged her, but knew better.

She fumbled with the doorknob before pushing the door open and falling face first into her bed. She weakly rolled onto her back as her body quickly grew several degrees too hot. She closed her eyes to calm down her senses, but when she opened them, she found a wooden door.

"Are you trying to kill me?" Clarice yelled angrily into the darkness. She stopped immediately when she heard her father's voice talking to someone on the other side. "What the hell?" she muttered, as she reached out to open the door....

Sophie had no idea that she had passed out in the taxi. All she knew was that darkness surrounded her with no wooden door before her. A wicked laugh rumbled before her. She had an idea of who the unpleasant owner was. She took a deep breath and began walking towards the voice that was taunting her.

"You can't!" she heard her mini me cry, grabbing Sophie by the hand and pulling her back. The little girl stood with her long red hair swinging in a ponytail, and her training clothes on. Her eyes remained glaring and focused on the laughter ahead of them.

"The kid's right," said the teenage version of herself, standing before her with shorter red hair, black combat attire, and her arms crossed defensively in front of her chest. She, too, glared over her shoulder at the sound taunting Sophie to come to it.

"Something's not right," teenage Sophie said flatly.

Sophie rarely saw both versions of herself before her and knew that if they were, whatever lie ahead, was definitely not going to be good.

"He's not going to stop," she declared to them before walking on.

Teenage Sophie stuck her hand out and held onto Sophie's shoulder, not taking her eyes off of whatever was before them. "This isn't the way," she said, shaking her head. "This won't end well for us," she said, staring Sophie down with a pleading look.

"We can't," begged the little girl as she tugged on Sophie's hand violently and shook her head no.

Sophie looked wildly between them. "He's getting stronger. We have to do this now," she said in a motherly voice. "We're more prepared," she added.

"Not for this," the little girl warned.

Sophie yanked her hand out of her grasp. "I'm doing this," she said, firmly.

"We can't go with you then," teenage Sophie stated flatly. The little girl looked at her as if she had gone mad. "She's going, regardless. We need to stay safe," teenage Sophie shrugged and stepped aside.

Sophie nodded at them and continued on blindly.

"You won't win this way!" she heard the little girl plead, but Sophie was tired of running and continued on.

The laughter grew louder as she grew closer. Suddenly, a presidential sized wooden desk was before Sophie with a large red leather chair turned with its back to her. She saw a wooden door to the left of her, which gave her little comfort at the moment, but comfort all the same to see the familiar image.

"Nice of you to finally join me," the old man hissed with excitement oozing from his voice.

"Visiting and joining are two different things," Sophie said boldly.

"Interesting point of view," the old man laughed as he spun his chair around to face her.

Sophie did not react to the half-scarred face like everyone else. In fact, it appeared to not faze her at all. Interesting, he thought to himself.

"We have much to discuss, you and I," the old man stated as his left side curled up into a wicked smile.

"I seriously doubt that," Sophie heard her mother announce, before stepping in front of her daughter and holding her arms out to prevent her from getting any closer.

"Jess," the old man sneered.

"Algos," Jess growled back.

Sophie's temperature rose as she felt her mother's energy against her.

"I think we're missing someone, aren't we?" Algos asked casually.

Sophie heard the doorknob turn and jerked her head to see who was coming as her stomach churned nervously. But the person who entered wasn't at all who Sophie was expecting.

Clarice nearly fell through the door. She looked around the room, clearly not aware of where she was or what was happening. Her head bounced back between the old man and Jess.

"Now the family's all here!" Algos clapped and smiled the same way he did after pushing his little brother into his death.

"Not quite," Jack said, stepping in next to Sophie and wrapping his arm around her waist tightly.

"Family?" Sophie asked, feeling vomit threating to come up through her throat.

Algos crossed his arms in annoyance. "Jack," he muttered.

"What do you want?" Jess demanded, cutting into Sophie's confusion.

"I have every right to talk to my granddaughter," Algos stated flatly.

"What?" Sophie whispered weakly as her head spun out of

control.

"Yes, Dear," Algos smiled. "You belong to me," he said with pride.

"She belongs to no one," Jack declared, but squeezed Sophie, trying to keep her grounded at the alarming announcement.

"Oh, but doesn't she?" Algos said, tilting his head and hauntingly inspecting Sophie as if she was suddenly a new test subject for him. His eyes were dark, dilated, and soulless.

"What the hell?" Clarice asked, trying to figure out how she was caught in such a horrible dream. She looked to Jess for answers, but Jess never took her eyes off of her father.

"You can't have her!" Jess demanded as she fought to keep the animal in her in check.

Sophie's body temperature increased to the point of being unbearable. She could feel the anger emanating from her mother, and it was scorching.

Algos laughed the laugh of a predator.

"I already have her," he hissed at Jess, and went to take a step forward.

Clarice froze, unable to move. She began desperately gasping for air as some unknown, invisible creature seemed to have grabbed her by the throat and was trying to crush her windpipe. Algos paid her no attention and began striding towards Sophie.

"Not this time!" Jack declared and pushed his hand on his daughter's forehead, forcing her spiraling into darkness.

Sophie did not see what happened to her parents. She did not see what happened to Clarice or Algos. She shocked everyone as she sat up, inhaling as much oxygen as she could force into her lungs.

"I know who he is," Sophie gasped.

"Who?" Ben demanded as they rushed to get closer to her.

"My grandfather," Sophie breathed out. "Clarice is my aunt."

Then Sophie's eyes rolled to the back of her head, and her body seized.

"Ben!" she heard James scream as he yanked Sophie's convulsing body into his arms.

"Hold her down!" she heard Ben order.

"She's going to bite her tongue off!" Tina yelled as Sophie felt someone pry her mouth open to shove something hard into it.

"What's wrong?" she heard James demanded furiously.

"I don't know!" she heard Ben scream back in frustration.

Sophie felt her body temperature continue to rise as she convulsed on the bed. She heard her friends cry out to her. She felt their tears as they fell onto her skin.

Someone picked her up and put her into freezing water. Most likely trying to lower her temperature as quickly as possible. Sophie heard the water splash violently around her. Then the darkness took her and swallowed her completely.

Sophie felt the life slowly leave her physical body. She felt her lungs fill up with what felt like water as she slowly drowned in nothingness. She couldn't move, no matter how hard she tried. She screamed, but nothing came out as she continued to fall deeper and deeper.

Suddenly, she hit the ground hard with a thud.

"Ugh," Sophie grunted when she landed.

She attempted to open her eyes and see where she was. An image floated before her out of focus, then she finally saw the child version of Eddie sitting on the ground, staring at her curiously.

"Do you want to play a game?" the little boy asked innocently. "Chess is my favorite...."

Did you enjoy this book?

Your feedback helps me provide the best quality books and helps other readers like you discover great books.

It would mean the world to me if you took 2 minutes to share your thoughts about this book as a review. Scan the code below to get quick access on leaving a review.

If you want early access to future books be sure to subscribe to my newsletter at:
www.chasingstormi.rocks

Summer '22

Fall '22

Dead Draw

Book Three of the Sophie Lee Saga

Dead Draw

Sophie was barely breathing. Ben grew pale as he checked her vitals.

"She's barely got a pulse," he whispered.

"We need to get her to the hospital!" James called out in panic.

"No," Tina ordered. "If he hasn't found her yet, he will definitely find her there. She won't stand a chance," she whispered softly as she stared at her friend.

"What do you mean if he hasn't found her yet?" Ben asked his wife in alarm.

Tina remained silent.

"What do you know?" James quickly challenged.

"I don't know anything," Tina lied, still staring at Sophie's barely breathing body.

"What. Do. You. Know?!" James demanded.

Before Tina could respond, her eyes rolled back, and her knees buckled under her. Ben raced to catch his wife before she fully hit the ground.

"What the hell is going on?" Ben yelled, looking at James with wild eyes, but James was too busy stumbling to the bed to catch himself before he fell into his own dark spell. "A little help here!" Ben yelled in frustration at the ceiling. There was no reply.

Tina opened her eyes to a wooden door. Her stomach jumped, and she put a protective hand over it.

"You're safe," she heard Jess assure. "Please open it."

Tina took a deep breath and pushed open the door. She shielded her eyes as they adjusted to the flooding white light around her.

"Hello, Tina," Jess whispered with a smile. She sat on a couch in the middle of what looked like a log cabin living room warming up to a fire.

"Jessica," Tina replied nervously.

"I'm not here to harm you," Jess assured. "But we do need to talk," she said in her motherly voice. "Come," Jess said, patting the cushion next to her. "Have a seat."

Tina hesitated, but made her way to the couch and took a seat.

"I don't know what's wrong with her," she blurted out.

"I know," Jess whispered softly. "This isn't about Sophie. This is about you."

Tina looked at her in panic, unsure of what she already knew. Jess kept her gaze directed towards the fireplace and gave a heavy sigh.

"Motherhood is both a glorious and difficult journey," Jess started slowly.

Tina tried desperately to swallow the panic forming in her throat.

"We do what we can to keep our children safe," Jess continued softly. "Even if that means making choices, others don't understand," she added, looking Tina straight in the eyes.

"I don't know what you're talking about," Tina lied, looking into the fire.

"You will be forced to choose a side, unfortunately," Jess continued, as if Tina hadn't responded. "We understand you have to choose what is best for you," she said, still staring Tina down. "We won't think less of you either way. But they do deserve to know."

Tina looked at Jess as her eyes quickly filled with tears.

"We need to save Sophie," Tina said with great determination. "It will do no good to know the mistakes I've made. It will only distract them."

Jess' heartbreak showed through her eyes. She reached out and gently put her hand on Tina's thigh.

"Your secrets are safe with us, but they still need to know," Jess shared.

"My life can't be saved," Tina said, looking guilty as she stared at the floor.

Jess tilted her head suddenly at the girl, who had already condemned herself to sacrifice before her.

"You fight for my daughter," Jess said, with authority. "Therefore, we fight for you."

"Clarice, is your sister?" Tina asked, looking at Jess in shock.

Jess took to staring back at the fire as Tina watched her attempt to blink away the heartache in her eyes.

"You can't save everyone," Jess sighed. "But you can always try," she added with a weary smile.

Jess jerked her head quickly to stare into Tina's soul once more.

"A mother should always put her child first," she said firmly.

Tina understood what Jess was saying. She knew what Jess wanted her to do.

"I will tell them," Tina resigned. "Together, we will save Sophie so she can save us all. With as little casualties as possible," she added as she put her hand over Jess'. Tina felt Jess squeeze her leg slightly as her body swelled up with comfort and love.

"So, tell me about this dreamcatcher theory you have," Jess said with a knowing smile.

Tina looked horrified, then shook her head and laugh.

"I don't know if it's a theory, really," Tina sighed.

"You're the smartest person I have come across in my lifetime," Jess said, smiling with encouragement. "That says a lot since I'm still existing amongst the living," she added with a wink. "Walk me through it."

Tina grabbed the paper and pencil that appeared on the table next to her. She scribbled and describe to Jess the images that came to her last night.

"That's interesting," Jess said, once Tina was finished, deep in thought. "Why do you think Sophie needs this?"

"Do you not know?" Tina asked in surprise.

"Know what?" Jess questioned; not sure she was ready for the answer.

"Sophie thinks he has found a way to access her mind and control her," Tina replied hesitantly.

Fear flooded Jess' eyes, and panic filled her heart and lungs.

"No," she whispered so softly, even Tina barely heard her.

"I thought you knew," Tina gasped in panic.

"We knew he was pushing in," Jess breathed out. "We didn't know he could get control."

Jess grabbed her stomach and began gasping desperately for air to get into her lungs. Tina grabbed Jess by the arms.

"Breathe!" Tina ordered her.

"We can't find her," Jess sobbed. "Her life is too low." She violently shook her head and scrambled out of Tina's arms.

"What does that mean?" Tina asked, as fear paralyzed her.

Jess backed herself up against a wall.

"Jess! What. Does. That. Mean?" Tina demanded.

"We thought she turned herself off," Jess choked out.

"Maybe she did!" Tina offered in desperation.

Jess looked at Tina, making Tina shiver to her core. It was like she could see the insanity take control over Jess, and Sophie's mother was no longer present.

"He's done it," Jess whispered as she slid slowly down the wall. She held out her hand as a light shoved Tina through to the other side of the door.

Tina woke up gasping for air, and Ben grabbed her and pulled her into his arms.

"What's wrong?" he asked in panic, but Tina couldn't breathe.

She looked desperately at the only person who was going to be able to save them all. Tina grabbed Sophie's limp hand and placed it over her belly as she sobbed uncontrollably for the life that was going to be sacrificed before she ever got to hold it.

Acknowledgements

The Sophie Lee Saga would never have existed if it hadn't been for several people in my life. My mother, for putting the original seed of writing a fiction book into my crazy head. It was her comment that I later mentioned to Shyera McCollough when I was so desperate to find balance in a world that was quickly spiraling out of control due to the Covid-19 pandemic.

When discussing possible writing topics, I mentioned a story that had been started and never finished in middle school. I laughed, telling her that my mother mentioned that my writing draws people in and I could be like Nora Roberts with a fiction novel. She was immediately invested and insisting that this story needed to be told.

Once a few pages were written, I shared it with my friend, Mario. He insisted it needed to be a saga. I couldn't believe he thought it was going to last that long when it wasn't even a full chapter yet! However, the thought intrigued me way too much to pass it up.

I found myself leaving "Easter Eggs" for what I envisioned to come as Sophie continued her journey. Writing *The Key* allowed me to have another thing to bond over with my father. He was the first to read the rough draft of *The Key* with my mother a close second. Before I knew it, my mother was offering ideas to wrap up the Saga with *The Key* not even being completed yet! Thus, my parents quickly became my creative writing team.

When it was time to get started on *The Protector,* we sat around the dining room table and tossed around ideas and what I was stuck on. It is truly a blessing to have such a supportive team for my current journey. I love that my father is still sending me text messages of their ideas that never stop flowing!

You, my readers, also keep me going. I wasn't sure if you were going to love the story as much as I did, but you eagerly proved me wrong! At first, your excitement was a little overwhelming. It made me want to write an even better second book. I hope you enjoy it as much as I enjoyed writing it.

This story took an unexpected turn, as usual when the story is writing itself. I found myself diving deeper into the world that Jack and Jess remain to keep Sophie safe. The world Algos wants to crumble in order to gain total control of Sophie and her abilities. This new inspiration is thanks to the OG Storm Chaser.

It is a difficult journey to be on when the person who supported you the most is slipping before your very eyes. The woman that never hesitated to tell me how proud of me she was and how much she loved me now has a time clock that seems to be running out quicker and quicker as the days pass. I strongly believe that loved ones never truly leave us when they pass on to another plane, but I wasn't quite ready to be done hearing her stories or praises.

Thus, the dream realm unintentionally grew. Rules became more defined as you meet the Counsel of Death, and learn the ultimate punishment for breaking the rules of this sacred place. Although it has become another battle ground to face off Algos, it was inspired by the beloved OG Storm Chaser. The woman that will always hold my heart, and never be far away, even when the clock runs out. She may never fully understand how much she has inspired this story to grow, but I will always be grateful for everything she is and more.

Lightning Source UK Ltd.
Milton Keynes UK
UKHW021959140622
404445UK00009B/188/J

9 798985 699913